BOUND AT THE SUGAR MILL MARKETPLACE

Sugar Mill Marketplace Book 3

BECKY CLARK

Foreword

RAT RACE is the prequel novella that bridges Becky Clark's Mystery Writer's mysteries and the Sugar Mill Marketplace mysteries.

Read RAT RACE before you read BOOKED, PLOTTED, and BOUND as it sets the stage for some action that occurs in those early books in the Sugar Mill Marketplace series.

You can buy RAT RACE for 99c or download it for free when you subscribe to Becky Clark's newsletter, *So Seldom It's Shameful News.*

Subscribers also receive FICTION CAN BE MURDER—the first book in the Mystery Writer's series—as well as some related short stories and a Christmas play.

Dena

"OH NO, you don't. No phone for you!"

Dena Russo's phone was plucked from her hand before she knew what was happening. She was still groggy from sleep. The sun hadn't even come up yet.

Twist stood by her side, ears perked.

Dena had come to know Twist better the last few weeks and found out that in addition to her bad habit of stealing socks, Twist had another bad habit. She didn't bark when danger was near.

Like now, for instance.

Twist could be excused, of course, because until this very moment Dena didn't realize she was in danger.

Dena watched as pocket chaff fell from a coat pocket into the Mexican pottery planter Charlee had given her as a housewarming present when she moved to Sugar Springs in December. It had continued to remain empty until Dena could decide what to plant in it.

Apparently, at the moment, it looked like a trash can.

"Get your coat, it's cold out."

"Where are we going?" Dena's hands shook as she

shrugged into the parka held out to her. She zipped it up over her fleece lounge pants with the cartoon tacos printed all over them and a threadbare t-shirt that had approximately four more launderings before it disintegrated into the memory of a shirt.

"You'll find out soon enough. Get some boots on, too."

"Can I put real clothes on first?"

"No."

Dena stepped into her snow boots, left by the door, and pulled them up. As she straightened, pink fuzzy handcuffs clamped on her wrists before she was pushed out her front door into the snowstorm.

Charlee

CHARLEE RUSSO CHECKED THE TIME. Not too early to call her mom, especially when she had good news to share.

"When you talk to your mom, ask her if she wants to go to the Dark Dagger Awards with us. We could make a weekend of it." Charlee's boyfriend Ozzi started to brew a pot of coffee and popped two pieces of bread in the toaster.

Charlee was grateful he and her mother got along so well. She'd heard horror stories from her friends about terrible in-law fighting. She blushed. Not that Dena was Ozzi's mother-in-law any time soon.

"What's the matter?" Ozzi asked.

"Nothing. Just hot."

"You won't be for long. Sounds like the storm coming in will be bad."

Charlee turned away and fanned herself. She refused to be one of those hyper-vigilant girlfriends, always dancing on the knife edge of marriage proposals. They'd never talked about it, not seriously anyway. Both of them were perfectly happy with their relationship as it was.

"They're predicting a bunch of snow down south, but I don't think Denver is supposed to get hit with much," Charlee said.

"Hope not. Those March storms can be a real mess." Ozzi buttered the toast and held one of the slices out to her. "Want one?"

"No, go ahead. I want to talk to Mom first."

Ozzi poured coffee and handed her a cup. He sat with his toast and coffee at the kitchen table and began scrolling through his phone.

Charlee took her coffee to the couch and dialed. After a minute she dropped the phone next to her. "That's weird."

"What?" Ozzi asked.

"Mom's phone went straight to voice mail. Some message about contacting the Sugar Mill Marketplace offices in the event of an emergency. Since when did they get offices there?"

"Didn't you tell me she got an assistant? That's probably all it is. Trying to sound all professional and whatnot."

"I guess. It's just weird she has her phone off."

"What makes you think her phone is off?" Ozzi asked.

"Because it went straight to voice mail."

"It would do that if she was already talking on it."

"Oh, that's right. Probably Lance."

"May as well dial again." Ozzi laughed. "Your brother isn't one to talk on the phone longer than he has to. Especially this early in the morning."

"Unless he's on shift."

"Then he *really* won't want to talk on the phone. Might let some perp get away while he's making small talk with his mom."

"He'd have to get her to explain it to his chief." Charlee smiled at the thought her brother the cop would let his mommy bail him out of a jam. She dialed Dena again. Still voice mail. Weird. This time she left a message. "Hey Mom, why aren't you answering your phone? Anyway, I wanted to tell you my news. I've been nominated for a Dark Dagger! That's the same one Rodolfo Lapaglia won and all those online photos helped me solve …. Never mind. Call me back before you get busy at the bookstore and I'll give you all the deets. Ozzi and I want you to come to the ceremony with us if you can. Okay. Bye. Call me!"

Evelyn

WEARING a mint green cardigan and matching polyester pants, Evelyn Milligan stood at the two-story Sugar Mill Marketplace window overlooking the snowy parking lot. Their car was the lonely sentinel. Both of Evelyn's hands clutched her lower back. Her husband Max crossed the promenade in front of their photo studio and joined her.

"Back acting up again?" he asked.

"If anyone would have told me how complicated getting old was, I'm not sure I would have believed them." She made fists and kneaded her back.

"Beats the alternative, though." Max massaged Evelyn's shoulders.

"That it does. But wouldn't it be better if when we got to be eighty, we got less achy? Let the kids deal with aches and pains."

"You figure out how to do that and I'll be first in line." They stood quietly and watched the big fat flakes of snow.

Balaam, their smoke-colored Persian cat, wound his way around Evelyn's feet.

"Starting to really come down," Max said.

"Remind me. Why'd we come in today, anyway?" Evelyn said.

Balaam stopped his figure eights around Evelyn to peer at Max through slitted copper- hued eyes.

"Balaam wants to know too."

"Because, my dearest kitty cats, we are responsible businesspeople who run their business responsibly. Plus, we have nothing better to do," Max said with a smirk.

"Speak for yourself. I could have been …." Evelyn trailed off.

"Exactly."

They both watched as Kober got out of her car and Skyler parked next to her.

"We won't get any customers today. Probably should have stayed home." Evelyn turned toward Max with a smirk. "You could have taken the opportunity to learn how to bake bread or something."

"Honestly, woman. Isn't it enough I do the laundry and cook your meals?"

Evelyn knew Max was joking. There was a time, though, and not too long ago, when they were confounded by having to switch jobs at the photography studio they had launched. Everything had been mapped out. Their business plan written, chiseled in stone. All scenarios envisioned. Except one. They were both stunned when it turned out Evelyn was the better photographer. She clearly had the better artistic eye and understood the equipment almost intuitively. Max had to take over the business side of things—dealing with money, scheduling, even laundering the costumes their customers dressed up in. It was one of the biggest rifts in their long marriage, second only to that disaster with their son.

Kober held the door for Skyler and they both stomped the snow off their boots and joined them at the window.

"I'm thinking sourdough," Evelyn mused.

"You're going to make bread?" Skyler asked.

"Max is."

"No, he's not," Kober said without even looking up.

Max gave a loud harumph.

Kober looked up. "You are?"

"Probably not. But would it kill you to think that I could?"

Kober reorganized the pile of hair haphazardly arranged atop her head. "It might." She draped her coat over her arm and squinted, staring out the window. "What are you guys looking at?"

"The snow." Evelyn looked at Kober. "Are you okay, dear? It looks like you put your mascara on with a garden trowel."

Kober ran both index fingers under red-rimmed eyes. "Must not be waterproof. Coming down pretty hard out there."

Evelyn didn't buy that for a minute but kept her mouth shut. If Kober didn't want to talk about whatever it was making her cry, then she'd mind her own beeswax. Evelyn turned back to the window. "Every time there's a huge storm like this, I always think of the Native Americans and the pioneers here so long ago. Everything they did had to relate to their survival. Can you imagine being out in a storm like this without a sturdy structure around you? I've never worried about our farmhouse, even though it's old and creaky—"

"Just like Max." Kober nudged him good-naturedly in the ribs. He gave her a hip check in return.

"—and the Marketplace," Evelyn continued. "Can you imagine this place ever blowing over in the wind?" Everyone murmured. "Today we completely take our survival for granted. At least from a blizzard."

Kober stared out the window. "I wonder how much I'm supposed to bake today. I can't imagine anyone will come in."

"I was wondering the same thing," Skyler said.

"At least you can keep all your cheese and whatnot in the refrigerator and only cut off hunks if someone comes in and asks for it," Kober said. "But if anyone braves this storm today, they will skin me alive if they schlep all the way here for a brownie and I don't have any."

"Tell you what, Kober." Max buttoned the top button of his golf shirt and snapped his red suspenders. "You bake up a storm in here and if the storm is so bad out there you don't sell anything, Ev and I will buy it all up and we'll throw ourselves a big 'ol pity party."

Evelyn said, "We will?" at the same time Kober said, "Deal."

"Brownies are the key to survival, Ev, I thought you knew that." Max winked at his wife.

They all watched the snow falling for a while longer before wandering away to open their shops and begin their day.

Evelyn and Max walked all the way through *Step Into History*, their photography studio.

"Ow!" Evelyn rubbed her shin where she barked it on the corner of one of the boxes. "That's the third time I've done that in the last two weeks. Today might be the perfect day to open these up and then get rid of them."

"Hugo should do it. He's the one who let somebody abandon them here," Max grumped.

Evelyn sighed. "I know. I think people mean well, donating clothes they think we can use for costumes, but—"

"They're just lazy and you know it. We're much closer

than the drop-off place for the thrift store in Colorado Springs," Max said.

"You know how I hate to admit you're right, right?"

"I do. But I'm always looking forward to hearing it." Max leaned toward her expectantly, a comical look of anticipation on his face.

Evelyn wrinkled her nose. "Nah." She shoved the boxes closer to the wall. "Did Hugo ever say who dropped these off?"

Max shrugged. "Some middle-aged woman, which to him could cover a spread from forty to ninety. Nobody he recognized. He was first to the Marketplace that day. He told me she was waiting in her car for someone to unlock the doors. Said she seemed nervous."

"Probably because she knew we didn't want her old crap."

"You know the saying," Max said. "One man's trash is another's man's old crap."

Charlee

"STILL NO ANSWER from my mom. That's so weird."

"Yeah," Ozzi said with a smile. "To think your mother might have a life that doesn't revolve around her grown children. So weird."

"Just because you and your mom have a perfectly functional relationship is no reason to mock me." Charlee snapped the kitchen towel at him.

Ozzi scooped her in his arms and danced her around the kitchen. "I'm so proud of your Dark Dagger nomination. And once your mother returns from her secret trip to the Bahamas, so will she."

Charlee laughed. "Can you imagine? My mother jetting off to the Bahamas? I mean, she makes hasty decisions all the time, but not like that. On the other hand, her life really should revolve around me and Lance, so I'd make the argument she should take us with her." She ran her hands through Ozzi's longish hair. "I'd lobby for her to include you too. Even though you need a trim."

Ozzi kissed her goodbye then gathered his things for work. At her apartment door he stopped. "Let me know if you decide to book a flight to the Bahamas to meet up with your mom, okay? I'll have to make different plans for dinner. Maybe squeeze in a haircut."

"You'll be the first to know."

As Ozzi closed the door behind him, though, Charlee began wondering about her mother again. Maybe Dena took Twist on an early walk before work and didn't take her phone. Maybe she's already at the bookstore and turned off her phone, or worse, forgot it. It's happened before. She really, really wanted to tell her mother the good news. None of her thrillers had ever been nominated for such a prestigious book award before. Charlee smiled, envisioning the display table Dena would create in the bookstore. Even though her mom's Thrice Sold Tales was a used bookstore, she had a round table right in the center prominently showcasing piles of Charlee's books, the only new books offered for sale in the store. Dena proudly plugged them to everyone who walked in. "Or at least that's what she told you," Lance had pointed out to her as only a big brother could. He said he couldn't believe it until he could confirm it independently. Always the cop.

Charlee wanted to get to her desk and start writing, though. An interruption, even a welcome return call from her mother, would derail her flow and knock her out of the zone. She had a couple of tough scenes to write today so she really needed to focus.

She tried Dena's cell again, which, just like before, went straight to voice mail. She called the direct line to Thrice Sold Tales. No answer there either, just the recording that came on after four rings advising of the hours and location, but if it was an emergency, to call the Sugar Mill Marketplace offices.

Charlee jotted down the number, unaware the Marketplace even had an office until she'd heard these outgoing messages on her mother's phones. It wasn't an emergency to tell Dena about the Dark Dagger nomination, but she was pretty sure she'd be forgiven.

Charlee dialed, expecting the number to route back around to one of Dena's phone numbers. When a woman answered before the second ring, Charlee was momentarily speechless.

"Hello?" the woman repeated, this time impatiently.

"Oh, I'm sorry. I was looking for Dena Russo."

"She owns Thrice Sold Tales. I can give you that number to call directly. But the store doesn't open until ten."

"I'm her daughter, Charlee. I called her cell and the store number, but she's not answering."

"I can't help you."

"What's your name?"

"Kateri Warcloud. Why?"

"It's just weird we haven't met. My mom didn't tell me the Marketplace had an office staff now."

"What's so weird about that?"

Charlee took a breath. She wasn't making a good impression. "Kateri, I don't want to bother you or anything, but are you actually, physically at the Marketplace?"

"How else would I answer the phone?"

"I didn't know if you worked remotely—never mind. Could you go over to the bookstore and tell my mom I'm trying to reach her?"

"Is this an emergency?"

"Well … no, but I think she might have forgotten her phone or lost it or something, and I—"

"I thought you said you called the bookstore directly."

"I did, but—"

"If she was there, she would have answered."

"But, could you just peek——"

"I'm sure she's busy with something and she'll return your call when she's able."

Before Charlee could respond, her phone went dark. She bared her teeth at her phone. Kateri Warcloud hadn't made a very good impression either. "I hope Mom didn't hire that snippy … rapscallion." Charlee jotted that word down. She was channeling one of the characters from her work-in-progress and that would be the perfect thing for him to say.

She dialed Dena's cell and the bookstore numbers again. Still no answer. This time she also added a few words about how rude and unhelpful Kateri the Marketplace phone answerer was.

Charlee sat at the table with another cup of coffee and the English muffin Ozzi had put in the toaster for her. All the nooks and crannies were crispy, exactly how she liked it. She drained her cup and finished both halves, licking melted butter off her fingers, all the while willing her phone to light up.

Charlee looked up the number for the Sugar Springs Bakery, the shop right next to Dena's bookstore in the Marketplace, and dialed.

A loud voice answered. "Isn't it a little late to apologize to——"

"Pardon me? Is this the Sugar Springs Bakery?"

"Oh. Sorry. I thought you were someone else. Yes, this is the bakery. What can I do for you?"

"Kober? I don't know if you remember me. This is Charlee, Dena's daughter."

"Oh, hi! What's up?"

"I'm just having trouble reaching my mom. She probably lost her phone or something. I don't want to bother you or anything, but could you run next door and see if she's there? I asked Kateri, that gal in the office—what's her deal, anyway?—but she blew me off."

Kober snorted. "She's kind of a piece of work. Not what you'd call a people person. I haven't quite figured her out yet. But yeah, hang on a sec, I'll go check for you."

Charlee heard indistinct noises, then Kober's muffled voice bellowing, "Dena, your kid is trying to stalk you. Answer your phone!" Charlee smiled as she pictured her mother jumping out of her skin when Kober barged into the bookstore and startled her.

In a few moments Kober came back on the line. "She's not there. It's all locked up."

"Oh. Doesn't that seem weird to you?"

"Not really," Kober said. "It's early. Store doesn't open for a couple of hours."

"But I've been calling her cell and she's not answering that either." Kober started to say something, but Charlee cut her off. "Normally I wouldn't worry. But I left her a message about this big-deal award I was nominated for—"

"Congratulations!"

"Thank you. And normally she would have called me back by now. You know how she is."

"Indeed I do."

"It's been plenty of time to see my text or listen to my message if she took the dog on a walk or was in the shower or something. And if she was in the middle of something and couldn't talk, she'd give me a thumbs up and say *TTYL, Bug* or something so I'd know she saw it.

"She calls you Bug?"

"Yeah."

"Like Volkswagen?"

"No. Like Doodle. But there's been nothing from her. I'm getting worried." Charlee was quiet for a moment. "She lives alone, you know. Maybe she fell or something."

It was Kober's turn to be quiet. Finally, she said, "The weather is brutal here today. The kids have a snow day. I'll have Jain go over to Dena's house and tell her to turn on her stupid phone."

"I don't want to be an imposition…"

"Nah. Jain likes any excuse to go over and play with Twist. And she's probably ready to get some time away from her brothers. I mean, it's been more than ten minutes and I'm sure they're all feral by now. And if Dena slept through her alarm or something, then she'll probably appreciate Jain waking her up and getting her to the bookstore in time to open. Not that we'll have any customers today, though."

Kober congratulated her again on the Dark Dagger before disconnecting.

Charlee made sure her phone was turned up loud and began clearing away the breakfast dishes.

Kober

KOBER DIALED HER SIXTEEN-YEAR-OLD DAUGHTER. "Jain, can you please go over to Dena's house and tell her that her daughter is trying to call her but can't get through?"

"Sure. I've gotta get dressed first."

"Always a good idea."

Kober returned to mixing up her sugar cookie dough. If anyone did come into the bakery today, they'd definitely want sugar cookies and cocoa. Unless they wanted brownies and cocoa. Luckily cookies and brownies had somewhat of a shelf-life, but Kober wished she could predict what the traffic at the bakery would be like on a day like this. Oh, well. She'd find out soon enough. And maybe that pity party of Max's would be fun. It would at least be a diversion from what had happened between her and Nic this morning. Even though she was alone, she blushed, embarrassed to have assumed it was Nic calling to apologize when it had been Charlee calling.

Kober knew that the more time elapsed, it would be much less likely that Nic would apologize. Or even call.

The growing knot in her stomach hardened with every tick of the clock.

She should have taken a snow day herself and spent it with the kids. But she hadn't been able to stop crying until she reached her favorite parking space in the Marketplace lot and managed to pull herself together. Her kids didn't need to see all that. She could take the day to compose herself and decide what to tell them. And the kids could sit around all day and eat junk food and watch TV, as was protocol for a proper snow day. They'd regroup later.

Jain called back thirty minutes later. "Mom? Dena's not here. Twist was racing around all crazy doing the potty dance, though, so I let her out. And now she's telling me she's starving. Should I give her some food?"

"Sure, why not. How'd you get in the house?"

"The front door was unlocked. I knocked and rang the bell, and Twist was barking up a storm, so I didn't think I'd surprise her if I just came in. I made sure she wasn't in the shower, though."

They both had a laugh at Dena's expense, remembering when Dena had barged in on Kober in the shower recently. Kober had gotten over the shock and embarrassment within a couple of days, but Dena might never recover.

"I'm going to stay here for a while and play with Twist, if you think that'd be okay. When I left, the boys were having a fart contest. I was happy to get out of there."

"Ew. I don't blame you." Kober had witnessed her fair share of those contests. She coveted her win during the Spit Bubble contest, but drew the line at belches and farts, truly the domain of young boys. "I'm sure Dena wouldn't mind if you stayed to keep Twist company. When she gets home, though, tell her to call her daughter."

After Kober disconnected from Jain, she called Charlee

and relayed what Jain had said. Kober was distracted and wanted to get back to her baking and formulating what to tell the kids about Nic. "Dena probably just went for a walk or something."

"It's not snowing there?" Charlee asked.

"Oh. Yeah. Maybe the grocery store then."

"Was her car there?"

Kober and Jain hadn't discussed that, but she didn't want to say so and cause Charlee any further worry. Dena was fine. Probably just slipped next door to have coffee with her neighbor or something. Kober felt her jaw tense. Maybe Dena was still on a date. Perhaps she had a grown-up sleepover. She decided to keep that thought to herself. "Jain didn't see her car." Technically not a lie. Kober was trying not to … embellish her conversation so much anymore and was satisfied with her statement. The little white lie of omission might not hold up under scrutiny, but it would do for now.

Kober unclenched her jaw. Not every man was Nic. If Dena found someone to have a sleepover with, Kober would try to be supportive. Her curiosity got the better of her and she couldn't wait to find out who Dena was with all night. A bit of racy gossip would be a welcome diversion from thinking about her own love life.

It wasn't her place to plant that seed in Charlee's brain, however. Sleepovers and cheating husbands were topics for Dena and Kober alone.

"Charlee, Jain is going to play with Twist while she avoids her three younger brothers. I told her to tell Dena to call you the minute she gets home."

Boyd

"I'M GOING to be the best neighbah they've ever had," Boyd Drummond said to one of his brand-new, never-been-used, price-tag-still-attached snow shovels.

He knew his Colorado neighbors weren't too wild about some loud-mouthed transplant from Boston popping the top of his mid-century ranch house. It wasn't ugly, but it sure didn't match anything else in the neighborhood, so he tried to make it up to them. He took around pints of his fresh-made ice cream to each house, along with coupons redeemable for more from his shop, Scoops Ice Creamery, at the Sugar Mill Marketplace. About half the coupons had been redeemed in the last couple of weeks, so he knew he was making a dent in the hard feelings they still might harbor. He'd also given away some of the oversized plush ice cream cones he'd ordered as decorations for his shop. They were easily five times bigger than he'd expected and he'd ordered too many, so giving them away seemed to be a good idea. The smiles on the faces of those who received them confirmed it.

There might still be some holdouts, however, and today he'd win them over too.

In one of his many spare rooms, he rummaged through boxes of clothing he still hadn't unpacked until he found a coat. He was a big guy and didn't get cold very easily, but he knew he needed something over his signature outfit of Hawaiian shirt and cargo shorts, if only because he'd look nuts going outside without one. He couldn't find any boots, and honestly couldn't remember if he even owned any. Before he settled on living in Sugar Springs, he'd been in apartment buildings where other people dealt with the snow.

"Score!" Boyd found some gardening clogs and slipped them on over a pair of socks. He glanced in the mirror and laughed his loud, infectious laugh before heading to the garage with both snow shovels. "Sawks and clogs togethah. Wicked awesome fashion sense." He pressed the button to raise his overhead door.

He had bought two different kinds of snow shovels when he got to Sugar Springs, at the urging of Swede, the hardware store owner. Actually, Swede had tried to get him to buy a snow blower, but Boyd had laughed. "You saying I'm a loafa? Out of shape? I'm a snow shoveling monstah, you'll see." One shovel was wide and ergonomic with a plastic scoop, allowing you to walk behind and simply push the snow out of the way. The other was smaller and more old-fashioned, with a metal blade, the kind where you scoop and toss. Both had their uses, he assumed, hoping he'd figure it out when he needed to.

Boyd stared from his garage down the driveway as the heavy, wet snow fell, swirling and dancing in the wind.

"The fun starts now!" he bellowed into the storm.

He tried to find the most pragmatic way to deal with the snow piling up, finally deciding to use the wide shovel and clear a path down one side of the driveway, allowing him to forge a path to the sidewalk.

Boyd pushed the shovel in front of him until it stopped short, after about six inches. He tried again. Another six inches, but the blade was packed with snow. It felt like he was pushing concrete. He planted his feet and bent his knees, struggling to lift the full shovel, eventually managing an awkward toss of the accumulated snow onto his lawn. He tried again. This time he was able to figure out a better angle and pushed the shovel a bit further. He expected he'd be able to clear a swath all the way to the street.

The snow had other ideas.

He knew there was much more humidity in Boston than in Colorado, so he expected the snow to be drier here, more lightweight than this was proving to be. Colorado snow didn't seem to cooperate as well as Boston snow. Of course, when he'd shoveled Boston snow, he'd been many years younger and many pounds lighter.

He exchanged the wide ergonomic shovel for the smaller old-fashioned one. Scoop, toss, scoop, toss. Boyd established a rhythm and found himself at the bottom of his driveway in no time. He determined where the sidewalk was, under all that snow, and turned the corner, scooping and tossing as he went.

He scooped and tossed along the sidewalk in front of his house and continued past his neighbor's house as well. He saw his neighbor standing in his picture window sipping from a mug while watching Boyd.

Boyd stopped long enough to wave at him. The man raised one hand in reply. Boyd kept going, past the next house and the next until he got to the corner where he turned around. He was dismayed that a couple of inches had fallen on his recently cleared path, but he scooped and tossed on the return trip back toward his own house.

When he got there, he had worked up a sweat and briefly toyed with the idea of shedding his coat and leaving it draped over his car in the garage. He decided against it, though. His uncovered legs were keeping him as cool as could be expected. He was pleased by the traction his clogs gave and knew they had already become a beloved part of his snow shoveling outfit.

Scoop, toss, scoop, toss.

Boyd made his way past his neighbors' houses on the other side. One woman opened her front door and yelled, "What in the world do you think you're doing out there, you maniac? The storm's not even over!"

"Just getting a jumpstart on it. Don't you worry, I'll have this done quicker'n you can count to fawty!"

The woman shook her head and said something to her husband before shutting the door. They both stood in their front window and stared as Boyd shoveled.

He began panting and stopped to rub his upper arm. The scoop-and-toss was beginning to take its toll on him.

When Boyd got to the next corner, again he turned around to find another two inches of snow had covered his newly-cleared sidewalk. Again, he scooped and tossed his way back. When he got to his own driveway, he could barely determine the strip he'd cleared from the garage down to the sidewalk. He scooped and tossed that path again. When he got to the garage, he opened the back of his SUV and sat down on the tailgate to catch his breath.

This time he did remove his coat, in an attempt to cool down a bit.

As Boyd sat rubbing his arm, panting, and sweating, he pulled out his phone and typed in "heart attack symptoms." He scrolled through them. "Huh."

He dialed his phone. "Hey, Hugo. Do me a favah and come over to my house."

"Have you looked outside?"

"I am outside."

"What are you doing outside?"

"I'm shoveling snow for my neighbahs."

"You're an idiot." Hugo snorted. "Everyone knows you wait until the storm is over before you start shoveling. Then you hope someone in the neighborhood with a snowblower makes the rounds before you go out. Then you gift them with the ceremonial bottle of bourbon to thank them. Town charter says you have twenty-four hours after the snow stops to clear public right-of-ways."

"I'm getting a jumpstart."

"Wait. You're serious? You called me to come over and help you shovel snow?" Hugo snorted again.

"No, I called you to come over just in case I'm having a hawt attack."

"What? You're having a heart attack?"

"Probably not. I mean, I'm exercising, doing repetitive movements. *Of course* I'm going to sweat and my arms will ache. But come ovah, just in case. I wouldn't want my neighbahs to have to deal with it. I'm trying to make a good impression on them."

"Boyd. Hang up and call 911 right now. Or get to the hospital!"

"No! People *die* in hospitals! I'm a survivor! Just come ovah. Yell at me to my face."

"Boyd—"

"Quit worrying. I'm a little rusty, but I've shoveled mountains of snow in Boston."

"But you haven't shoveled mountains of snow *in* the mountains! You're at eight thousand feet here, not sea level."

"Like I could forget." Boyd barked out a laugh. "I still brown out when I tie my shoes."

"You don't wear shoes."

"Figure of speech."

"Are you really not going to call anyone?" Hugo asked.

"I called you."

Hugo made an unidentifiable noise in his throat. "I'll be right there."

While Boyd waited for Hugo, he tried using the ergonomic shovel again on his driveway and was pleased that it was a bit easier. "I just needed to get that first layer off," he said through ragged breaths. By the time he got down the driveway to the sidewalk again, though, the path he'd cleared earlier with the small metal-bladed shovel while scooping and tossing wasn't as wide as the shovel he used now. It began to bog down too. He leaned on it, contemplating his next step to tackle the snow.

Hugo slid around the corner in his metallic red Range Rover and came to a stop in the middle of Boyd's driveway.

Boyd hadn't yet figured out how to ask Hugo how much that car cost. He was sure it was upwards of a hundred thousand dollars. He knew it was rude, but when someone drives such an expensive car, maybe what they want is for someone to ask. "Hey, Hugo—"

"Oh, good grief, Boyd." Hugo emerged from the car already speaking. "I'd almost convinced myself you were pulling my leg, but here you are, wearing garden shoes and shorts in a blizzard." Hugo grabbed the snow shovel from Boyd and marched him into the garage. "Go get your wallet. We're going to the hospital."

Boyd waved him off and entered the house.

Hugo followed. Once inside, he stood, hands on hips, staring at Boyd. "What are your symptoms?"

Boyd started gyrating and singing "Addicted to Love" in his booming baritone.

"Not funny."

Then he launched into an even louder rendition of "Simply Irresistible."

Hugo stared at him. "Robert Palmer is turning over in his grave. And the irony that he died of a massive heart attack should not be lost on you."

Boyd waved away his concern. "This is just a false alarm. In my overzealous attempt to be adored and admired by my neighbahs, I simply overdid it out there. I'm not as young as I used to be. I shouldn't have bothered you, but now that you're here, let me make you breakfast—you like stuffed French toast?—then we'll go to work."

"Go to work … shoveling snow?"

Boyd brightened. "You're gonna help me?"

"No! Twenty-four hours until *after* the snow stops, remember?"

"Fine. I meant go to work at the Marketplace anyway."

Boyd became self-conscious when he noticed Hugo staring at him like Balaam stared into his ice cream case. Boyd gathered supplies to make breakfast, but before he could crack an egg, Hugo stopped him.

"You know what? I'm going to make you breakfast, Boyd. You deserve it after trying to help all your neighbors like that."

Boyd guffawed. "I see right through you, kid. You want something healthier than French toast, doncha?"

"Well…"

"Fine. Do what you want." Boyd sat down and put his feet on the chair opposite. "Make me healthy."

Hugo and Boyd chatted about nothing while Hugo whipped up a couple of egg white omelets with broccoli and mushrooms. Boyd protested that the mushrooms were for spaghetti and meatballs and the broccoli was for something he called Cheesy Potato Quiche. Hugo simply rolled his eyes.

"You making me breakfast makes me want to do something nice for you." Boyd thought for a moment then snapped his fingers. "Got it. I'll help you woo Skylah."

"What? Unnecessary and uncool. Besides, who do you think you are, Cyrano de Bergerac?" Hugo flipped the omelet. "Besides, if memory serves, that story did not end happily for Christian, so thank you no. Butt out and eat your breakfast. No thanks necessary."

"Fine. But I'd make a good Cyrano." Boyd accepted the plate Hugo held out to him.

Hugo watched while Boyd took a bite.

Boyd nodded while he chewed. "Not bad. But you know what would make this even bettah?"

"Fresh cilantro," Hugo said confidently. "But you didn't—"

"A side of stuffed French toast."

Charlee

CHARLEE COULDN'T CONCENTRATE. The thrilling climax she was supposed to be writing sounded more like Dr Seuss, full of made-up words and nonsense phrases. She'd tried to use "rapscallion" in four different places, only to delete it each time. Her mind kept wandering to her mother back in Sugar Springs.

Kober at the bakery didn't seem worried, so Charlee tried not to, but it wasn't going well. Something just didn't seem right.

Dena wouldn't up and leave without making sure someone was taking care of Twist.

Perhaps Kober's daughter misunderstood the situation and Twist pulled a fast one on her, pretending to be starving. Peter O'Drool, Barb and Don's devious pug in the upstairs apartment, did stuff like that all the time. Dogs seem to have a tiny manipulative bone, maybe in their tail, that fibbed to humans whenever their canine desires overwhelmed them. *You forgot my dinner! Where's my snack! Throw this ball!*

But Charlee fell for Peter's dramatics every time,

despite suspecting she was being manipulated. She couldn't even venture a guess as to how many times she stopped whatever she was doing when Peter pawed at her apartment door and looked at her with those baleful eyes. Then when she gave in to whatever he'd been demanding, Barb or Don would appear and laugh at how she'd been hoodwinked by a gassy little pug once again. She didn't care though, which was probably exactly how Jain felt with Twist this morning.

And yet. It was almost time for Dena to open the bookstore and she still hadn't called? Even if Dena did have errands to run early, and even if the snow added time to each one, Sugar Springs wasn't that big. She should be home by now.

There was still the possibility that something happened to Dena's phone. Charlee called Dena's cell and then the bookstore number again. Nothing.

She didn't want to bother Kober for a second time, but thought she'd try the other tenants at the Marketplace. Maybe one of them knew something that Kober didn't.

Charlee looked up the number for the cheese shop and dialed.

"Really Grate Cheese, this is Skyler."

"Hi Skyler, this is Charlee Russo, Dena's daughter."

"Oh hi! How nice to hear from you."

Charlee hadn't met Skyler before, but she sounded just as perky and blond as her mother had described.

"Hey, have you heard from my mother this morning?"

"No. Was I supposed to?"

Charlee had to process that bizarre question for a minute. "Um … I don't know. It's just that I've been calling and calling her this morning and she's not answering, so I was just hoping you might know something."

"Something like what?"

"Like if she had to go somewhere at the last minute or if her phone is on the fritz or .... I don't know. Something."

"Sorry, Charlee." Skyler giggled.

Charlee did not. It was a phrase that amused everyone but her, especially when they uttered it accidentally. "Can you let me know if you hear from her?"

They hung up and Charlee dialed the number for Zoet Chocolates. No answer. She called Step Into History.

"Hello, dear. This is Evelyn. We met when you and your mom came to Sugar Springs, remember?"

Charlee was taken aback. "How did you know it was me?"

"Because Kober told us that you'd called earlier and the phone just rang for Skyler and then for Hugo. I made an educated guess."

Charlee smiled. She'd liked Evelyn and Max the minute she'd met them at Corky's Corner Sandwich Shop. Kober had been there too, and they'd all had a fun and lively lunch together. They were the ones who mentioned to Dena that the Marketplace was seeking tenants.

"Then you probably know what I'm going to say, too," Charlee said.

"You're worried about your mom."

"I am. It's just that she—"

"Why don't you hop in your car and drive down here? Put your mind at ease. By the time you get here, you and Dena can have a nice lunch together."

Charlee did some quick calculations. Two and a half hours, in good weather, but maybe a nice dinner. "You know what, Evelyn? I might just do that. I'm not getting any work done anyway."

"Oh, are you supposed to be writing? Maybe you

should keep pounding on that keyboard. Max and I are all caught up on your books, chomping at the bit for another."

"That's so kind of you, but you wouldn't say it if you'd read the drivel I wrote this morning."

"I find that highly doubtful, dear."

Charlee refrained from reading some of the passages as proof. She never wanted to draw back the curtain entirely for her readers and fans. She wanted them to know it was complicated and difficult to write a book, but she didn't want to actually show that particular sausage being made. "You're very generous, Evelyn. Please let me know if you talk to my mom."

"It'll be nice to see you again, dear. Be careful driving down here. And take the interstate, it'll be plowed."

Charlee called her brother. "Hey, Lance, feel like a trip to Sugar Springs?"

"I've got a shift. Why?"

Charlee didn't want to worry him so she simply said, "I just wanted to drive down and see Mom."

"Why don't you wait until the weather is better? I think the storm is heading this way."

"No, I checked. It's going south. By the time I get to Sugar Springs, it should be well into New Mexico."

"Whatev, Space Case. Don't get stuck in a snow drift."

Charlee smiled at his regular endearment for her. "Thanks for the tip. I'll do my best."

Next she called Ozzi. "Are you busy? Wanna go with me to my mom's?"

"I'd love to, but can you wait for the weekend? I can arrange for some time off then."

"No, I really wanted to go today." She and Ozzi had almost the identical conversation as she had with Lance, but the endearments were more endearing, and Ozzi knew she was worried.

Charlee grabbed some essentials for the trip: snacks, water, change of clothes, snacks, computer, power cords, snacks, car phone charger, blanket, snacks. Then she added some snacks.

Before she left, she ran upstairs and asked Barb and Don if they needed anything before she headed out of town. They didn't. Barb pressed a wrapped loaf of banana bread into her arms, for the trip. "Can't have too many road snacks!"

"Truer words were never spoken, my friend."

Kober

KOBER GLARED at the item "wedding cakes" on her menu board. "I'd rather starve and have this place fail than be complicit in one more marriage. I mean, wedding. I refuse to base my bakery's survival on that!" She muttered in staccato while she rinsed and wrung out a rag. She stared at the menu board as she wrapped a corner of it around her index finger. She was tempted to erase the entire board but opted for placing her finger on the W of "wedding cakes." She knew in her fury she'd make a mess of the surrounding menu items and would be forced to confess what she'd done—and why—then beg Skyler to work her artistic magic over the whole thing again.

Maybe she could manage the tiny erasure when she calmed down. Perhaps several years from now.

All morning she'd been expecting her husband Nic to call her, begging for forgiveness. *I don't know what I was thinking*, he'd say. *It was a momentary lapse! I didn't mean it!*

Alas. The only phone calls today—because she didn't count when the twins called to tattle on Wyatt—involved Dena's daughter. At least that was something of a diversion. But now it had been several hours without a peep from Nic.

She was moving through the stages—perhaps not of grief, but of something equally overwhelming. She began late last night sick to her stomach when Nic abruptly packed a bag and told her, "If I'm going to be snowed in, I want it to be with her."

"Her" turned out to be someone he worked with. Could it get any more cliché than that? She couldn't hear most of what he had said to her after that due to the drumbeat in her head that pounded the refrain *he's leaving us, he's leaving us, he's leaving us.*

She didn't even wonder until after she had vomited twice who Nic's floozie was. A client? His secretary? CEO of the company? It finally explained his late nights and how he "got busy with work" in Denver and had to stay there even when he was expected home in Sugar Springs. Kober felt a twinge of vindication that she wasn't crazy after all when her thoughts had drifted in that direction over these last few months.

Was this probably-too-young-for-him harlot even aware Nic had a wife and four kids tucked away in Sugar Springs? Did he tell her he was single? Did this long-legged bimbo engage in late night pillow talk with Nic? Did he regale her with stories about every little irritating thing Kober did that Nic never liked? Did this homewrecking side piece laugh demurely with a hand fluttering up to her throat, whispering to him that he was a saint—a saint—for putting up with a fishwife like Kober? Did this emaciated skank really not see any of Nic's faults? The way he snored? The back hair? The way he clipped his nails at the kitchen table?

The kids were sound asleep and hadn't heard any of it. He left for Denver with them none the wiser, leaving it up to Kober to break the news to them, the coward. She spent the rest of the night crying and vomiting and planning his murder, but in the morning couldn't bear to say anything to the kids. She woke them briefly to tell them the radio just announced a snow day and they could go back to sleep. She'd see them after work, expecting that while she was at the bakery she could work out just the right words to say to them. But *were* there right words to tell someone their entire world had shattered while they were sleeping and that nothing would ever be the same again?

By mid-morning it seemed she had made her way all the way through to fury—which surely *must* be the last stage—by yelling at a pan of brownies before slamming it into the oven. "So typical. Leaving me for a younger woman. The man never did have any imagination."

Kober had no idea if this woman was younger, fitter, blonde, long-legged, or half his age, but it made her feel better to think that Nic was the cliché and not herself.

She was a little miffed at Dena as well. Where was she? Didn't she know Kober needed to talk to her about all this? If nothing else, she wanted to hear her say out loud that Kober hadn't imagined all the things Dena had been promising were only figments of her imagination. "Reading too much into the situation" was how she remembered Dena describing Kober's concerns.

Kober unwrapped one of the enormous peanut butter cookies in the display case and took a big bite. By the time she'd eaten half of it, she felt decidedly calmer. Ah, the power of eating your feelings. It really worked. No wonder it was such a popular pastime.

Kober stared at the huge half-eaten cookie. How had she managed to get out of the house this morning with that fake smile plastered on her face without having eaten one of these? Thank goodness the kids had a snow day.

That meant they wouldn't troop over here after school. Kober knew she had the entire day to organize herself and come to grips with this turn of events.

But where was Dena? Kober had been talking to her over the last couple of months about Nic. She caromed back and forth with her emotions and Dena had helped her keep things in perspective, something she sorely needed at the moment.

She finished the peanut butter cookie, then eyed some others on the tray. Which would help her deal most expeditiously with this new batch of feelings? Cinnamon hazelnut biscotti? Oatmeal raisin? Snickerdoodle? Molasses?

She reached for a chocolate chocolate chunk and tore off the wrapper like it was Nic's face.

Hugo

HUGO HELPED Boyd clean the kitchen, all the while casting surreptitious glances at Boyd in a continuous effort to gauge his heart health.

He wasn't sneaky enough though, because finally Boyd said, "Sheesh, I'm fine already. The pain is almost gone."

"Almost?" Hugo asked, alarmed.

"Don't you ever get pains when you overdo something? You're acting like you haven't."

Hugo shrugged. "I've never had a heart attack before."

"Me neither. And I'm not now, for the record. My hawt is perfectly fine."

"I'd feel better if we called a doctor."

"And I'd feel worse. Guess that makes it a standoff." Boyd held up his hands. "Look, Hugo. Thank you for coming ovah. You didn't have to do that."

"You're right."

"But you did, we had a nice breakfast—even though it wasn't stuffed French toast—and now we can go to work. I've learned my lesson. Don't shovel snow until the storm is ovah—"

"Um … that wasn't technically the lesson."

"Whatever. Let's go to work."

"Let's call your doctor first."

"I don't have a doctor. I just moved here last month, remembah?"

"How could I forget? That would be like forgetting you were outside in the middle of a whiteout." Hugo smirked.

"Hey! That's a wicked good name for a new flavah! Wintah Whiteout." Boyd moved his hands across the air, creating a marquee only he could see. "Coconut ice cream with bits of peppermint. No … vanilla with bits of coconut. No! With gummy penguins. Or maybe something crunchy to evoke icicles." Boyd stood. "C'mon. Gotta get over there and get some of these ideas whipped up."

"You think people are coming to the Marketplace for ice cream on a day like this?"

"You think people will be there for chocolates?"

"More likely than ice cream."

"Care to make a small bet?" Boyd asked.

Hugo stared at Boyd while he contemplated. "We'll keep track of the number of customers who come in and actually buy something. Each transaction. Like if a mother comes in with ten kids and buys each one an ice cream cone, that just counts as one."

"And if someone comes in and orders a box of truffles to be delivered to their wife every month for seven years, that just counts as one also."

"Geez, wouldn't that be wonderful? That's a good idea. Maybe I'll work on some package delivery deals like that," Hugo mused.

"Focus, dude. And if I win, you have to let me make you some stuffed French toast."

Hugo nodded slowly. "Okay. And if I win, you have to go to the doctor."

"Hey, that's not—"

"Those are my terms. Take it or leave it." Hugo folded the dish towel and hung it over the handle of the oven.

Boyd stared hard and then clapped Hugo on the back, causing him to lose his balance. "You got yourself a deal!"

Boyd began getting ready to go to the Marketplace.

"Whoa, whoa, whoa." Hugo raised a hand to stop him. "You are not wearing flip flops and shorts in this blizzard."

Boyd sighed melodramatically. "Yes, Mommy." He returned, still wearing his shorts and Hawaiian shirt, but now he wore the gardening clogs he had on earlier.

"Try again."

Boyd shrugged. "Fat guys wear shorts. What can I tell ya?"

Hugo pointed at his feet. "Put on shoes."

"These are shoes."

"They are not."

"I don't have anything else."

"Liar." Hugo went into the spare room where the boxes labeled CLOTHES were stacked up. He rummaged through until he found a pair of sneakers. "Geez, you weren't kidding. But these will have to do."

Boyd began shoving his feet in them.

"With socks," Hugo commanded.

As they left the house, Hugo said, "I'm amending the bet. If I win, you go to the doctor *and* you go shopping for appropriate Colorado clothes."

"Ah, yer killin' me way worse than any hawt attack ever could."

———

Hugo and Boyd made it the short distance to the Marketplace in Hugo's expensive Land Rover, the vehicle of choice for the royal family, some of the Kardashians, and all the chocolatiers living in Sugar Springs. Hugo knew Boyd was dying to ask about the car, especially the 22-way heated and ventilated leather massage seats. Because everyone was. Max asked vague questions about how it handled the very first time he saw it. Kober was more direct and yelled across the parking lot, "Son of a manufacturer's suggested retail price, Ritchie Rich!"

"Just ask, already."

"You mean it?" Boyd said.

Hugo nodded. "It was a gift from my par—"

"Can I borrow it sometime?"

"Oh. That's not what I—Yes, as soon as you go to the doctor."

The snow had piled up impressively on unplowed streets, and Hugo concentrated on not spinning out. It probably wouldn't have mattered much if he had, since they only saw one other car driving around.

When they saw the parking lot devoid of any cars other than the tenants, they both let out a laugh.

"Let the wagering begin!" Boyd stepped out of the car and waved his arm in a regal manner.

"What happens if neither of us have any customers?" Hugo asked. "Who wins then?"

"I guess neither of us."

They went to their respective shops on opposite ends of the Marketplace. Despite the distance, Hugo heard Boyd singing, presumably while he created his Winter Whiteout ice cream concoction.

Crazy, Hugo thought as he peered into his chocolate case. He had only been in business a few months, but he knew he didn't need to make any more goodies for today's shoppers. If he had any customers at all today, he'd be surprised.

He saw the light flashing on the store's landline, which made him laugh. He barely remembered he had a phone there. He punched the button and listened to Dena's daughter ask if he'd seen Dena today.

Hugo walked through the vendor room to Dena's back door. He turned the knob and was surprised it was still locked. Typically, as soon as they got to the Marketplace, all the tenants rolled up their front security gates and unlocked their back doors into the common vendor area. He couldn't remember a time when anyone left the door locked.

Hugo walked into the cheese shop and asked Skyler, "Where's Dena?"

Skyler's eyes widened. "Nobody knows."

"Really? That's weird."

"Right?"

Hugo shrugged. "She probably went into Colorado Springs after work yesterday and decided not to drive back in the storm."

"Maybe. But wouldn't she have called one of us to take care of Twist? And when Jain went over there, she said the front door was unlocked."

"That doesn't prove much. Half this town doesn't lock their doors, I bet."

"But leaving Twist?"

"Yeah, I guess that is weird," Hugo agreed. "And no phone call? Who can't get to a phone these days?"

As if on cue, Skyler's phone rang. Hugo knew it was Jake her cheese supplier calling because of the way her voice went up two octaves.

Hugo gave her a wave and left the cheese shop. He did not feel like listening to her flirt with Jake.

Kateri

KATERI SAT in the Marketplace office, temporarily situated next to Hugo's chocolate shop. It was spacious, but wasn't much of an office, to tell the truth, consisting mostly of a battered old desk Evelyn and Max fished out of their basement. She expected she'd be relegated upstairs to one of the broom closets as soon as they were able to lease out this space.

She did have a new rolling pneumatic-lift chair and a Marketplace-business-only laptop, compliments of the newly-formed Sugar Mill Marketplace LLC, comprised of Evelyn, Max, Hugo, Skyler, Kober, and Dena. She was their first employee and her supplies were the first purchases the new company had made. Before she was hired, it seemed Dena had been trying to do everything. Which, of course, meant that not much had gotten done.

Kateri hadn't been on the job long, and really hadn't done much, except advocate for the laptop instead of a desktop computer so she could take it home. It would come in handy on those days when she couldn't get to the Marketplace because her grandmother needed her.

She hadn't made a big show of the relief she felt when Dena told her she could have flexible hours to care for her grandmother. She had promised she wouldn't abuse the privilege and trust that had been extended to her, but it seemed today would have been an excellent day to work from home. Because she was new, though, she felt pressure to avoid taking any advantages. She didn't want anyone to think she was a shirker, or wasn't executing her duties.

That said, she still wasn't entirely sure what her duties actually were. Not only was she new, the Marketplace Manager position was also new and nobody truly knew what all it entailed. She'd been expecting all the tenants to come together for a big meeting, hammering out what she was responsible for, but that hadn't happened yet. Maybe it never would. Everyone was so busy with their shops that they didn't have time to organize her job. Short-sighted of them, but oh well.

Kateri had busied herself with the obvious work to do. She knew she'd be responsible for seeking out and vetting businesses as potential tenants for the Marketplace, so she gathered up all the contracts and checklists and various paperwork she could find. After perusing it all, she compiled all the important bits into one document, cutting and pasting from each one until she felt she had template forms containing everything necessary to provide an informative packet for prospective tenants.

One thing she'd always hated was reinventing the proverbial wheel. Why cogitate on something over and over when you only needed to think it through once? That was something she learned in her previous life. Fat lot of good it did her, though.

The paperwork for Boyd Drummond and his Scoops Ice Creamery was a particular mess. She tried to make sense of it but couldn't. Exasperated, she went to the ice cream parlor.

"Mr Drummond—"

"Boyd!" he bellowed. "Call me Boyd. You want some ice cream?" He hurried over to the freezer case. "I just made this batch. I'm calling it Wintah Whiteout. Or maybe Snowstorm Surprise. It's got—"

"Explain this paperwork to me." She held out a stapled packet to him.

He didn't take it from her, just offered a big belly laugh, and began to scoop ice cream. "I'm not in a paperwork mood. Besides, it's a snow day!" He handed her a cup of ice cream.

She ignored it. "If it's a snow day, why are we all at work?" She stepped closer, almost touching his belly with the papers. "I don't understand why there are two of these contracts, but your signature isn't on either one." He still didn't take them from her. She flipped a few pages. "And it doesn't look like this got notarized properly."

They stared at each other for a bit.

"So... you don't want any ice cream?" Boyd asked, perplexed.

Kateri felt heat rise up her chest, toward her neck. She knew her face would quickly redden, something she decidedly did not want to happen at this moment. "I do not." She turned on her heel and marched back to her office, slamming the door behind her. She took big gulps of air. "How do they expect me to take care of things around here if they're not willing to meet me halfway?" she fumed. "Ice cream, indeed."

Kateri used her new template forms to recreate everything for Boyd Drummond and Scoops Ice Creamery. She marched back to the ice cream parlor and had Boyd sign all of it. By the time she had finished with him, his file was half the size with twice the information. She pounded her notary stamp harder than was necessary, but she felt she needed to illustrate the seriousness of proper paperwork.

After he signed everything, Boyd pushed an ice cream cone into her hand. She ate it at her desk. When she'd finished, she couldn't remember if she thanked him for it.

The heat rose up her chest again.

She wiped her mouth with a paper napkin and turned back to her computer.

She knew they used Mr Finster, the only attorney in Sugar Springs, for their legal work. She emailed him the contract templates she created and made sure to get his input about them. He seemed thrilled by her work and told her if she ever wanted to leave the Marketplace, she could come work for him. She'd seen his messy office before, however, and knew she would not be making that career change. Besides, she was secretly hoping that working as the Marketplace manager might be the new beginning she'd needed.

Kateri's stomach growled. She knew she shouldn't have had that ice cream. It somehow made her hungrier than before. She'd skipped breakfast, telling her grandmother she wasn't hungry as she placed a bowl of oatmeal in front of her. She knew she had to get to the grocery store soon, but her last paycheck was supposed to stretch across the pile of "past due" notices and wasn't quite that elastic. The calculations Kateri had jotted down on the back of one of the envelopes before bed last night helped set her mind at ease so she could eventually fall asleep. Next month she'd be all caught up, she predicted. Maybe the one after. But certainly before summer.

At her desk this morning, she pulled out the envelope. She knew she was alone in her office, but quickly folded it so the angry red "past due" stamp wasn't visible. The calculations seemed correct in the light of day too, so she opened the faded and warped plasticware she dug up from the back of a kitchen cabinet to use as her lunchbox. She nibbled on half the peanut butter sandwich she'd brought for lunch. It was only mid-morning, but she was starving. On any other day Kateri would have saved it to eat on her way home so she could truthfully tell her grandmother she'd just eaten. That way Grandmother would be more likely to accept a larger portion of the soup Kateri had planned for dinner.

Maybe this was the week they got back on track, at least as far as the pantry was concerned.

Or maybe not.

This was also the week she'd hoped to pin down Dena about some of the questions and concerns she was having about her position at the Marketplace, but it seemed she had taken off on a trip somewhere.

When Dena's daughter called, Kateri had been brusque, she knew, but she was terrified that Dena had mentioned this vacation of hers and Kateri had just forgotten. As the new Marketplace manager, she didn't want that to be one of her first official deeds. Or it might be one of her last, a gracious swan song of blunder.

As soon as Kateri had hung up with Dena's daughter, she scrambled, checking everywhere for any information from or about Dena. Relief coursed through her when she felt satisfied that Dena hadn't mentioned it. No emails, no voice mails, no texts, no sticky notes.

As she returned the rest of her sandwich to the faded and warped plasticware, she felt a pang of regret she hadn't been more helpful to Dena's daughter. Technically, keeping track of Dena was probably not part of her job description, but still. Perhaps she could have been less … like herself.

This Marketplace gig was new and it had been quite a while since she'd been thrust into the world. *Fake it til you make it* had worked for her once before. Until it had failed spectacularly.

Maybe this time it would be different.

Maybe this time she would be different.

Evelyn

EVELYN AND MAX were playing gin rummy in the studio, using the boxes they were going to empty and throw away as a makeshift card table. They both had cups of coffee and one of Kober's huge oatmeal cookies next to them. Evelyn had tried to be the grown-up and suggested to Max they could split one of the cookies. But when Max pointed out they were made of healthy oatmeal and it was still breakfast time if you squinted, how could she argue?

She calculated the last hand. "That's five hundred. I win."

"Five hundred? That can't be right." Max pulled the notepad and pencil toward him. He added a large one in front of each of his scores and recalculated. "Sorry. I beat you by more than three thousand points."

Evelyn sighed melodramatically. "It's going to be a long day snowed in with you. Are you sure you don't want to go spend the day with your girlfriend? Maybe she made pot roast."

Max jumped up, pulling Evelyn to her feet. He danced her around while singing "I Only Have Eyes For You." He dipped her at one point, long enough for her to take a bite of her cookie and offer one to him.

They both started breathing heavily when they heard a woman's voice.

"Are you open?"

Evelyn and Max waltzed toward the front of the studio and stopped in front of a harried-looking woman and a teenage girl covered in snow, at the end of a trail of snowy footprints. The girl's eyes looked like they could shoot a stream of venom clear across the room. Max took a skittish step backward from her as she suddenly yanked a knit cap from her head exposing flyaway red hair that seemed as angry as she was.

"I guess we are," Evelyn said warmly. "But we're a bit surprised anyone braved this storm to come in today."

The woman nodded. "Yeah, it's a mess out there, but we're staying at the inn and Deondra here is furious with me because her dad and brother went ahead to Aspen, but I wanted one more night here in Sugar Springs with my favorite daughter—"

"Only daughter," Deondra snapped.

"And I thought it would be fun to have one-on-one time with her." The woman brushed snow off her daughter's shoulders. "But I didn't know this storm was coming and now we're—"

"Trapped." Deondra and Evelyn finished together. Deondra's eyes flickered with surprise.

"Yes … trapped," her mother agreed sadly. "But before we killed each other in that lovely bed-and-breakfast room, I remembered hearing about this place, so here we are, untrapped and ready for a photographic adventure."

The way she said it, Evelyn knew that a photographic adventure was the last thing this woman wanted. But she also knew for a fact there was no beach or ski slope in

Sugar Springs and very iffy wifi at the bed-and-breakfast so they'd have to make do with what they could find at the Marketplace.

"Ugh," Evelyn said to Deondra. "You could be skiing in Aspen right now if it wasn't for your terrible mother wanting to spend time with you." Evelyn rolled her eyes teenage-style, then smiled. She held out her hand toward Deondra, as an invitation toward the back of the studio. "Let's find the perfect costume for you." Evelyn winked at the woman over her shoulder as she and the girl walked toward the clothing racks. "You look through these and pull out anything that strikes your fancy. Give me a holler when you're ready."

Evelyn walked back to the woman and Max. "We'll give you a memorable photo shoot. I promise."

"It's already been memorable," the woman said. "I'm Janet, by the way. And thank you. I don't know what we would have done if you hadn't been here."

"Probably killed each other," Max said.

"Probably." Janet glanced at Deondra as she angrily flung hangers across the metal rod. "So how does this work exactly? I give you all my money and we leave here in bright sunshine full of peace and harmony and the love and gratitude a daughter should have for her mother who's giving it her very best shot today?"

Max laughed. "Ah, you've been reading our promotional materials."

Evelyn pointed at the poster on the wall showing the package prices. Max explained the nuances of the different packages.

Janet's eyes began to glaze over. "Do I have to decide right now?"

"Absolutely not." Evelyn waved an arm around the empty studio. "If I had to guess, I'd say you had all day to decide. Maybe tomorrow as well. Do you want to be in the picture too?"

Janet shrugged and tipped her chin toward her daughter. "Let's just play that by ear, shall we?"

The two women walked over to where Deondra was still furiously sorting through the costumes.

Evelyn feigned a look of outrage. "What did these clothes ever do to you?"

Deondra got to the end of the assortment of women's clothes. "Poodle skirts? Flappers? Saloon girls? Pirate wench? Prim prairie wife?" She narrowed her eyes at Evelyn. "Where are the good female role models?"

Evelyn stared at the teenager. After a bit, a slow smile spread across Evelyn's face. She walked over to a separate rack and pulled out a simple beige-and-brown patterned knee-length shift with two-inch-wide straps at the shoulders. The stripes on the bodice ran horizontal. The skirt's matching vertical stripes hung in loose layers.

Deondra's eyes widened. "Is that made out of ... snakes?"

"Have I got a role model for you!"

Balaam

BALAAM PADDED QUIETLY into the photo studio, stopping before he reached Evelyn and Max. They were talking to a woman and Balaam had no interest in hearing their conversation. It likely had nothing to do with him, and she wore gloves which meant there were no treats at the ready, so what was the point?

He sat regally in his favorite spot where the sun lit up a square of carpet. He liked to pretend it was his castle and the rest of the carpet was where all the peasants lived. Sometimes he pretended the carpet was a moat and he pictured the peasants crying out for help to be saved from the vacuum cleaners he'd stocked it with. His tail flicked with nonchalance at their plight, then curled around his feet.

"Oh, that's Balaam," he heard Max say. "The evil one."

Balaam looked up from his daydream and the moat turned back into boring old carpet.

"Persian, right?" the woman said. "He's beautiful."

Finally. Someone who knows a quality feline on sight.

"Yes. And a bit evil," Evelyn said.

Balaam narrowed his eyes at her.

Evelyn shrugged at him. "You know it's true."

Balaam began grooming himself with tiny yet signifi-cant flicks of his pink tongue. He'd forgive them soon enough. Humans knew so little. But they did control the food.

Most of the food, anyway. He'd already made the rounds of the Marketplace. He'd snagged half a sesame encrusted cracker from the cheese shop, bacon bits from the bakery, and a cashew from the chocolate shop. Balaam knew enough to stay away from Hugo's dangerously toxic chocolate but was always curious when he saw Max nibbling a truffle or something. Perhaps he'd succumb to his curiosity one of these days. But you know what they say about that.

Balaam had finished his daily toilette and looked up to find Evelyn and the woman gone, and Max holding out a bite of cookie to him. Without wanting to appear too eager for Max's seemingly contrite apology, Balaam stared for a moment, then ran his tongue around his whiskers, unable to control himself any longer. He swiftly covered the ground between his carpet square and Max. He plucked the morsel from Max's hand with tiny front teeth, but before he could get away, Max scooped him up and kissed him on the top of his head. There was no way he could hiss at Max without dropping the cookie, so he simply wiggled in humiliating desperation until Max let him down.

Balaam chewed the cookie then turned to Max and hissed.

"Nice try, old bean. You know you love me."

Balaam stalked away, annoyed when Max was right about anything.

He would never admit it, but Max had also been right about Twist, too. Just out of the blue one day while Balaam had been staring at the dog curled up in her bed in the bookstore, Max had come up behind him. "Cats and dogs, man. They don't have to be enemies."

At the time, Balaam had thought that Max knew nothing about the world. Cats and dogs certainly did have to be enemies. Especially when the cat was him and the dog was an overly friendly white German shepherd with ears that transmitted her every thought and who had the gall—the utter gall—to boop him on the nose.

More than once.

The only other creature who had ever tried such nonsense was that stupid puppy someone had brought over to Max and Evelyn's house. "Isn't he cute, Balaam?" Evelyn had simpered.

As his reply, Balaam had slashed at his widdle puppy face with razor-sharp claws. It had done the job to teach the incessantly rowdy creature to keep away from him, but Balaam had a twinge of regret as he thought about it now. He wouldn't act the same way today. Especially because that creature was at least five times his size by now.

Would that dog boop Balaam the same way Twist had? He shuddered. What was the world coming to, anyway, when a clearly superior cat couldn't command respect?

Balaam strutted through the studio where he came upon a teenage girl emitting the kind of pheromones that warned off predators. Not on my watch, honey. The only pheromones in here will be emitted by yours truly. He hissed at her. She looked down at him. They stared at each other. Balaam hissed again. The girl hissed back, showing her teeth.

Balaam hurried away, glad to have put her in her place.

Balaam and Twist had come to a sort of détente too,

much like he had with the girl. Balaam would continue to hiss at Twist, while Twist would continue to boop Balaam and allow him to snuggle up in the cozy dog bed with her. It would be Even Steven, a mutually agreed upon contract. He still needed to get Twist's buy-in to the plan, though.

Balaam wandered over to the bookstore, puzzled when he found the security gate closed and the cozy dog bed empty.

Where was Twist?

Twist

JAIN HAD MIRACULOUSLY APPEARED JUST when Twist thought she was going to piddle on the carpet, something she hadn't done since she was a puppy. Dena had left in such a hurry, she hadn't pulled the board from the doggy door to the back yard. She had begun keeping it closed at night ever since the unfortunate turn of events that had occurred in the yard recently.

Twist's concern for Dena had taken a back seat to her urinary discomfort. She forgot about Dena entirely when she saw Jain pour an entire bowlful of kibble instead of the two tiny scoops Dena allowed. Dena said it was the veterinarian approved amount for her size, but Twist knew differently.

But now that she'd gobbled it down and made another foray into the yard, Twist began to worry about Dena again.

Just when she was thinking some resolute and careful investigation was in order, her attention was redirected to Jain who had produced a small bottle of something bright red from her coat pocket. Jain gave it several sturdy poundings against her palm then swept the brush across a couple of her own fingernails. "Fingernail polish," she explained. "Touching up."

Jain looked at Twist sitting there watching her. "Shake." Twist lifted a paw. While Jain studied her long claws, Twist sat still for a bit before demurely pulling away.

"Please?" Jain said. "It goes on toes too." She pulled off her own boots and socks to show Twist the pedicure on her own feet. "It won't hurt a bit. And it will kill some time until Dena gets back. I'll give you a treat when we're done."

Twist had to acknowledge that the red color made a splendid contrast against her snowy white fur. And Jain *had* offered bacon treats ....

After a moment of careful deliberation, Twist placed a delicate paw on Jain's knee, happy enough to oblige, under the circumstances.

After Twist's nails were all painted and dried, her treat consumed, and her dazzling toes marveled over, the boys showed up at Dena's house too. They stomped inside, tracking snow everywhere. Jain scolded them, requiring a clean-up of their mess.

Twist's flicker of concern about Dena again disappeared while she romped with the four kids. They even raced her around outside in the storm and built a snowman, which the twins promptly knocked over and used to duck behind as they lobbed snowballs at their older siblings.

Twist had a delightful time trying to nab a snowball in midair. Her prize for success, unfortunately, was a face full of wet snow. That part of the game was over. Instead, she concentrated on knocking down the kids as they ran around. They'd collapse in a drift, giggling helplessly as they tried to stand again, wearing more clothes than Twist had ever seen a person wear.

Thoughts about Dena niggled in her brain and she began to slow down, eventually sitting near the back door while the kids romped.

When they finally returned to the house, they shed their layers of clothing in a heap near the door, with their wet socks on top.

Twist nudged half-heartedly at the socks a couple of times, but due to her worry, couldn't summon the energy to pile them up somewhere. Perhaps later she'd put them with the socks Dena had given her, the red ones with the cartoon bones on them.

Where was Dena? Why'd she leave in the pitch black night? Was she ever coming back?

Dena

THE SUN HAD JUST BEGUN to lighten the sky. Normally when there was this much snow on the ground, it was as bright as day even in the middle of the night. But during this active blizzard, with snow blowing and swirling around the streetlights and in a trajectory straight at the headlights on their car, everything was a bit disorienting. Daylight would be a welcome turn of events, Dena thought. She wasn't even sure where they were.

Georgia had been yammering on and on about her water aerobics class and her boyfriend, but Dena had stopped listening. Instead, she kept trying to figure out what was going on. Dena hadn't worked out exactly why Georgia had kidnapped her or where they were going. And what could be the explanation behind the pink fuzzy handcuffs?

Dena abruptly interrupted Georgia's story. "This doesn't seem like some kind of weird sorority hazing prank, since we're at least fifty years out of college—well, you are. I'm only forty years out. Plus, I'm pretty sure I haven't tried to pledge any group lately. So ... I'm wondering. Did Beige Ann, Sue and/or Cassandra put you up to this? Are they still harping on the stupid hike we went on? I've told you—and them—a million times that I had nothing to do with what happened on that trail."

Georgia ignored Dena, but suddenly dove a hand into her bra and pulled out her phone. With her other hand she punched the buttons to answer it.

As far as Dena could tell, it hadn't even rung.

"Uh huh … yep … I am … is it? … okay." Georgia dropped the phone back into her cleavage and came out with a blue tablet she immediately popped into her mouth.

"What was that?" Dena asked sharply. "And would it be possible for you to keep two hands on the wheel in this storm?"

Georgia continued to ignore her, just kept traveling much too fast in the blizzard. After a swig from her water bottle, Dena was happy to see her place both hands appropriately on the steering wheel.

The gigantic Ikea store on the outskirts of Denver caught Dena's eye and she squinted out the passenger window. She gestured wildly at Georgia using both hands because it was impossible not to, what with the pink fuzzy handcuffs attached to her wrists. "This is almost where you get off to go to Charlee's apartment." Dena smiled. "Oh! Are you guys surprising me? It's not even my birthday." She relaxed and settled into her seat. She'd heard about pranks like this, but usually they were perpetrated on some unsuspecting workaholic who couldn't be bothered to take a family vacation.

Dena had been busy with her new bookstore these last few months, certainly, but if anyone would have offered her a day off for an adventure, she'd have immediately handed over the keys to the store. Dena frowned. To whom, though? Who exactly would be available to accept the keys to Thrice Sold Tales? She didn't have any employees, nor any prospects at the moment. But even if she did, she didn't have the money to pay them to work for her.

Today, in this storm, chances were good the Marketplace would be empty and it wouldn't matter if the bookstore was locked up tight or not. But the minute she returned to Sugar Springs after her adventure with Georgia and Charlee, and maybe Lance and Ozzi too, she'd have to crunch all her numbers to see when—or if—it would ever be financially viable to hire an employee.

She wondered what the plan was for today, and why Georgia and Charlee felt the need for this sham kidnapping. She hoped whatever plans they'd made wouldn't get thwarted by the snow.

Dena looked hopefully out her window as they neared the freeway exit she knew would take them toward Charlee's apartment complex. But when Georgia passed right by it, Dena's hope frittered away. Dena gazed longingly in the direction of Charlee's apartment.

"Why didn't you take Charlee's exit? Are we going to Lance's? Will you *please* tell me what you're doing?"

Dena's questions remained unspoken because at that moment Georgia slammed on the brakes and slid across the slippery highway toward the shoulder. Dena screeched and held on to the dashboard until the car came to a stop.

Before Dena could formulate words that weren't colorful expletives, Georgia had whipped out her phone. She dialed then spoke into it. "I'm going the wrong way. And it's snowing. What should I do?" She nodded along to whatever the person on the other end was saying to her, making occasional mm-hmm noises. "Okay." She shoved her phone back into her bra, but with a puzzled look brought out a different phone and stared at it.

"That's mine," Dena reminded her. "Can I have it back now? I'll call Charlee."

"No phone for you!" she said in a singsong voice, tucking it back into her bra.

Dena glanced behind them and shrieked. "You're not even off the road! You're gonna get us killed!"

"Pshaw. Don't be such a drama queen. My boyfriend says drama queens are the worst."

"That may well be, but if you want to see him again, you better either get moving or pull all the way off the road."

Georgia gave the car a little gas and the back end fishtailed a bit. She gave it some more gas and it fishtailed a lot.

Dena stuck her knuckles against her mouth to stifle the unhelpful scream that she knew was bubbling up.

Georgia floored it and her car shot back on to the highway across both lanes before she regained control in the fast lane. "There. All that nonsense for nothing." She'd only driven about ten feet when she shouted, "Oops!" and veered all the way across the highway again. With inches to spare, she took the exit. As they reached the intersection at the bottom of the exit, they slid right through. Thank goodness there were no cars coming because Georgia simply twisted her steering wheel and shot into the intersection, turning left, then returning to the freeway on the opposite side. When they were back on the interstate, Georgia plucked out her phone and yelled into it, "We're going the right way now!"

Dena didn't even think she'd dialed.

"We're not going to Charlee's?" Dena said, perplexed. "We drove all this way and we're not stopping to see her? Or Lance? Where *are* we going then? What exactly is your plan?" Dena held tight to the dashboard.

"I'm doing it." Georgia gave her a perplexed look. "I was supposed to get off at the exit and turn around."

"Says who?"

Georgia squinted through the snow blowing straight at the windshield. "My boyfriend."

Dena didn't mention how silly it sounded that her seventy-two-year-old friend called someone her boyfriend. Although this was not the time or place to attempt to come up with a more appropriate label. "Is that who you were talking to just now?"

"Of course. We talk all the time."

Dena listened as Georgia launched into a rambling, disjointed story about said boyfriend. The entire time they'd been in the car, starting hours before the sun had barely considered squeezing above the horizon in Sugar Springs, Georgia had been talking about him. At times she was as giddy as a schoolgirl, but at other times she sounded like she'd just boiled up a bunny.

For the first hour of their trip Dena had been asking Georgia questions. Where are we going? Why am I hand-cuffed? Why didn't you call me before you came all the way from Santa Fe? Aren't you driving a tad erratically? Could you slow down, you realize this is a blizzard, right? Can I have my phone? How 'bout we call Charlee or Lance? Maybe they can meet us and drive the rest of the way.

On a good day, in perfect weather, under optimal circumstances, Georgia was barely a proficient driver. But Dena had suspected that Georgia was on some kind of drug, and now, after seeing the blue pill, was sure of it.

And here they were, driving through a wet, relentless March snowstorm.

"What was that pill, Georgia? Is it because of your brain injury?"

"Quit interrupting me. I was telling a story."

"You've been talking pretty much nonstop since we got in the car. But you still haven't told me anything about what we're doing here, and why you felt the need to hand-cuff me."

Instead of answering her, Georgia launched into yet another story about her water aerobics class.

Every few miles, Dena offered to drive, but Georgia simply kept on with whatever story she was telling, ignoring Dena completely.

It made her too nervous to watch Georgia drive, only paying half as much attention to the road as Dena thought prudent. Instead she turned her head and stared out the passenger window.

March was typically Colorado's snowiest month and it wouldn't surprise Dena if this storm broke records.

But she still didn't know why they were out in it. It was becoming clear, though, that she wasn't being taken on an adventure with her kids.

Georgia hadn't answered one of Dena's questions on the drive, no matter how she worded them. Dena's questions simply seemed to remind Georgia of some water aerobics or boyfriend anecdote, often both. Sometimes Georgia answered with a simple raised eyebrow or quirk of her mouth. But mostly she ignored them.

She did, however, keep talking periodically to someone on the phone. Each time she did, her driving became even more erratic and scarier, if that was possible. Their conversations were cryptic to Dena. It seemed Georgia mostly listened. A couple of times, Dena wasn't even convinced there was anyone on the other end of the phone.

If Dena had an inkling that Georgia was not in her right mind when she showed up at her house in the middle of the night, she was absolutely sure of it now. Dena assumed her friend's state of mind—perhaps enhanced by too many prescriptions—had something to do with the injury she sustained on that hiking trip they'd taken a couple of months earlier, the last time Dena was in Santa Fe.

Georgia had been in the hospital for a long time, and then continued her recuperation at her enormous house in Santa Fe. Dena had tried to contact her repeatedly from Sugar Springs with no response. But then suddenly, Georgia had begun to initiate video chats with Dena.

While the contact was welcome, Dena still felt like something was wrong. Video chatting wasn't perfect, but their connections were decent enough to see that Georgia hadn't seemed like herself on any of their calls. Dena also had the impression someone was always there with Georgia, but they kept silent and out of camera range.

It had creeped Dena out more than once. The final time it happened Dena decided it must all be some prank Georgia was playing on her, perhaps with a friend, because Georgia had accused Dena of pushing her off that trail on purpose. It was so far-fetched, it had to be a prank.

Now it didn't seem that way at all.

Before Georgia had slapped the handcuffs on Dena, she had tried to get Georgia to go to the 24-hour clinic in Sugar Springs with her, but Georgia refused, adamant she was perfectly fine. Dena really wanted a medical professional to take a look at Georgia, but what was Dena supposed to do—pick her up, throw her in the trunk, and drive her to the clinic? Tie her to a chair and call 911? How do you give people help when they don't want it? Every idea Dena came up with was accompanied by the image of her son Lance, the cop, frowning and shaking his head, repeating, "That's a felony. That's a felony. That's a felony."

Eventually Dena capitulated, giving up on all the felony scenarios.

"Now that we're heading south, can I assume we're not on our way back to Sugar Springs and perhaps we're going to Santa Fe?"

"You know what happens when you assume."

"So we're not going to Santa Fe?"

"Did I say that?"

Dena took a deep breath. It wouldn't help if she lost her temper completely. Theoretically, she was a prisoner. That never ended well in the movies.

"Georgia," Dena said in a smooth, controlled voice. "When we get to Santa Fe, can we go to your water aerobics class?"

Georgia grinned and bounced in her seat. "I would love that!" She clamped a hand over her mouth. "You tricked me!"

"I'm not a complete idiot. I would have figured it out soon enough."

"I suppose. But I wanted it to be a surprise."

"Why?"

Georgia thought for a minute. "I don't remember."

Dena settled back in her seat. They were on their way to Santa Fe. If Georgia was excited about taking Dena to her water aerobics class, maybe she'd agree to visit her doctor's office as well. If nothing else, perhaps Dena could finally get Georgia's friends in Santa Fe to admit something might be terribly wrong with her.

"Can I have my phone?"

"Nope."

"I need to call the Marketplace and tell them I won't be in today."

"Don't be a ninny. Nobody is going to the Marketplace today. Snow day, knucklehead!"

"I need to call someone to take care of Twist. With the … um … surprise visit, I forgot to open her doggie door. And she'll be hungry."

Georgia didn't respond.

Dena kicked herself for not arguing more forcefully with Georgia about letting someone know where she was going. She could have easily overpowered Georgia, but knowing Georgia wasn't in her right mind changed everything. Dena was less concerned about herself and more concerned about Georgia.

But now the scales were beginning to balance.

Worry for Georgia had become worry for herself, Twist, and now her house. When Georgia had hustled her out to the car, Dena hadn't turned back to look, but now she worried that Georgia hadn't pulled her front door closed all the way. Was snow blowing in and piling up in her living room? Had Twist gotten out? Was she now lost and hungry in this storm?

"Do you remember closing my front door?"

"I don't remember my middle name most days," Georgia said sadly.

That was not a good sign, but Dena decided to believe Georgia had indeed closed her front door. I mean, it would be a habit, right? Everyone always closed their door when they left their house. Even when it wasn't their door or their house. But it would be like trying to remember if you brushed your teeth. Everyone on earth had to go feel the bristles to be certain.

Of course her front door was closed and Twist was safe inside. Doing the potty dance, probably, but safe.

Maybe when she didn't show up at the Marketplace someone would go look for her and find Twist alone. Poor Twist. Abandoned by Duke Bughata and now by her. Dena hoped there'd be a chance to make it up to her.

Would she bark like Lassie and raise an alarm? Would they figure out that Timmy wasn't in a well, but Dena was in a car careening down a slippery highway toward Santa Fe? Those odds seemed slim.

Dena eyed Georgia's chest. She contemplated diving into her bra and grabbing her phone nestled in Georgia's bra. Dena knew it was in Georgia's right cup, while Georgia's own phone lived in her left. She tried to remember if her phone was powered on or not. Had she shut it down last night? She couldn't remember. Maybe if someone called Dena's phone, Georgia would answer it by mistake, at which point Dena could make a ruckus and get rescued.

As they made their way south toward Santa Fe, Georgia began repeating stories she'd already told about her water aerobics class. It was so disjointed and rambling Dena couldn't even follow the anecdote she'd already heard.

Wait. Would a seventy-two-year-old woman just out of the hospital after a medically-induced coma and broken bones even be allowed to take a water aerobics class? Highly unlikely, Dena thought.

As Georgia hummed an atonal but robust version of "Bohemian Rhapsody," Dena's mind wandered to the Marketplace. If someone checked on Twist, would someone open the bookstore too? Dena didn't really think there'd be many customers on a day like this, but it didn't look good to have one store in the Marketplace shuttered while everyone else was open. Assuming everyone else made it into their shops.

Dena groaned. If nobody went into the Marketplace today, nobody would even notice that Dena wasn't there. How many days would pass before someone missed her?

Dena couldn't take the humming anymore. "When did

you start taking water aerobics? I don't remember you doing that."

"I started after I got out of the hospital. Said it would be good therapy and increase my stamina and whatnot. Oh! And look how strong I am!" Georgia took her hands off the steering wheel and flexed for Dena, first with goal-post arms, then by gripping the fingers of both hands together.

The car veered into the other lane causing Dena to close her eyes and squeal.

Georgia grabbed the wheel again and rolled her eyes at Dena. "You're such a baby. There's nobody around."

"All the more reason to worry about getting buried in a snowbank!"

"You should start taking water aerobics. Calm yourself down."

"I am calm!" Dena shouted.

Georgia looked sideways at her. "Riiiight."

It was clear to Dena that Georgia was in the throes of a mental health crisis of some kind and maybe talking to her wasn't the best idea, but she really wanted to know what Georgia planned to do back in Santa Fe.

"I'm assuming we're going to your house. What's going to happen when we get there?"

Georgia grinned. "You'll see."

At any other time, Dena would assume Georgia was kidnapping her for a surprise party or like that time Georgia took her on a trip to Joshua Tree to a wellness spa where she didn't want to be stuck alone with her carp pedicure and seaweed bath. Either a party or a spa would be perfectly fine with Dena. But again, the odds didn't seem to be with her.

After every twenty miles or so Georgia checked in again with whoever was on the other end of her phone, many times popping a blue tablet in her mouth. Every time she hung up, her driving became faster and more erratic, if that was possible.

Dena was a much more cautious driver in the snow, and, as she gripped the dashboard, she realized she was also a much more cautious passenger.

"If you take off these ridiculous handcuffs, I could drive and you could rest." Dena adopted a calm, reasonable, hardly scared-out-of-her-wits-at-all tone.

"I was told to keep you cuffed."

"By who?"

"Whom."

"By whom?"

"I was also told not to tell you that."

"By whom?"

Georgia giggled. "Nice try."

Dena glanced at the pink fuzzy cuffs around her wrists. They looked like they came from the party store, maybe favors for a … what? … bachelorette party? She gave yet another quick pull against them, but they didn't break. They didn't even squeak. Much sturdier than they looked. "You know, there's really no reason for these handcuffs anyway. I came with you willingly."

"Yeah, that was stupid of you."

Hugo

HUGO SAT with Boyd at one of the tables in the vendor room at the Marketplace. He kept shooting him worried glances out of the corner of his eye until Boyd caught him.

"Will you stop that, already? I'm perfectly fine."

"Then why do you keep struggling to take a deep breath?"

"Because I'm secretly in love with you and this is how I profess my undying devotion to you."

Hugo stared at him for a minute. "Yes, I can see that."

They sat in silence, sipping coffee and nibbling from a small plate of the healthiest dark chocolate truffles Hugo could find.

"Think we'll get any customers today with this storm?" Boyd asked.

"If you're asking if you should go make more ice cream, I can't imagine even the hardiest folks in Sugar Springs would trudge through a blizzard for a double scoop."

"Only because they haven't tasted it." Boyd boomed

out a laugh, then licked the piece of chocolate he held between two fingers.

Suddenly, voices and laughter reverberated through the Marketplace. It sounded as if a school bus just opened its doors.

Hugo and Boyd hurried through the chocolate shop into the promenade. Coming around the corner was a swarm of kids—at least a dozen—most of whom looked to be teenagers, but a few younger and a few older. One of the older ones pushed an Asian man in a wheelchair. Two of the younger kids pushed a teenager in a wheelchair. The children were all nationalities, sizes, shapes, and colors, moving as one, with purpose, like a school of fish. All carried a box or basket or tote bag. All were talking and laughing.

Hugo and Boyd stepped back, out of the way.

The man in the wheelchair waved his arm and spoke to the youngster pushing him. Immediately the wheelchair pivoted and rolled to a stop in front of Hugo and Boyd.

"Hello," he said. "I'm Pham. Which shop is mine?" The man spoke with a slight Asian accent.

Hugo and Boyd looked at each other.

"No idea," Hugo said. Pointing at the management office next to the chocolate shop, he added, "But Kateri probably knows. I'll—"

"I'll take it from here." Kateri had emerged from her office and brushed past Hugo and Boyd. "I'm Kateri Warcloud," she said to Pham. "Follow me."

The parade of people fell in line behind her as she marched into the shop between the management office and Boyd's ice cream shop. The security gate had already been raised. The noise hadn't abated one bit as Hugo and Boyd brought up the rear.

"Did you know they got another tenant?" Hugo whispered to Boyd.

"Nope. But I'm glad to finally have a neighbah. I was getting lonely all by myself at this end of the Marketplace."

They craned their necks to see into the packed shop. All the kids emptied their hands, stacking and stashing whatever they had carried in. As each put down their load, they turned and headed back out to the promenade, passing Hugo and Boyd. They offered a smile and pleasant greeting to them as they passed.

Hugo then knew what it felt like to be a flight attendant as people filtered off an airplane.

"Hi … hello … hi … hi, there…"

The shop had cleared out enough for Hugo and Boyd to make their way inside. Kateri was pointing things out to Pham, reading from a list she carried. Finally, she handed the page to him and said, "The code for your security gate is written on there. You can change it whenever you want, but you need to let me know what it is. There are times when someone might need to raise or lower it if you're not here."

Like today with Dena, Hugo thought, annoyed. Everyone else managed to get to the Marketplace to open in the storm. It was her idea to have rules about their hours in the first place and she couldn't even be bothered to follow them. Sheesh.

"This is Hugo Dekker and Boyd Drummond. Boyd owns the ice cream parlor next to you, and Hugo has the chocolate shop at the other end. If you need anything else, I'm in the office on the other side of you. Or text me. My number is on that paperwork." Kateri pointed at the paper Pham held, then turned and strode back to her office.

Hugo was always a bit put off by Kateri's brusque

manner. He thought it was rude, but Skyler had told him she thought it was just businesslike because Kateri had so much work to do. Hugo protested she couldn't have more work to do than the rest of them and they managed to be pleasant to each other. Skyler had no response to that.

Hugo stuck out his hand to Pham. "I'm sorry about her," indicating the direction Kateri had gone. "She's always … busy."

The older teen who had been pushing Pham's wheelchair bent to rearrange the blanket on Pham's lap. "I'll go help them get the rest of the stuff. You'll be okay?"

Pham waved him away. "I'll be fine." He smiled at Hugo and Boyd and said, "My kids act like I'm an invalid or something."

"Those are all your kids?" Boyd asked.

Before Pham could speak, though, they all swarmed back into the shop, carrying more boxes and bags. They began opening everything and pulling out items, asking and telling each other where things should go.

They reminded Hugo of locusts. A productive swarm of locusts.

Hugo, Boyd, and Pham watched as stock pots, wok pans, utensils, cutting boards, plastic prep containers, squirters, hot plates, and chopsticks appeared. Several stacks of two-toned lacquered bowls were carefully placed on a long communal table that four boys had carried in. Right after them, the largest boys hauled in what looked to Hugo like long pieces of plywood.

Hugo walked over and picked up one of the two-tone bowls, admiring it. It was shiny black on the outside with red lacquer inside. One side of each bowl had a dip, while on the opposite side, about half an inch from the rim, there were two holes. Hugo stared at it, trying to figure it out. After a bit, Pham rolled over to a pile of matching red chopsticks and picked up two. He rolled back to Hugo and placed a chopstick in each hole and rested the other end on the dip at the rim of the bowl.

"Ingenious!" Boyd bellowed, startling Pham.

"Those are beautiful," Hugo said. "But you're going to serve ramen or something in those? People will probably steal them."

Boyd indicated the long table. "Not if they only eat in here."

Pham cocked his head. "I thought lots of people sat at the little bistro tables around the Marketplace to eat. I figured they'd do the same with my noodles."

"Oh, they will," Hugo laughed. "And then they'll steal your beautiful bowls."

"No, people are good," Pham said.

"Are they?" Hugo asked pointedly.

"Pops, can you get out of our way?" one of the teenage girls asked.

Pham looked around the crowded shop, buzzing with activity, at a loss as to where 'out of the way' might be.

"C'mon." Boyd grabbed the handles of Pham's wheelchair and began pushing him toward the back door into the vendor room. "We'll get you a cup of coffee. You drink coffee?"

"I do. As soon as it's unpacked, I'll brew some Vietnamese coffee for you both."

"Until then, we'll have to make do with our boring stuff," Boyd said with a laugh.

Hugo moved a chair out of the way and Pham rolled up to the table. Boyd filled a cup and placed it in front of Pham, topping off the cups he and Hugo had been sipping from earlier.

Boyd settled his bulky frame into a chair. "So, you

never answered me," he said to Pham. "Those are all your kids?"

"Yep!" he said proudly. "I got a million more … all adopted or fostered."

"Wow," Hugo said. He tried to imagine the kind of person who would offer a home to that many children, but could only conjure the image of his own parents who had barely wanted him.

"So that's why they were all calling you Pops." Boyd nodded, as if it was the most natural thing in the world for a Vietnamese man in a wheelchair to be father to dozens of foster children. "You married?"

Pham nodded. "I was. To Mai. She died, last year. No, it's coming up on two years." For the first time, Pham's smile faded. "I still can't believe she's gone."

"I'm sorry," Hugo said.

"That must be hawd," Boyd said.

Pham brightened. "But the kids are my world now."

"They seem very helpful," Hugo said.

"Thank goodness for this snow day," Pham said. "They all wanted to help get Pham's House of Noodles," he flashed his hands with every word, like a neon sign, "set up. I wasn't sure how I was going to do it. Somebody always has something going on—basketball practice, play rehearsal, dance class, guitar lessons—but they all wanted to help. I almost resorted to a lottery."

"You could have brought them all ovah each day when they were free," Boyd said. "Spread out the work ovah two weeks or something."

Pham laughed. "You don't know these kids. They're all very driven, self-directed, highly organized. Many of them act that way because it's exactly what was missing from their homes. The others do it so they can keep up. In fact, I'm surprised they're not already done back there."

He tipped his head toward the back door of the noodle shop.

Hugo stood and sauntered over to the door to peek in. It was only fifteen years or so since he'd been a high school kid, so he felt confident he'd see them all goofing off back there. He stuck his head in and stared, wide-eyed.

There was now a wooden platform with ramps at either end giving Pham wheelchair access to the stove and one side of the prep table. They must have made it at home in pre-fab sections which they quickly assembled here.

The big pots were on the stove, steam already drifting toward the ceiling. Several kids manned the cutting boards, each with a pile of produce in front of them: carrots, zucchini, onions, mushrooms, celery. One of the girls filled the plastic prep containers after labeling each with neat handwriting. Two boys carefully concentrated as they filled squirters labeled *miso, soy, sweet,* and *hot.* Hugo didn't see any drips running down the sides. The taller boys and girls arranged decorative bamboo and rattan on the walls, along with vaguely Asian art they placed in groupings of three all around the shop. Tall teak shelves appeared along one wall, filled with the beautiful red and black serving bowls Hugo had admired earlier. The long communal table now had eight chairs around it, three on each side and one at each end.

Hugo gave a low whistle.

One of the older boys turned toward him and smiled. "Like it?"

"You've done a great job. I'm impressed."

"Pops deserves it," one of the girls said, to murmurs and nods of agreement.

Hugo returned to the table with Boyd and Pham.

"How's it going in there?" Boyd asked.

"It looks like they're almost done," Hugo said with surprise.

Pham didn't seem surprised at all. "They're good kids. Hard workers."

Pham had shed his coat and Hugo saw he wore a red, white, and blue patriotic t-shirt. "How long have you been here?" Hugo asked.

"Mai and I moved to Sugar Springs ... let's see ... twelve years ago. Maybe thirteen."

"And before that?"

Pham smiled at Hugo. "I've been around. Denver. California. Ramstein Air Base."

"You were in the military?"

Pham shook his head. "I was at the hospital. Got airlifted from Vietnam."

"You fought in the war?" Boyd asked, surprised.

"How I ended up in this." Pham rolled his wheelchair back and forth. He started to say more, but the kids burst through the door into the vendor room.

"Cool, a ping pong table!" one of the younger boys exclaimed.

"Go ahead and play," Boyd bellowed.

Four of them clamored for paddles and began slamming the orange ball back and forth.

"Come see, Pops!" One of the girls began pushing Pham toward his new restaurant, quickly abandoning him when she saw Balaam stroll in from the back door of the photography studio. "Oooh!" she squealed. "What a pretty kitty!" She stepped toward him.

Balaam took one look at the crowd and shot back the direction he came.

The girl was disappointed, but Hugo said, "You're not missing much. He's cranky."

Pham had rolled himself into his shop. "Kids! This is

beautiful! It's better than I even imagined." He wiped a tear that had slipped down his cheek. He held out his arms and each child in turn received a heartfelt hug.

Hugo watched, moved. He hoped these kids knew how lucky they were.

He suddenly felt quite jealous.

Kateri

"HI, GRANDMA. IS EVERYTHING OKAY?" Kateri moved her phone from her right hand to her left.

"Of course it is. You just talked to me an hour ago."

"I'm just worried the power will go off in this storm."

"Nope. Power is fine."

"What are you watching?" Kateri asked.

"What makes you think I'm watching anything?"

"Because I can hear the TV."

"Oh. Monk marathon. He's a pip, that one."

"Have you eaten anything? I left you the rest of that stew we had last night. And I'm making soup when I get home."

"I saw it. I'm not hungry. You can have it when you get home. No reason to make soup."

"Grandma …."

"Don't take that tone with me, young lady. I'm the one who *taught* you that tone. That's *my* tone!"

Kateri laughed. "Fine. But eat the stew. We have a new ramen place here. I'll—"

"What's ramen?"

"Asian soup. I'll have some of that and you can finish the stew."

"Are you sure?"

"Of course I'm sure. Now eat some lunch while you watch Monk. Call me if you need anything."

All the talk about the stew made Kateri's stomach grumble. She'd had to thin it down this morning before she left for the Marketplace because it barely filled half the bowl. She didn't want her grandmother to think there wasn't enough to eat. After her grandfather died, Kateri had learned how to stretch a dollar so far you could use it to fly a kite. It was simply another thing she'd taught herself. It happened to be the one thing she was sure wouldn't fail her, unlike her so-called friend and partner.

She shook her head, refusing to travel that path of memory. Nothing good ever came of that. Instead, she tried to ignore her growling stomach while she busied herself with organizing and finalizing the rest of Pham's paperwork. She'd take it over to him as soon as she checked over her figures for the Profit and Loss statement, and the projected budget for the next quarter. She wanted to finish all that so she'd have a clean desk to brainstorm some marketing ideas for the next few months.

She knew her survival depended on making herself indispensable around here.

Boyd

BOYD RAN INTO MAX, who asked him if Pham was moving in today. Boyd told him all about Pham's kids scurrying around to help him.

Max nodded. "Pham is really an inspirational guy. I'm so glad it worked out for him to open up at the Marketplace. Tell him Evelyn and I will come over later and say hi. We have a couple of customers I think will be here for a while."

"Customahs, you say?" Boyd thought about the bet he'd made with Hugo. A bet he desperately wanted to win.

"Yeah, probably the only ones today. Mother and teenage daughter. Got stuck in town because of the snow."

"Hey, do me a favah, Max. Don't tell Hugo about them." At Max's raised eyebrows, Boyd added, "We have a bet I'm trying to win."

"I don't think I want to know what you two have cooked up. Just make sure to stay out of Evelyn's way. I think she's about to drop some knowledge on these two."

Boyd hurried back to his shop and dug around for his best coupons and one of the last oversized plush ice cream cones he had left. Rocky Road. Max had told him the fabric marshmallows looked a bit like snowman snot and Boyd hadn't been able to get the image out of his head.

He stood in front of the ice cream counter debating whether to bring samples as well. But if he gave them samples, maybe they wouldn't want to buy more ice cream. Weren't mothers and teenage girls always watching their weight? He decided not to risk it. Just the coupons and plushie.

He peeked into the promenade and didn't see Hugo so he hurried around the corner the opposite direction from the chocolate shop. The ice cream parlor was exactly diagonal from the photo studio, but going this way took him by Kober's corner bakery. She had two security gates but had only opened the one in the front. He leaned against the side gate to catch his breath, making it rattle.

"Boyd? What are you doing over there?" Kober bellowed.

"Nothing!" he bellowed back. As he rounded the corner, he shook the plush ice cream cone over his head. "You never saw me!"

"If only I were so lucky!"

Boyd hurried past the bookstore and then the cheese shop. Skyler didn't look up. When he reached the edge of it, he stopped to catch his breath again.

When his breathing returned to a somewhat normal pattern, he sauntered past the studio. When he saw Evelyn with the two customers, he pretended like they had just given him an idea.

He presented the plushie to the girl. "Might you like this?" he asked her.

She gave it the onceover. "Um ... no?"

Boyd heard Max stifle a laugh.

"Are you sure?"

"Very," she said. "I'm fifteen, not three." The disdain in her voice did nothing to dissuade Boyd.

"I've had many, many fifteen-year-olds covet these ice cream cones. One even told me having it was her dream come true."

"It would be my nightmare."

"Deondra!" Janet scolded.

"Well, it would." She glared at her mother. "Don't you always tell me the truth shall set me free?"

"Yes, but—"

"Just practicing what you preach, Mom." Deondra shrugged. "What's that supposed to be anyway? Snot ice cream?"

"Yes, it is," Boyd said.

Deondra was taken aback.

"Well, it's not a giraffe! Of course it's ice cream," Boyd bellowed.

Deondra finally understood what was happening. "I didn't say *it's not ice cream*. I said it looks like snot ice cream."

Janet turned to Boyd and whispered. "I'm sorry about …" She waved an arm in her daughter's direction. "We're having kind of a rough day."

Boyd leaned in and pressed the coupons in her hand. "Then one or both of you are going to need ice cream at some point. There's nothing on this earth that ice cream can't fix. And I make the best." He tipped his chin in the direction of his shop. "Just on the othah side of the Marketplace there."

"Thank you," Janet said. "I think I saw a chocolate shop too. We might need both, after a day like this."

Boyd tried to keep his face neutral. He wanted to yell, "No, no, no! No chocolates! I'm trying to win a bet here!"

But he didn't. It took Herculean strength of will for him to say, "Yes, chocolates are good too."

He held out the big ice cream cone to Janet. "For you, good madame."

"I couldn't possibly. We flew and that wouldn't fit in our luggage. But thanks for the coupons!"

Boyd sighed and returned to his shop where he propped the plushie in the corner. "I expected more from you, Rocky Road."

Hugo

HUGO SAW Boyd sneaking around with a fistful of coupons and one of his stuffed ice cream cones, the ugly one Max always teased him about.

He's probably trying to bribe someone with it, Hugo thought. He tiptoed out to the promenade and followed Boyd to the photo studio. He couldn't hear what was being said, but saw a woman and a teenager both refuse the plushie. Boyd stuffed coupons in the woman's hand, though.

Hugo scurried back to the chocolate shop. He filled a bowl with assorted treats—chocolate-and-sea-salt-covered pretzels, truffles, chocolate-covered cherries, peanut clusters—then hurried across the vendor room, tucking the bowl into his torso like a football player so Boyd wouldn't see. He went in the back door of the photo studio, beginning to talk before he saw anyone.

"Max? Evelyn? Could I impose upon you to do a quick taste test for me?" He pretended to be startled when he saw the woman and teenager standing with them. "Oh, I'm sorry! I didn't know there were customers here."

"You're a lousy liar," Max told him, reaching for the bowl.

Hugo held it tight. "I was just wondering which of these go the best together. I'm going to test some new multi-treat packaging."

Max rolled his eyes.

Hugo began to offer the bowl around, explaining about each item, when Evelyn cut him off by grabbing the bowl.

"We're in the middle of something here, Hugo. Leave this with me and we'll let you know." She shooed him from the studio.

He left through the back door.

Boyd was leaning against the wall in the vendor room, grinning. "Cheatah, cheatah, pants on fire."

"Takes one to know one."

Dena

"GEORGIA, look. There's a truck stop at the next exit." Dena pointed at a sign. "We have to stop. I'm starving and I have to pee." It wasn't a lie, but in addition to her bodily needs, Dena was becoming very anxious about what trouble might be waiting for her when they got to Santa Fe. This truck stop might be her very last opportunity to summon help, not only for herself, but also for Georgia who became more manic with every passing mile. The blue pills didn't seem to help. "Seriously. I have to pee."

Georgia stared across at her as if she didn't believe her, which was rich, since she had teased Dena about her doll-sized bladder at least three times a week for the last fifteen years.

Regret wasn't nearly a big enough word for what Dena was feeling at this moment. When Georgia showed up at her house, she realized now that she should have picked her up, thrown her in the trunk, and driven her to the Sugar Springs Medical Clinic without a second thought, regardless of the fact it was probably a felony. No jury would convict her.

Georgia was clearly in the middle of a medical crisis and Dena had blown it. At the time, Dena thought she was helping Georgia by going along with her, assuming she'd see reason. But with every passing mile—and every blue pill she popped—Georgia got further from reality, and closer to whatever nefarious plot she had in store for Dena.

Back in Sugar Springs, Dena didn't even consider there was a nefarious plot in her immediate future. Now the thought filled her with dread.

The passenger side tires were suddenly driving well into the shoulder. Or at least what Dena assumed was the shoulder. It was impossible to tell with that much snow on the road. "Eyes on the road, please!"

Georgia jerked the steering wheel and slid straight across their lane and into the other.

Dena twisted in her seat, relieved there were no cars around them. "Take the next exit. Please?"

"Fine. But only because I have to pee too."

It officially worried Dena that there was no mocking of her tiny bladder. No comparing her to a lentil. No asking if she was part leprechaun. No teaspoon jokes.

Something really was off with Georgia.

Even though Dena truly did need a burger, fries, and the facilities, she also decided that getting all the way to Santa Fe with Georgia in this state might be impossible. She must get some help at the truck stop. Georgia wouldn't like it, but that's how it had to be. Enough was enough, and this was getting more dangerous by the minute ... for both of them.

Georgia took the off-ramp much too fast for conditions and almost landed them in a ditch. At the last minute she turned the wheel hard into the skid and by some miracle, they found themselves going the correct direction on the correct side of the road.

The truck stop, Dena was happy to discover, was one of the big ones.

"Sit still and be quiet," Georgia commanded. She pulled her phone from her bra, punched a couple of keys, listened for a bit, then began talking. "We are. We just got here." Georgia glanced around the parking lot. "Three semis, and … four cars, including mine." She giggled. Two of the trucks began moving across the parking lot. "Make that one semi. The other two are leaving." Georgia was silent, nodding and listening.

It was the quietest Georgia had been all day.

Dena wished she knew who was on the other end. She strained to hear their conversation, leaning as far as she could toward Georgia.

Georgia gave her a dirty look, switched the phone to her other ear, and rested her head against the window. "Good idea. Okay." She popped her phone back into her bra and dug around until she found Dena's. She pulled it out and put it on the dashboard in front of her. "Just in case you get any ideas in there." Georgia dug around in her bra some more and after a performance of wild contortions, said, "Aha!" and held up a key.

"Don't you carry a purse anymore?" Dena asked.

"This seems safer." Georgia gestured for Dena's handcuffs.

Dena held out her wrists, thrilled that she was going to be released. She was sure now she could get some help.

Georgia's hands trembled.

"Look at that shake you have going on. That's not normal. I'm sure it's because of those pills you keep popping. After we pee, let's get you to a doctor. Or maybe we can call 911 and they'll come to us so you don't have to drive anywhere."

Grunting a non-response, Georgia jabbed the key at

the handcuffs at least three times before coming close to the lock. Only after Dena wrapped her fingers around Georgia's wrist was she able to poke the key into the mechanism. She twisted it back and forth, first gently, then much more violently. Dena tried to help by thrusting her wrists apart, over and over.

They refused to budge. In fact, it seemed to Dena that they might have gotten tighter. It could have been panic swelling her wrists, however.

Georgia gave up. "Sorry." She dropped the key back in her bra.

"You're just going to leave these on me?"

"Looks like it." Georgia opened her car door.

"But—"

"You can stay here or come with. Up to you."

Dena huffed out a sigh. When Georgia glared at her, she wished she could take it back. She *was* handcuffed after all. "It's just … you know … hard." Dena struggled more than she needed to with the door handle.

It seemed like Georgia wanted to say something but changed her mind. Dena vowed to be as docile as possible until she could do something to fix this situation and get Georgia the help she obviously needed.

They began to walk toward the truck stop entrance. Georgia saw Dena glance around the parking lot.

"Oh. Almost forgot." Georgia pulled the scarf from around her neck and arranged it over the handcuffs, looping and tying so it would stay. After she finished, she smiled in a creepy, threatening way Dena had never seen before in all their years of friendship. "Behave yourself."

Now what? Part of Dena's plan was to flash the fact she was handcuffed to anyone she encountered.

Georgia pulled open both sets of glass doors at the entrance and ushered Dena inside. They stood, assessing the area. Dena was looking for other people, but Georgia only had her mind on the restroom because she pointed at the sign and began walking quickly in that direction.

They had to walk through the center of the gift shop. Nobody was shopping, and when Dena saw the "Closed" sign on the counter near the cash register, she realized nobody was working, either.

Dena followed Georgia into the women's room. She wasn't surprised to find it empty as well.

Georgia was in and out of her stall and washing her hands before Dena had barely managed anything.

"Um … Georgia?"

"What?"

"I … need some help."

"With what?"

"Everything?"

"You've gotta be kidding me."

Dena slid open the lock on her stall. She shrugged and held out her handcuffed wrists. "I can only do this." Dena hooked her thumbs at the very front of her fleece lounge pants and pulled them down about three inches. She glanced up at Georgia with a sickly, mortified smile. "You have to do it." Even the cartoon tacos seemed embarrassed.

"Oh my—No!"

"Then your only other option is to take these handcuffs off. And believe you me, whichever you choose, you better hurry."

At the look of impending emergency on Dena's face, Georgia plunged her hand into her bra and pulled out the key which she frantically jammed in the handcuffs. She tried to open them every-which-way, but still couldn't do it. She stared at the key. "Maybe I brought the wrong one."

"How many handcuff keys do you have?" Dena hopped from foot to foot. "C'mon, Georgia!"

"Turn around."

Dena spun.

Georgia yanked down her pants and was out of the stall before Dena even sat down.

"Thank you!" Dena called, relieved in a couple different ways. "But don't go anywhere. Your work here is not done."

When they finally left the restroom, and Georgia had washed her hands two more times and replaced the scarf over Dena's wrists, they began hunting for food. That is, Georgia hunted for food. Dena was hunting for a rescuer.

"Restaurant!" Georgia shouted and headed toward the sign. But it had a "Closed" sign near the cash register too.

They stood like meercats, heads swiveling in all directions.

"There's someone." Dena lifted both hands to point and the scarf slipped. Georgia hadn't looped and tied it like she had earlier.

"You wait here," Georgia said sternly.

That was fine with Dena because if there was anyone in here who could help her, this is where she'd find them. The person she'd seen was the cashier for the gas pumps and the market. With many of the roadside services and restaurants closed, this would be the crossroads of humanity, assuming there was any humanity to be found in a truck stop miles from everything besieged by a raging blizzard.

Dena's spirits lifted when she saw an orange trucker hat bobbing toward her, over the merchandise racks, coming from the direction of the restrooms. She stood behind a round freestanding rack of colorful sweatshirts that said "Mountains aren't funny ... they're hill areas" while she wiggled and maneuvered the scarf. Finally, it fell to her feet. She kicked it aside and took a few steps toward the man.

Startled at her sudden presence, he jumped when he saw her, but his friendly face turned to outright disgust when he saw the pink fuzzy handcuffs she held out to him. "Sir, I really need you right now."

"I don't know what you've heard about truckers, young lady, but this is beyond the pale!" He stomped off toward the cashier.

In a panic, Dena realized what it looked like she was offering the man. She began to hurry after him. "No, wait!" she called softly after him. He might be her only chance. She peeked around the rack of sweatshirts, but didn't see Georgia. The trucker was now at the register and Dena heard him talking to the cashier. She couldn't hear exactly what he said, but did catch the phrase, "unsavory clientele today" so she figured they were talking about her. She also heard him say, "funniest video montage I've ever seen," and then the unmistakable theme music from "The Simpson's."

She still couldn't put eyes on Georgia, so she began creeping forward toward the front register. She'd have to be quiet so Georgia couldn't hear her explaining that they needed to call 911 and get an ambulance out here for Georgia. If she thought the paramedics were coming for her, she'd certainly bolt. And who knew where she'd go or how much more erratically she'd start driving.

Dena heard the volume on the Simpson's video increase, which she was thankful for as it would cover any noise she made when she reached the trucker and the cashier.

The trucker spoke loudly over the sound of the video and said something to the cashier about the state patrol closing the highway. Dena relaxed a bit. Even if the trucker still believed she was unsavory and therefore unworthy of any help, at least with the highway closed, that meant there would be a police presence and a concentration of travelers waiting at a shelter of some kind, a church basement or school gym perhaps. More help for both Dena and Georgia.

Dena had made it up to the last row of shelves she could hide behind before she reached the front counter. She again peered all around. With no sign of Georgia, Dena began to tiptoe forward, trying to formulate what she'd say to get them to ignore the fuzzy pink handcuffs and take her seriously.

Suddenly a tight hand grabbed Dena's upper arm like a vice and pulled her backward, toward the door. Packages of chips, pretzels, beef jerky, and a gigantic bag of M&Ms were sent skittering behind them. Georgia hissed in her ear. "What do you think you're doing? I told you to behave."

"Wait! Help! I'm being kidnapped!" Dena called out frantically over the sound of "The Simpson's." But not before Georgia had hustled her outside.

Georgia was right, Dena thought ruefully. That water aerobics was really working for her.

Kober

KOBER'S personal life was overwhelmingly distracting, but not so much that she couldn't hear the cacophony from what she expected were a thousand voices. She left through the front of her shop into the promenade, and stood listening, trying to determine its origin. If her children were here, she might have ignored the noise altogether, assuming they were the cause of it. But her kids were at Dena's, playing with Twist. Or maybe they were home by now; she wasn't sure.

Her bakery took up the northeast corner of the Marketplace and she stared down the long expanse toward Evelyn and Max's *Step Into History* studio. Nobody in the promenade. Curiosity got the better of her and she turned the corner to reach the opposite side of the Marketplace.

Not a soul was in Boyd's ice cream parlor, but the space next to his—which had been unrented, as far as she knew—teemed with children of every size, age, and ethnicity. She peeked in the door and saw the space had been magically transformed into an Asian restaurant. She saw two boys holding up a sign being hammered in place, which read *Pham's House of Noodles.*

She walked through the site admiring the décor. Everyone greeted her politely and she nodded back, becoming confused as to whether this was some kind of school project or something. Had they rented space to one of those hands-on learning labs or something? If so, she didn't remember voting on it.

The back of the noodle shop was open and Kober stepped in the vendor area. The door to the management office was closed. Hugo measured coffee into the machine.

"Hey, did you know a bunch of kids were opening a ramen place here?" she asked him.

Hugo laughed and used the coffee scoop to point at a man in a wheelchair at the other end of the room sitting next to Boyd. "Kober, meet Pham." Hugo raised his voice. "Pham, this is Kober, she owns the bakery." Hugo used the scoop to point at the back door of the bakery.

Kober stood in the center of the vendor room, staring dumbly. Finally, the jumble all fell into place, like a magical jigsaw puzzle. "Oh," she said, "that makes more sense. You're the guy Max told us about. You have that big place out by the highway." She walked over and shook Pham's hand. "Nice to meet you. You've sure got a hard-working crew over there."

"Get this, Kobes—" Boyd said.

"Don't ever call me that again."

"Oh. Yeah. Sorry. But get this … those are all Pham's kids."

"Seriously?" Kober asked Pham. "I only have four and I'm a wreck."

Pham smiled. "They have their moments."

"They're all yours?" Kober was again having trouble understanding.

"Most are foster kids. Some I've adopted. And some have aged out of the system and had nowhere else to go." Pham shrugged. "What am I gonna do? Kick 'em out? If they don't mind sharing bedrooms and bathrooms, then I don't mind their company."

"Are they going to be here every day?" Kober asked.

"Oh, no, no, no. They all have school and work. They're just here today because everything's closed. I'll be here alone most days. Just like the rest of you."

"Kober's kids descend on this place like a bunch of balloons after school every day," Hugo said.

"That sounds nice," Pham said.

"Oh, then I didn't paint quite the right picture. You know how you let the air out of a balloon and it goes shrieking around the room? That's what I meant." Hugo grinned.

Kober made a face at Hugo, then shook her head at Pham. "They're perfectly lovely children. Nary a shriek in sight."

"If they're anything like their charming mother, I cannot wait to meet them."

Kober pointed at Pham. "You, I like." She pointed at Hugo. "You, not so much." Walking backwards toward the door to the bakery she said, "See you around, Pham. Welcome to the Sugar Mill Marketplace." Five minutes later, she had plated a bunch of goodies and walked through the vendor room to Pham's House of Noodles to deliver them to Pham's brood.

A few minutes later she sat at one of her bistro tables and nibbled a lemon bar, thinking about all those kids. Pham's and hers.

They were all dealt such a bad hand. She didn't know the story of any of Pham's kids, but if they were in the foster system, there had to have been some pretty terrible times for them.

Her own kids had two loving parents, who had the ability to care for them. At least until now. She felt her throat constrict and she forced herself to swallow another bite of the tart lemon bar.

It was lunchtime—maybe even past—and still her husband hadn't called. If only he'd call, maybe she'd never have to tell her kids anything. She had an entire scene in her head that she expected to be played out. It would be gauzy, like on a shimmery August day. In a meadow. Nic would run toward her in slow motion through a field of wisteria vines. She knew wisteria didn't grow in Sugar Springs—or anywhere in Colorado—but she always thought it would be perfect. If daisies were the friendliest flower, surely wisteria was the most romantic. Nic would be calling her name. She'd languidly turn her head, perhaps moving aside some of the wisteria vine, where she'd show her best side. When Nic reached her, she'd see tears in his eyes. He'd fall into her arms apologizing. "I've made a huge mistake," he'd say. "I can't survive without you." He'd beg her forgiveness, but she wouldn't say a word. She'd simply place one finger across his lips. Then he'd scoop her in his arms, as if she weighed no more than a feather from a swan—

Ah, who was she kidding. He hadn't even called to explain anything more matter-of-factly, forget the gauze and the teary eyes. Not even a text. Where was he going? Would he ever be back? What should she do with his clothes still hanging in the closet? If he never got around to telling her, then he couldn't be mad when she had a ritual bonfire for them. She made a mental note.

Kober stared at her lemon square and felt bile rising in

her throat. Her kids were not in the foster system, but they didn't have two parents any longer.

Hugo

AFTER PHAM'S kids got Pham's House of Noodles organized, they walked Pham through where they stashed everything, including his extra set of crutches. Hugo and Boyd had tagged along and took the tour with Pham.

Pham's kids were all so sweet and helpful to one another that Hugo got a lump in his throat and had to turn away.

He realized that was the difference between the family you chose and the family you were born into.

After the tour, Pham shooed all the children away from the Marketplace to go build a snowman or something. They piled in the vans with promises to drive carefully and to go straight home and stay there. One of the boys asked when he should be back to pick up Pham, but before he could answer, Hugo interrupted, saying, "I'll bring him home. No reason for you to come back out in the storm."

Pham thanked Hugo and when it was just Boyd, Hugo, and Pham in the noodle shop, Pham began to rearrange some things. "Sit down," he said to Hugo and Boyd. "Let me just get everything situated and I'll make us some phở. It's the least I can do since you've been so welcoming."

Boyd laughed. "All we did was sit around."

"No," Pham said. "You sat around with *me*, which made me feel welcome."

They watched while Pham effortlessly moved his wheelchair around the shop, up and over the ramp to the stove, down again to get more prep containers from the refrigerator. It didn't take long before they'd forgotten he was even in a wheelchair.

As Pham worked—boiling meat and bones, charring vegetables over a direct flame, toasting spices—their conversation flitted effortlessly around an entire landscape of free-ranging topics.

"It's almost ready," Pham said to Hugo. "Go see if Kateri and Kober would like to join us. There's plenty."

"I'll see if Evelyn and Max are still here."

"They have a customer," Boyd called after Hugo. To Pham he said, "Max said for me to tell you he'd stop by latah. I take it you've known him and Evelyn a while?"

"Ever since Mai and I moved here."

Hugo went next door. "Kateri, Pham made some soup. Come join us in his shop. You won't believe how fast those kids got it all set up."

Kateri chewed her bottom lip. "Tell him I already ate some stew I brought from home. But thanks."

"I'll tell him." Hugo didn't quite know what to make of Kateri. He saw her when she walked in this morning and she hadn't been carrying anything. The stew from home seemed to be a lie. It was possible she had allergies or just didn't like soup, or ethnic food, but why not just say that?

Hugo crossed over to the photo studio. He heard Evelyn talking, like she was telling a story. He listened from the back for a moment, but decided not to interrupt. Max, a woman, and a teenager were all listening to Evelyn with rapt attention.

At the bakery Hugo asked Kober if she wanted to try some of Pham's soup.

"Another day, perhaps."

That's all she said. And her voice wasn't like an airhorn.

"Aren't you feeling well?" he asked. "Maybe soup is exactly what you need."

"Soup can't cure my problems. Tell him thanks, though. And shut that door behind you."

Hugo frowned. None of them ever closed their back door. Kateri must have started a trend.

Hugo didn't like it.

"No takers," he said when he got back to Pham's. "Kateri already ate, Evelyn and Max have customers, and Kober thinks she might be coming down with something."

"More for us!" Boyd bellowed from the head of the communal table.

Hugo sat next him, but popped right back up when Pham placed a tray across his lap in the wheelchair and loaded it with three full bowls of soup. He used the beautiful lacquered bowls, poking a pair of chopsticks into the two holes, as well as placing a large ceramic spoon into each bowl.

"Sit down," Pham said. "I got this."

Pham placed a bowl in front of Hugo and one in front of Boyd, then rolled his chair into the space across from Hugo.

Hugo and Boyd both dug into the soup with the spoon.

"This is delicious," Hugo said. The broth was sublime and fragrant, meaty and smoky. The rice noodles were slightly chewy, providing texture and structure to the dish. The scallion, bean sprout, basil, and lime garnishes all balanced perfectly. And the spices! Hugo tried to identify them. He tasted fennel, cloves, coriander, and cinnamon, and of course the ginger he'd watched being charred, but Hugo knew he hadn't identified a couple. He asked Pham what flavors he was missing.

"I have a few secrets, but I can tell you about the star anise and cardamom."

"I don't care what's in it … it's wicked awesome!" Boyd offered a thumbs-up.

The three of them spooned broth and twirled long noodles on chopsticks while they chatted some more about inconsequentials—the storm, the Colorado sports teams, Sugar Springs gardening tips for when spring finally made an appearance.

Hugo and Pham had finished their soup, but Boyd had pushed his chair a bit away from the table and was using his napkin to mop his brow.

"What's the matter?" Hugo asked quickly.

"I guess that soup was too spicy," Boyd said.

"That soup was not spicy at all, and you know it," Hugo said. When Boyd began rubbing his left arm, Hugo stood. "I don't care what you say. I'm calling 911."

Boyd didn't argue this time.

Hugo stepped away while jabbing at his phone. "Medical. Yes. We're at the Sugar Mill Marketplace and there's a man here having a heart attack. No, he's sitting. No, we don't have a defibrillator here." Hugo listened for a moment. "Are you kidding me? Okay, we're on our way." Hugo stashed his phone. "One ambulance is stuck and the other one is out on a call. I'm driving you to the hospital."

"The clinic here in town?" Boyd asked with a grimace.

"No. The one in Colorado Springs. C'mon. We've gotta hustle."

Pham rolled over to where his crutches hung on the

wall. "I'm going with you." As he pushed himself up, the blanket fell from his lap. Hugo saw one of his legs was gone just above the knee. Pham grabbed the crutches, then gave his empty wheelchair a shove toward Hugo. "Put him in this."

Neither Hugo nor Boyd argued.

Evelyn

EVELYN OFFERED Janet and her daughter Deondra seats on the props in the photo studio. The women sat on bales of "hay" made of lightweight plastic, while the teenager sat astride a saddle mounted on a wooden sawhorse. Max had rolled his office chair nearby.

"You are absolutely right that some of these costumes are stereotypes, Deondra. But remember your history. One of the most famous pirates was Grace O'Malley, an Irishwoman. A redhead like you. Known as the Pirate Queen. As fierce and protective as any man. She saved her family home from marauders. And there was Sadie Farrell, an American river pirate. She got her ear bitten off in a skirmish and forever after that wore it in a locket around her neck."

"Ew."

"And, of course, Charlotte de Berry who was said to disguise herself as a man and rose through the ranks to captain the ship. Anne Bonny disguised herself as a man, too, but was found out when it became obvious she was pregnant. But I think my favorite pirate was Lady Mary

Killigrew, whose husband was hired by the Queen to stop piracy. While he was away, though, Lady Mary would indulge in piracy herself, using the staff at her castle as her crew. That's some kind of nerve, right?" Evelyn laughed. "But there were many fewer female pirates around the world. Of course, their stories seem much more glamorous than being a saloon girl or pioneer woman here on the prairie. Many of these women of the American West had rich, full lives with just as much adventure as someone on the high seas."

Deondra looked dubious.

"It's true. I want you to know about Rattlesnake Kate. She was definitely no stereotype. In fact, you'd be hard-pressed to find anyone—man or woman—equal to her accomplishments."

Evelyn handed the dress to the girl.

Deondra leaned closer and studied the dress. "It *is* made out of snakes!" She peered at it with wide eyes.

Janet wrinkled her nose. "I bet that was hard to iron," she joked.

"Almost everything about Kate's life was hard," Evelyn said. She looked at Deondra. "The first thing you need to know about Rattlesnake Kate is that she was a real person who was born in 1893, near Longmont, which is a bit north of Denver. This, however, is not her real dress, but it is an almost exact replica. A lot of what we know about Kate comes from letters to and from her, as well as the story she wrote about the rattlesnakes for a writing contest."

Evelyn started to settle on to the fake bale of hay prop, but then popped back up. "You know what? Let's go to the bakery. I could use something sweet. My treat."

Deondra's eyes lit up and she looked for a place to hang the dress.

"Bring it," Evelyn said. She turned to Max. "You're okay with minding the fort, aren't you? Unless you're desperate to hear this story for the ten-thousandth time. Maybe you could deal with those boxes."

"Dang it. I would, but I have an appointment." Max waved a fat book at them. "Got me an important meeting with Eleanor and Franklin. But bring me back something."

"Another great woman, Eleanor Roosevelt," Evelyn murmured, waving at Max from the promenade. "She'd empty those boxes." She led them into the bakery.

"Hi Kober. This is Janet and her daughter Deondra. They got caught in Sugar Springs because of the storm, so I'm treating them to whatever they want before our photo shoot. If you don't mind, we're going to have a little chat in here where it's more comfy." Evelyn took a big cartoon sniff. "And if those are brownies, you may as well bring me the pan."

"I take it you'll be here for a while?" Kober asked with a smile.

Deondra said, "She's going to tell us about Rattlesnake Kate. I'm dying to know about the rattlesnakes."

"Me too," Janet said.

"Everyone does. It was really what made Kate famous, but in the greater scheme of things, that was just one of many ways she proved to be a survivor," Evelyn said.

"Now I want to know too," Kober said. "I didn't know until this very minute how much I wanted to know about Rattlesnake Kate. I'll just be doing my thing back here, but you speak up so I can hear too. I'll make you up a little plate of assorted goodies. Hot chocolate too?"

"Yes, please," they all said.

They settled into one of the tables and Evelyn began. "Little bit of context first. Kate's mom died when she was only a few years old so she never had a mother to speak of.

Her dad raised her to be rootin' and tootin' … like another son, so she grew up fairly rough-and-tumble, strong, self-sufficient, never felt like she was weak. She refused the concept of femininity as it existed back then. She wanted so much more for herself—a family, financial success, fame, independence. She took off when she wasn't much older than you, Deondra, supporting herself and bouncing around the west. When she was still a teenager, she fell in love with a man she wasn't allowed to marry—"

"No fair! Why?" Deondra asked.

"Because she was too young," Janet answered quickly.

"She was awfully young," Evelyn agreed, "but that happened all the time in those days. It's different now. And we don't really know why Kate didn't marry him. A few years later, she did get married, but they divorced not too long after. But then … *then* she met Jack Slaughterback, and took his name. He was everything she ever wanted. They got married, homesteaded, adopted a little boy named Ernie. Unfortunately, Jack was a gambler and their relationship was volatile."

"What does that mean?" Deondra asked.

"Unpredictable," her mother said. "Like how you go from hot to cold, one minute hating me and one minute laughing with me."

"I don't hate you," Deondra mumbled, picking at a fingernail.

"Well, Jack and Kate didn't hate each other either," Evelyn said. "They'd fight—mostly about money and the way he tried to gamble it all away—but they'd make up, then fight again and he'd leave, then he'd come back. They did this over and over again."

"This doesn't make her sound much like a survivor. More like an enabler," Kober grumbled, carrying a tray with three cups, a carafe, and a plate piled high with brownies, lemon bars, gingersnaps, and coconut macaroons.

"Maybe I'm not telling it right," Evelyn said, "but because Kate couldn't ever depend on Jack, she had to take matters into her own hands constantly. She had to figure out how to make a go of it on their dryland farm—"

"What's that?" Deondra asked.

"A dryland farm—which is what they had, up near Greeley—didn't use irrigation, like they do now. They didn't have those enormous sprinklers you see in fields these days. It was a tough, tough life because it didn't rain much there and because they didn't use irrigation, they'd plow the water under, literally. When it rained or snowed, they'd be out there with their plows, burying the water so it wouldn't evaporate. In the 1930s, when they were trying to make a go of the farm, there was a terrible drought in Colorado. You've studied the Dust Bowl?"

Deondra nodded.

"Well, it hit Colorado hard. Between her husband Jack leaving her alone for so much of the time, and the difficult farming conditions, Kate had to resort to all kinds of creative ways to earn money for her and Ernie, the little boy they adopted. Luckily, she was pretty savvy. One of the things she did was brew up moonshine, which was illegal. They called it bootlegging."

"Like in *The Great Gatsby*. Didn't he get rich from that?" Deondra said.

"Wow. Impressive," Janet said.

Deondra blushed.

"Lots of people got rich because of Prohibition. Kate wasn't one of them, but she was always able to pay her bills. Eventually, though, she was arrested for brewing up hooch, even though the story goes that she hid her still in her goat pen to cover up the smell. But I guess they found it anyway. She wouldn't leave Ernie, though, so they let her take him to jail with her."

"Can you imagine?" Janet said with wide eyes.

"It was only overnight, but yes, it was another example of Kate doing things her way." Evelyn reached for a brownie and took a bite.

"But what about the snakes?" Deondra asked impatiently.

Evelyn smiled while she chewed, knowing she'd hooked her with Kate's story. Trying to draw out Deondra's anticipation a bit longer, she slowly took another bite. Crumbs rained down.

Where was Balaam when she needed him?

Balaam

BALAAM STROLLED the Marketplace looking for Evelyn. The place was a bore today. No Twist to ignore. Hardly anyone around, for that matter, and because of that, no surprise treats.

He never knew what the day would bring, food-wise, except for the can Evelyn opened every morning at home and the kibble tossed in his bowl in the back of the studio.

Almost always, though, creatures in those wheeled conveyances—strollers, Evelyn called them—dropped tasty tidbits. Balaam could follow them all around the marketplace, cleaning up after them. He considered it a favor to the custodians who came in to work their magic every night.

That, in addition to picking up anything that dropped inside the shops, was his constant devotion.

It was unfortunate that it often ruined his appetite for dinner and worried Evelyn, but that was a small price to pay.

He strutted through the studio, glad that horrible girl

who hissed at him earlier wasn't there any longer. But neither was Evelyn. Just Max.

"Hey, devil cat," Max said. "What's shakin'?"

Balaam was offended that Max believed anything on him would do anything as crass as *shake*. He was in control of his limbs at all times. Once in a while his fur would puff, which was humiliating when it signaled he got spooked, but what could he do? To know him was to love him, even when he looked like a dandelion gone to seed.

He lifted a paw and licked it, all the while staring at Max's fingers. Was he holding treats of any kind?

"I'm fine, thanks for asking. And you?" Max said.

Balaam wasn't sure if Max truly cared whether he was fine or not so he continued to stare up at him, piercing through Max's very core with narrowed copper-colored eyes. He did not understand how Max could be so oblivious to his entreaty, but no tidbits magically fell from Max's fingers.

Balaam walked on, convinced he would not survive this day.

He wound his way through the cheese shop where Skyler stared at that shiny box she always carried around. Today it was speaking to her about making mozzarella from just two ingredients. Didn't she know she had mozzarella right in her display case?

Nothing on the floor. Such a lazy woman. Had she been staring at that screen the entire day?

Balaam circled the vendor room for leftover bites of sandwiches or a cheese puff. He'd recently discovered their infinite delights. The airy crunch. The fact they were both a delicious treat *and* a toy. The powdered cheese that coated his whiskers also offered a snack for later.

Alas, nothing.

He meandered through the back of the bakery, always

good for a nibble or two. That woman was a mess, constantly dropping deliciousness on the floor. Balaam had begun to wonder if she did it on purpose. Today he found half a macaroon and proudly carried it between tiny front teeth while he walked through the customer area in the front of the bakery.

Ack! The girl from earlier was sitting at a table with Evelyn and the other woman.

Balaam dropped the cookie and shot out of the bakery before he turned into a dandelion puff. He hoped Evelyn could save herself.

Evelyn

EVELYN LAUGHED. "Okay, the snakes. Have I described for you a solid example of a tough western gal?"

Deondra and Janet both nodded.

"Good. So, she and Ernie, who was about three, were on horseback out riding on the prairie heading somewhere, I don't remember. But she had to get off the horse to open a gate and when she did, she heard, and then saw a rattlesnake nearby ready to pounce on her. So she shot it. Then she saw another and another. Shot them too. She was feeling pretty smug that she had her rifle handy. But then she saw like twenty or thirty coming her way and knew she didn't have enough bullets for all of them."

Deondra's hand fluttered to her mouth.

"Exactly! Just try and picture being in that situation." Evelyn lowered her gaze at Deondra. "It gets worse. She sees these thirty angry rattlesnakes coming her way and knows her gun is going to be useless. But she sees a *No Hunting* sign which she yanks from the ground then uses it as a weapon. She kills all these snakes, but more keep coming. She's scared out of her wits, as you can imagine, but just keeps twirling and striking and killing her way out of them until she can get back to her horse, where Ernie has been sitting watching all this. It took her two hours to fight all of them. When she was done, there were," Evelyn paused for emphasis, "one hundred and forty dead rattlesnakes."

Janet and Deondra gasped. Kober had pulled up a chair and sat with them, listening raptly, munching on a gingersnap from the plate. Max had wandered in also and reached for a brownie.

Evelyn nodded gravely. "Rattlesnake Kate fought her way out of the middle of a rattlesnake migration and lived to tell the tale. I don't even think she got bitten. The news spread like wildfire across the community, as you can imagine, and before she knew it, there was a reporter there who took her picture in front of all the strung-up snakes. It made her famous."

Deondra stroked the replica dress on her lap and said with awe, "And she made a dress out of their skins."

"And a necklace from the rattles. And a pair of shoes, I think. I know the actual dress is on display at a museum in Greeley, if you have time to go see it."

The women all sipped their cocoa, nibbled treats and pondered the story for a few moments. Whenever Evelyn thought about Rattlesnake Kate, or relayed her story to someone—which she did with alarming frequency—she wondered what she would have done in a life-or-death situation like that. Not only did Kate need to survive herself, but her little boy was out there too, and she had to keep him safe. Parents could move mountains to save their children, this Evelyn knew from experience. But if the horse had been bitten, or if the migration took up a larger area, how would she and Ernie have made it the couple miles back to town?

"That's … amazing," Deondra said. "How terrifying that must have been."

"Kate faced a lot of snakes in her life," Evelyn said, "but most she couldn't make a dress out of. She was struck by lightning. She was attacked by one of her farmhands. She was beaten and robbed. She married and divorced three more times, for a total of six husbands. I think she searched all her life for a relationship that allowed her to be herself, where she could live exactly the way she wanted."

"What happened to her?" Janet asked.

"She died in 1969 from some illness. She was seventy-six."

Deondra stood and picked up the snake dress, holding it in front of her, as if she wore it. "You should have a million of these, and none of the prairie dresses or wench costumes."

Evelyn laughed. "I don't think that would work out too well, but I'll tell you what. I'll get a rattlesnake necklace and matching shoes, for a complete Rattlesnake Kate outfit."

"Deal. Can we go take our pictures now?"

"Absolutely."

"What are you going to wear, Mom?"

Janet looked at the ceiling while she contemplated. "I think I'll wear one of those prairie dresses—"

Deondra groaned.

"But I'll add the black cowboy boots I saw, a black hat, and a rifle. And maybe there's a moonshine jug around somewhere?"

Max's eyes lit up and he hurried toward the studio, calling, "I have just the thing!"

Evelyn said to Deondra, "So, that's the story of

Rattlesnake Kate … do you still think there weren't any good role models in the olden days?"

"You've convinced me. She's an excellent role model and the ultimate survivor. I approve."

"A perfect Colorado tale," Janet said. "I approve too."

They cleaned up their mess, carrying plates and mugs to the back of the bakery.

Kober jumped at the noise, then turned her head and swiped at her face with her apron.

It was clear to Evelyn that Kober's mind had been elsewhere, and equally clear she wiped away tears rather than wayward flour. When Kober turned back, she sported a broad grin, but she wasn't fooling Evelyn. She was worried about something.

"Thanks for letting us hang out here, Kober," Evelyn said.

"Are you kidding? I haven't been this entertained at work since that guy offered me roller blading lessons in exchange for a dozen blueberry streusel muffins."

Evelyn laughed. "We were all entertained that day, the way you careened down the promenade. I thought you were going to crash right through the plate glass!"

"I told him if he ever did that again, to *start* with the lesson on how to stop."

"I love roller blading," Janet said.

Deondra's eyes widened at her mother's statement. "*You* roller blade?"

"I led a rich and full life along Venice Beach back in the day. I was no Rattlesnake Kate, but I survived some adventures."

Deondra's face lit up with new respect for her mother.

What was it about kids? Evelyn wondered. Why did they think their parents had always only been their parents?

Evelyn thought back to when she was young and found out her own mother had dated several men before she got married. She'd been scandalized and told her mother so. Her mother had simply laughed at her. "Evelyn, my darling girl. How was I supposed to know who my prince was if I hadn't kissed all those toads?"

And her dad? Evelyn smiled now at the memory of him scooping Mom in his arms and dancing her around the house. He didn't know Evelyn was nearby and she'd heard him say, "This reminds me of *that* night. You know, the one that ended in the hay loft." The way Mom had blushed when Dad pinched her bottom had scandalized Evelyn and she ran upstairs before they discovered her there. She remembered writing pages and pages about it in her diary, trying to understand it all.

Of course, she and Max had probably scandalized their son several times too and never knew it.

Evelyn's face clouded at the thought of Oscar and she returned to listening to Janet and Kober discussing their various roller blading escapades.

"Shall we go take some photos?" Evelyn asked Janet and Deondra.

As they walked back to the studio Deondra said, "I think Rattlesnake Kate is amazeballs and I can't wait to tell all my friends about her."

"I saw a great musical in Denver about Rattlesnake Kate. It was written by two women, Neyla Pekarek and Karen Hartman. Keep an eye out for it, it was an astounding night of theatre. Even Max approved. I bet you can look it up on the internet."

"You know, all those prairie women are my role models," Janet said. "The Native women, the pioneer women, the farm wives. All of them endured so many things I can only imagine. They had to be smart, strong, and brave. They were survivors, through and through."

"Plenty of modern women are my role models, too," Evelyn said, dropping an arm around Janet's shoulder. "Some survive raising children."

Charlee

AFTER TOO MANY WHITE-KNUCKLE MILES, Charlee
finally reached Dena's house in mid-afternoon.

Before she left Denver, she had told both Lance and
Ozzi several times that the storm would be long south of
Sugar Springs by the time she got there, to alleviate their
concerns, and had even begun to believe it herself. At least
until the visibility became worse instead of better. She still
had not heard from her mother, so there was no way she
was turning around anyway.

The snowplows had done nothing, since the storm was
still raging, so Charlee carefully picked her way through
Sugar Springs with only one close call where she took a
curve and her wheels didn't respond. She righted the car
and rode the crest of adrenaline all the way into Dena's
driveway.

The snow in the driveway was pristine until she drove
on it. Before opening the car door, she gathered her purse
and stuck one arm in the sleeve of her coat, in too much of
a hurry to be bothered with both. She struggled through

the snow to one of the small garage windows, cupping her hands around her face and squinting as she peered inside. Relieved to see Dena's car in there, she felt a bit foolish driving all the way to Sugar Springs from Denver in a blizzard.

Charlee hurried to the front door. Thankful it was unlocked, she flung it open and stumbled and slid inside. As she shut the door behind her, she called, "Mom! Mom, it's me."

No answer.

Charlee kicked off her boots and dropped her coat on the floor, rushing toward the bedroom. Maybe she'd been here all along and needed help!

"Mom! Mom!" Charlee ran into the bedroom and saw Dena's unmade bed, but no Dena.

She then raced around the house, quickly scanning every inch.

No Dena.

No sign of a struggle.

Nothing out of place, as far as she could tell.

Charlee tried to control her breathing, taking a deep cleansing breath like her yoga instructor taught. Then she began a more systematic search.

Still nothing.

But on the kitchen table was a note. "Mrs Russo, we took Twist over to our house. We will play with her and take good care of her until you get back. We promise. We didn't want you to think we kidnapped her. Ha ha." It was signed by Jain, with a heart dotting the I; *Wyatt* in a sloppy looping cursive; and *Leo* and *Lincoln*, also with a heart dotting the I. "PS, I signed for the twins, but they promise too."

Kober had told Charlee that her kids had come over

when she'd called from Denver earlier this morning. If they still had Twist, that meant her mother had been gone all day.

And nobody knew where she was.

123

Evelyn

THE PHOTO SHOOT WENT WELL, but Janet and
Deondra decided to come back tomorrow for their
pictures. Evelyn showed Max their package of photos.

"Nice job," he said, shuffling through and admiring
them. "This one's fantastic. An excellent keepsake for the
time they got snowbound at the Sugar Mill Marketplace."
He slid them back into the envelope. "Wanna play some
more cards?"

"I do, but we really should get rid of the boxes."

"Then where will we play cards?"

"Maybe I never explained this thoroughly, but this—"
Evelyn waved her arm around the studio— "is our place
of business. People come in here and we take their pictures
and they give us money. Gin rummy, on the other hand, is
what people never give us money to do."

Max grinned. "Seems we should revise our business
plan."

"Come on, you old coot. Let's see what's in those
boxes."

They maneuvered them to the center of their

costume area. Evelyn pulled the strapping tape from the top of the first box. She began removing items of men's clothing and tossing them to Max, who listed them out loud.

"Pants, shirt, shirt, sweatshirt, pants, shirt, shirt—hey, this one is nice. I'm keeping it."

"For what era?" Evelyn asked without turning around.

"Not for here, for my personal use." He held a golf shirt to his torso, then turned toward the mirror.

"You have seventeen shirts that look exactly like that one."

"Nuh uh." He performed what he thought was a sexy dance, holding the shirt to his chest. "Looks good, eh?"

"Ohferpetes—" Evelyn returned to emptying the box. When there was nothing left inside, she sighed. "Nothing we can use."

"Speak for yourself." Max waggled his new favorite shirt at her.

"I stand corrected." She scooped up the pile and unceremoniously dumped it back into the box. She pulled the tape from the next box and began plucking out women's clothes and flipping them to Max.

Again, he narrated. "Dress, dress, t-shirt, sweater, dress, blouse, blouse, dress, pants, blouse—"

"Wait. Let me see that," Evelyn said. Max tossed it to her. She held it to her torso, checked herself in the mirror, then dropped the blouse into a different pile. She saw Max grinning at her. "What?" she said.

"Nothing."

Again, the box was emptied with nothing they could use for their costume collection.

Max pawed through the pile of clothing on the floor. "This kind of looks hippy-ish." He held up a vest that looked like it might have been macramé.

"First, that's hideous. Second, it would be our only item of hippy clothes."

"Collections have to start somewhere," Max said.

Evelyn plucked the vest from Max's hands. "True. But this one will have to start someplace else."

"Fine. I'm not sure how I'd wash it anyway."

"Duh. With your delicates." Evelyn toed the final box. "Shall we make a bet there's nothing useful in here?"

"That's a sucker's bet." Max cocked his head. "But wait. If the house always wins, and we're the house here, then …"

"Nope. Still a sucker's bet." Evelyn tore the tape off the top of the box. Before she opened it, she placed a palm flat against the top. "I say there's nothing worthwhile in here. If I'm right, you go get me another one of Kober's cookies."

"And I say it'll be another load of crap. If *I'm* right, then you have to get *me* another one of Kober's cookies."

They shook hands.

Evelyn opened the box and peered in. "Max! Look at this!"

Charlee

ON THE VERGE OF PANIC, Charlee tore out of the driveway and careened to the Marketplace. The parking lot was practically empty. Charlee burst into the promenade, stomped the snow from her boots while hurrying past the photo studio.

Relief almost buckled Charlee's knees when she saw the security gate was up at the bookstore. Thrice Sold Tales was open.

"Mom? Mom?"

Charlee tore through the stacks, then burst through the back, shouting for Dena in the vendor room.

Skyler came running from the cheese store.

Charlee stood dumbfounded in the center of the vendor room. Dena wasn't there. The restroom door stood open. "Where's my mom? She's still not here? Nobody has heard from her?" Charlee knew her voice sounded hysterical, but it perfectly matched how she was feeling so she didn't attempt to temper it.

By then Max, Evelyn, and Kober had joined them. A woman she didn't recognize stood across the room with her arms crossed. Probably Kateri, the office manager, Charlee thought.

"I can't find her anywhere. Her car is in her garage. She hasn't been here? She hasn't called? Why is the security gate open at the bookstore? Isn't she the only one who can open it? Was it open when you guys got here? Is it possible she got robbed late last night? Oh my—" Charlee scrambled to get back to the bookstore, but Max stopped her.

"Charlee, sit down." Max pushed her into a chair. "Take some deep breaths. We'll figure this out. Dena's cash register is locked up tight. There's been no foul play here. Nobody has been robbed." He glanced at Kober. "Can you get her a glass of water?"

Kober hurried from the vendor room.

"Why is the bookstore's security gate up if she's not here?"

Kober returned with a glass of water. As she handed it to Charlee, she said, "We opened it for her."

Charlee looked alarmed. "I thought there was a password on it. Is it possible there was some kind of security breach and all of Mom's codes got hacked?"

"How would Dena's security gate password do anything other than open her security gate?" Max asked quietly.

Charlee took a sip of water. "I don't know. I was just at her house. She wasn't there but her car was in the garage. I'm just really worried about her."

"Now we are too, dear," Evelyn said.

"Should we call the police?" Skyler asked.

Kober didn't answer, simply dialed her phone. "Sheriff Johnson? We need to report a missing person." She listened for a bit, then said, "Hang on, I'm putting you on speaker." Kober set her phone in the center of a table in the vendor room and everyone crowded around. Everyone except Kateri. "Okay, start over. Everyone's here."

"Everyone? Then who's missing?" the sheriff asked.

Charlee leaned closer to the phone. "Sheriff? This is Charlee Russo, Dena Russo's daughter. She owns Thrice Sold Tales? She's been missing all day … maybe longer. I've been trying to call her and she's not answering, and she left Twist alone at her house. I drove down here from Denver—"

"In this storm?"

"—and she's not at her house."

"She's a grown woman, Charlee. She can leave her house whenever she wants."

The sheriff's voice was softer than her words implied, but Charlee had to make her understand. "Sheriff, her car is still there. In the garage."

Sheriff Johnson was quiet for a moment. "That does seem odd. But there's not a lot we can do. Did you see anything unusual at her house?"

"You mean other than her not being there and her car in the garage?" Charlee's voiced notched up into squeaky territory.

"No," the sheriff said slowly. "Like signs of a break-in or a struggle."

"Nothing like that. The front door was unlocked."

"Is that unusual?"

Charlee glanced around the table, not knowing the answer.

Evelyn piped up. "Keisha, you know what it's like in Sugar Springs. Lots of us don't always lock our doors."

"But was that unusual for Dena?" the sheriff asked.

This time Evelyn glanced around the table. Everyone shrugged, unaware of Dena's habits.

"There's no way my mom would leave her door

unlocked. She was married to a cop and not too long ago, she had a … well … a stalker."

Evelyn's hand fluttered to her throat and Skyler's eyes widened.

Kober gasped loudly. "She never told me that!"

"Charlee," the sheriff said. "Get off speaker. I have some questions for you."

Charlee picked up Kober's phone and walked into the bookstore for some privacy. She realized when she reached the front counter that she probably should have shut the back door behind her, but if she closed it now it would look very conspicuous. She left it open. If the other tenants were going to eavesdrop, so be it.

"Okay, sheriff. I'm off speaker."

"Now tell me everything about this stalker."

"It didn't seem to be that big of a deal." Charlee stopped. "No, that's not what I meant. It didn't seem to *go on* very long, I guess is the thing. I don't know if she ever mentioned it, but my dad was a cop. This guy might have been someone he sent to prison. A few months ago, he pretended to be someone my mom went to high school with. They went out a few times before she found out."

"What did he do to her?" Sheriff Johnson asked quietly.

"Nothing, that's the thing. She figured it out and he just disappeared. She never heard from him again."

"Did she report it?"

"Yeah. The New Mexico cops said they'd talk to Colorado Corrections and see if they could figure out who it was. It seemed to me that there wouldn't be too many people my dad arrested or testified against who got out of prison within that time frame. But nobody ever contacted her about it. Maybe he was lying about it. I completely forgot about it until today."

"Unless it wasn't someone who had just been released." Sheriff Johnson mused for a bit then said, "I'll make some calls and see what I can find out. I'm sure it's unrelated or you would have seen signs of a struggle."

"I guess that's true."

"There's not a whole lot we can do right now with this storm, but I'll send Vince, er, Deputy Chavez out to look around. I know Dena likes to walk over by the river."

"That sounds ominous," Charlee said.

"No, no, no, that's not what I meant. But if she went out and then the storm hit and caught her by surprise, maybe she's just holed up at someone's house out that way."

"But she'd still answer her phone."

"Not if the battery ran down."

"She'd use someone's phone to at least call Kober or someone."

Sheriff Johnson was quiet. "Let's not jump to any conclusions, Charlee. Let me see what I can find out."

Charlee gave the sheriff her cell number then returned to the vendor room to give Kober's phone back. All the tenants were exactly where she'd left them.

"What'd she say?" Max asked.

"Not much. She'll send the deputy out to look around and she'll make some calls." Nobody said anything. "I guess I'll go look around the bookstore. See if there's any kind of clue in there. Will you guys all make sure your phones are on and turned up, just in case?"

Evelyn said, "Of course, dear." She and Max both checked theirs.

"Already done." Kober dropped hers into her apron pocket.

Charlee looked around the room. "Thank you, every-one. You've been so kind."

Skyler crossed the room and started toward the back door of the bookstore. "C'mon, I'll help you search."

Charlee followed her into the bookstore. "Thanks, but I can't imagine we're going to see anything that explains this."

"We'll just have to keep looking until we figure it out." Skyler strode to the front counter and worked methodically from one end to the other. She read every invoice and receipt, lifted objects to peer under them.

Charlee walked to the front and took in the entire store, then began walking back and forth up and down the stacks, covering every inch of carpet.

When Skyler had finished with the front counter, she mimicked Charlee's activities, but on the other side of the store. They ended up in the back.

"Nothing," Charlee said. "Not even a book cockeyed on the shelf."

Skyler sighed. "Where could she be? Is it possible she went to some book convention or sale or something?"

"Without her car? Without saying anything to any of you?" Charlee shook her head. "I guess I'll go back to her house and search there."

"I'll go with you. Let me get my coat."

———

They took Charlee's Chevy Sonic since Skyler's had about a thousand pounds of snow piled on top of it. As she slid into Dena's driveway once again, Charlee noticed her tire tracks from earlier had almost disappeared under newly fallen snow.

"Geez, it's really coming down." Charlee shuddered to think that her mother might actually be stuck out in the storm. When they got inside the house, the first thing she did was check the closet for Dena's coat and boots. Both were missing. At least that was something positive.

Skyler kicked off her boots and dropped her coat to the couch. "So … what are we looking for?"

Charlee removed her boots and coat too. "No idea."

"Where would she keep her suitcase? Maybe she took a trip and had someone pick her up."

Charlee went to Dena's bedroom and opened the closet.

"Does she normally make her bed every day?" Skyler stared at the tangled bedclothes.

Charlee thought for a minute, trying to remember occasions when she visited Dena. "No idea." She poked around the closet. No suitcase. But was that where she stored it? Charlee dropped to her knees and peered under the bed. Not tall enough for luggage.

She stood with her hands on her hips and surveyed the room. Skyler did the same.

"Nothing seems weird to me in here," Charlee finally said. She stepped into Dena's bathroom. Skyler followed her but Charlee closed the door. "Nature calls." When she came out, Skyler was sitting on Dena's bed.

"Well?"

"She doesn't wear much make-up, but it's all there. So is her toothbrush. I'm absolutely certain she didn't pack for a trip."

They moved to the pristine guest room: bed made neatly, pillows just so, tracks in the carpet showing vacuum marks.

Charlee pulled open the closet door. On the shelf were extra sheets and blankets. Formal dresses hung from the rod. On the floor was the vacuum and a set of lime green luggage.

"Wow. Can't lose those at baggage claim," Skyler noted. "Does she have another set?"

Charlee shook her head.

Skyler poked her head into the hallway bathroom. "Doesn't look like anyone has ever used this one. Perfectly neat."

They made their way down the hall back to the living room. Again, Charlee stood with her hands on her hips and surveyed the area. Twist's bed cozied near the fireplace. Throw blanket on the back of the couch. TV remotes, a Smithsonian Magazine, pile of red socks in the corner, and a neat stack of books on the coffee table. "A Killing at Cotton Hill" by Terry Shames which Charlee had given Dena because it was the first in a mystery series she knew Dena would enjoy. "Another Saturday Night and I Ain't Got No Body" by Jennie Marts. Charlee turned the cover over and could see why this was in Dena's reading pile. The cover was adorable and it looked like a funny romantic mystery. "White Trash Warlock" by David R Slayton was on the bottom of the stack. Dena loved nothing better than a good magical confrontation—at least in fiction—and Charlee loved that the cover had a colorful illustration of the D&F Tower, which was a Denver landmark not too far from where she lived. The real one didn't have tentacles, though.

"Nothing unusual in here."

Skyler pointed to the socks. "What about those?"

"Pretty sure they belong to Twist."

"Ah."

The kitchen was more of the same. Clean dishes in the drainer. Charlee checked them to see if any were still wet. Bone dry. Coffee pot empty and unplugged. Nothing on the stove. No towering piles of unopened mail, computer printouts, ransom notes.

Skyler pulled open the fridge. A whole chicken sat on the top shelf. She poked it and turned to Charlee. "Thawed."

Charlee looked at the weekly menu she knew her mother kept on the side of the refrigerator, attached with two magnets in the center. She slid them to each side. One magnet said *Emotionally attached to fictional characters*, and the other said *My weekend is all booked*. Charlee read the menu. "She was going to roast that tonight, then turn leftovers into chicken and dumplings."

Charlee opened cabinets until she found Dena's stash of shortbread. She plopped into a kitchen chair, tore open the package, and pulled out the tray. Buh bye, shortbread.

After she'd eaten three cookies, and Skyler had nibbled one, Charlee said, "I just don't get it. She didn't plan on going anywhere. There's nothing out of the ordinary here or at the bookstore. Where in the world is she?" Charlee didn't want to cry in front of Skyler so she shoved another cookie in her mouth.

"I wish I knew."

"Are you sure she didn't say anything to you about … anything?" Charlee asked.

"I've been racking my brain." Skyler nibbled another cookie, then spoke softly. "What about this … stalker?" She wouldn't meet Charlee's eyes.

Charlee shook her head. "That happened in November when she still lived in Santa Fe. This is March in Colorado. She would have told me and my brother—he's a cop—if the guy showed up again or called her or something. At the time, this guy told her he was just having fun, messing with the wife of the cop who put him away. He was never violent or anything. In fact, she actually enjoyed going out with him. At least until …." Charlee sighed. "He probably just skulked away and got on with his life after she figured him out." She ate two more cookies. "And even if he did somehow figure out that she moved to Sugar Springs and showed up here, she would have put up a fight. Look at this place." Charlee waved a hand behind her. "Not a pillow out of place."

They polished off the sleeve of shortbread without talking, each lost in their own thoughts, probably hoping the other one would suddenly have some sort of epiphany about it all. But no.

Charlee wadded up the shortbread wrapper, then glanced around for the trash can. Something caught her eye. In the corner of Dena's kitchen was the Mexican pottery planter Charlee had given her as a housewarming present. She knew Dena was waiting for summer to take it outside and plant something in it. So why was she using it for a trash can? Especially since she already had a kitchen trash can on the other side of the room?

She dropped the shortbread wrapper back on the table and squatted down next to the planter. Charlee began pulling items from the pot. Gas receipt. Power bar wrapper. Small zipper plastic bag full of orange peels.

"This is road trip trash," Charlee said excitedly. "I'd recognize that anywhere. But it wouldn't be Mom's. She'd throw it away at her destination."

Skyler came over to look closer. She picked up the receipt and squinted. "Looks like the thingy was getting low on ink, but I'm pretty sure that says Santa Fe." She handed it to Charlee who also squinted at it. "Maybe she was in Santa Fe recently and threw it out when she got home."

Charlee kept squinting and held it at various angles to read it better. Finally, she said, "That definitely says Santa Fe, but look at the date and time." She pointed at it and Skyler bent close.

Twist

THE CHANGE of scenery to Kober's house with the children was welcome. First there were many more socks laying around there and the treats were new and interesting. The boys kept flipping something they called "Doritos" into the air and cheered each time Twist snatched one from midair. They progressed to placing one on her snout and telling her to wait to eat it until they shouted, "Now!" That game was less fun, but she was growing fond of Doritos, so she played along.

The boys tired of it before she did, however, but then they invited her to come outside and play with them in the snow.

They couldn't possibly know, but Twist loved everything about the snow. She loved the cold air. She loved how the flakes landed on her eyelashes and snout, making her cross-eyed when she tried to look at them. She loved burrowing her nose into a deep pile then flinging snow into the air when she leaped back up. She loved digging in it, spraying it in a snowscape behind her. She loved rolling in it, making Dog Angels.

But what she didn't know until that very day was how much she loved chasing children and knocking them into snowdrifts.

Twist rammed into Jain for the fun of it, but also to explain she hadn't much liked having to sit still for so long while Jain painted her nails. Although, as she admired the glittery red flash as she ran, she had to admit she did feel very pretty. But still. Jain hadn't told the truth about how long it would take.

She raced around the yard dodging the twins until she was behind them. Then BOOM—over they went into the snow. Twist wasn't particularly adroit at math, but she stopped targeting them when she felt like she had toppled them at least as many times as they had put Doritos on her nose.

Then it was Wyatt's turn. Earlier Wyatt had eaten an entire sandwich while sitting on the floor in front of the television, mere inches from her face, and hadn't even offered her a nibble. For this he must pay. And now he was throwing balls of snow for her to fetch, but they disintegrated before she could reach them. She felt her frustration grow with every lob of his arm.

Twist stalked Wyatt around the yard. He'd grown weary of throwing the balls across the yard for her and instead began throwing them at his siblings. His aim was deteriorating, though, because the balls of snow disintegrated on their backs or heads rather than harmlessly in the yard. As he bent to scoop more snow, Twist ran at him full tilt. At exactly the right moment, she skidded to a stop, hip-checking him into the air. He landed face first and came up sputtering and laughing. He grabbed her around the neck and hugged her tight. "You're the best! I love playing in the snow with you!"

He scrambled to his feet. "C'mon ... let's go get Jain!"

Twist danced and frolicked at his side while he crept up on Jain flat on her back making a snow angel. Wyatt scooped handfuls of snow and dropped them directly on her face.

While Jain yelled at Wyatt and wiped snow off her face, Twist stood next to her and gave a mighty shake of her snowy fur, dousing Jain again.

Jain didn't yell at Twist, though. Instead she said, "I'm going inside. It's time for cookies."

Twist couldn't agree more. And maybe afterward Dena would come get her.

Balaam

BALAAM SAT in the promenade near the huge window of the Marketplace, tending to his toilette.

When he finished, he coughed politely and ran one paw across his whiskers, as the final act of a well-groomed cat.

He curled his tail around his feet and stared out the window at the lights of the parking lot, wondering why they were still there and not at home curled up in front of the fire. Or at least why *he* wasn't curled up in front of the fire.

What Max and Evelyn did was up to them.

He glanced backward at the photo studio, where he heard them talking.

C'mon, already. Let's go home.

Balaam was anxious to get home to his food bowl and his bed, which he'd be dragging in front of the fireplace no matter what Max said. He hadn't caught the house on fire yet and didn't think this time would be any different.

His anxiety stemmed from wondering how they were going to get him from the Marketplace into the house without having snow touch his perfectly groomed, and as yet, perfectly dry, fur.

Normally, he'd simply follow them out the door on his own dainty feet and hop in the back seat of their car. But even he knew that if he took one step out the Marketplace door, he'd be blown into Kansas and perhaps buried under three feet of snow. Probably forever.

He could only hope that today was the day Evelyn would swaddle him in the fuzziest blanket she could find until only his nose was visible. Then she'd nestle his burrito-ness into a waterproof tote which she'd carry to the pre-heated car under her coat. A purr-ito, if you will.

All day Balaam had been twirling around Evelyn's feet, hissing at Max, and otherwise trying to explain to them that he was of the opinion they should get out of here and in front of that fireplace. Had they not noticed the snow piling up all day?

But Evelyn was dealing with that annoying teenager he'd gotten into a hissing match with earlier, and Max said something about getting so much work done since nobody came into the Marketplace today.

You know what else didn't happen at the Marketplace today? Toddlers didn't drop Cheerios. Kober hadn't waited until the end of the day to sweep up her crumbs. Skyler wasn't around to offer nibbles of cheese.

A complete waste of a day.

Balaam groaned, but Evelyn thought he purred.

"Oh, there you are, my sweetums!" She picked him up and held him like he was a baby, rocking him gently.

He struggled, pretending he didn't like it, clawing his way to her shoulder.

"Ouch!" She plucked him off her mint green cardigan and held him at arm's length. "I will get you declawed, you little imp. Don't test me."

But then she booped him on the nose so he knew it was yet another empty threat. Like when she said she was never giving him any more salmon scraps if he continued to beg for them. Or that she was going to put him on a diet. Or when Max threatened to boot him to Kingdom Come, wherever that was. Come to think of it, he might really do that if Evelyn wasn't watching.

Evelyn placed Balaam back on his feet and returned to Max. Balaam heard her make some ripping noises and looked over to see the two of them diving into a large box.

Evelyn said, "Max! Look at this!"

Oh, great, Balaam thought. No swaddling. No fuzzy blanket. No waterproof tote. No pre-heated car. Exactly how he wanted this day to play out. He groaned again.

"Aren't you the sweetest, most contented kitty on the planet? Such purring today," Evelyn said as she tossed items from a box.

Why were humans so stupid?

But at least they saw the benefit of playing in boxes.

Kober

IT HAD BEEN a nice distraction to have Evelyn and the mother and daughter customers hanging out in the bakery while she worked. Kober wondered when—or if—she and Jain would ever take a trip, just the two of them. She sure wouldn't want to go someplace like Sugar Springs, though. Maybe a theatre trip to New York City. Or a Hawaiian resort where they'd lounge on the beach all day. Or a train trip across Canada.

Kober sighed. None of that was ever going to happen. Maybe it might have been a possibility previously, but not now. She forced her attention back to the present before she spun herself up with unanswerable questions and unknowable what-ifs.

She had listened to Evelyn's soothing voice regale them with the riveting tale of Rattlesnake Kate while keeping her hands busy mixing batter and dough she probably didn't even need. She could freeze some of it, she supposed, but right now it helped manage her stress.

As Evelyn's voice washed over her, Kober considered the life of Rattlesnake Kate and how she survived all those actual snakes plus all the metaphorical snakes in her life. And here Kober was faced with one single trauma and she was at her wit's end.

Why was she so weak? She never thought of herself as weak before, but look at her. What kind of example was she setting for her children? Jain would see her mother undone by a man who had an affair and made a fool out of her. The boys would see a woman who could not stand up to a man, who had her power stripped from her, less than a man.

She hated what she was so quickly becoming. One of those bitter divorcees whose life stopped the minute her husband walked out on her. Her only topics of conversation forevermore would be how to get a man, how to keep a man, and her life before when she had a man.

Kober didn't know very many divorced women. She could probably count on two hands her friends over the years who had divorced. And on one hand, the number of divorced women she knew in Sugar Springs. And on zero hands, the number of divorced women she could talk to about any of this.

Where was Dena? She could definitely talk to her. Even though Dena had been widowed and her husband had loved her up to the very end, Kober knew she'd have words of wisdom.

But even if Dena didn't have any wisdom to share, she could be counted on to kick Kober in the butt and tell her to quit feeling sorry for herself.

Once when Kober was fretting and talking constantly about some of her bakery items not selling as well as others, Dena had actually gone out and bought Kober a package of enormous white undies with a note that said, "Stop your whining and put on your Big Girl Pants. Check your recipes. Tweak as necessary. Lather, rinse, repeat."

Of course, Dena was absolutely right. Quit talking and do something.

Kober had changed some recipes and nixed some items altogether. She exchanged words for action.

But now she needed more wisdom from Dena.

Where in the world *was* she?

And what might *she* need?

Kober hated feeling helpless, but she was drowning in it right now.

Charlee

CHARLEE WAVED the gas receipt at Skyler. "See that? It's from just after midnight. And Mom's car is still in the garage. Someone she knew came from Santa Fe and she must have gone back with them. But who?"

"And why?"

"I don't know. Mom has been on the outs with her friends back there, but maybe they made up. But why a trip in the middle of the night, in a blizzard, no less? Without telling anyone?" Charlee was disappointed that the storm ruined any potential clues about the car that gassed up in Santa Fe. Even her own tire tracks had mostly disappeared under new snow. But maybe whoever came up from Santa Fe believed the storm was going the other direction. Wasn't that the same thing she told Ozzi and Lance?

Charlee took a picture of the gas receipt and texted it to Sheriff Johnson. Almost immediately Charlee's phone rang.

"What am I looking at?" the sheriff asked.

"It's a gas receipt I found at my mom's house in the trash."

"And ..."

"And it shows someone got gas in Santa Fe just after midnight. Plenty of time to get here before I even started calling my mom."

"Charlee, there's nothing I can do with this information. It's not illegal to get gas after midnight in Santa Fe. And there's no way to even tell whose car it was. For all you know, Dena was just being a good citizen and picked up some litter."

"Sheriff, you know my mom used to live in Santa Fe, right?"

"I do, but Charlee, none of this is an indication of any crime. I appreciate that you're worried, but I told you, it's not illegal for a grown woman to leave town without telling you. It's not—"

"She didn't take a suitcase. Or her toothbrush. This was not a planned trip."

"All the more reason she didn't have a chance to tell you about it. Some emergency came up and she's handling it."

The sheriff's calm, logical response did nothing to calm Charlee. "The last time my mom saw her stalker was in Santa Fe."

"Please don't jump to conclusions. You said yourself she hadn't had any contact with him since then and he was just playing some perverted game with her."

"Have you heard from either the Santa Fe cops who came out to take her statement or the Colorado Department of Corrections?"

"It's only been a little while, but I've called and am waiting on a response. Be patient."

"Would you be patient if your mother was missing?"

Sheriff Johnson sighed. "No, I guess not. But, Charlee, try to hold it together and let me do my job."

Frustration finally bubbled over. "Fine. Do your job." Charlee hung up on the sheriff but immediately dialed again. "Hey, Ozzi, I—yes, I'm fine. I'm here at my mom's and—the drive was fine, no problems. But it seems Mom headed down to Santa Fe for some kind of emergency. I'm going to go help her." She held the phone away from her ear, but she heard all the same arguments from both Ozzi on the phone and ten minutes earlier from Skyler in person. Stereo lecturing. Twin earbashing.

When Skyler had begun her lecture, Charlee had given her a glare so intense she'd need tweezers to remove it from her memory. It had served its purpose, though. Skyler had quit talking mid-sentence.

Ozzi, however, couldn't see Charlee's face and continued listing reasons she shouldn't go to Santa Fe. Nothing he said changed her mind, since she'd already told herself all the same things. Finally, she interrupted him. "Oz … Oz … hush up a sec. Thank you. I hear what you're saying, but if you were here, you'd do the same thing. And, really, the storm is almost over here—" Charlee shot Skyler a warning glance to keep quiet— "and I'm sure the highway has been plowed and is perfectly clear. I'll just zip down there, help my mom, and be back home tomorrow. Maybe the next day." Charlee listened, nodding and punctuating what Ozzi was saying with *mm-hmms* and *of courses* until he ran out of steam. "I made a list of all that and will follow it to a T …. Yes, it was a mental list, not actually written down …. Yes, I listened to all of it …. No, I barely rolled my eyes …. Only like five times …. I will. I love you too. Talk to you later."

After she hung up, she texted him. *Forgot. Don't say*

anything to Lance unless he asks. Probably be home before he misses me. You know brothers! Thx

"You can't drive to Santa Fe in this," Skyler said.

"Sure I can." Charlee went to Dena's bedroom and pulled out the lime green nested suitcases until she found an overnight bag. She rummaged through her mother's closet and drawers, pulling out sweaters and leggings. Either Dena would need them or Charlee would.

Skyler stared. "You're really going?"

"I am."

"You don't even know that's where she is!"

"It's the only explanation I can think of, and I have to do something. I can't just wait around here for someone to drive around town looking for her. You know as well as I do that she's not wandering the streets of Sugar Springs."

"What about Sheriff Johnson calling about that stalker?"

"She has my number but she's not going to find out anything. That guy is long gone. And I doubt Mom's little non-violent run-in with him rose to the top of anyone's list of things to worry about. I mean, read the paper. Much bigger stuff gets ignored every day."

"Maybe in Denver, but not Sugar Springs." Skyler's voice had an offended edge to it.

Charlee didn't respond as she zipped the bag and headed toward the kitchen. She grabbed one of Dena's canvas grocery bags and began filling it with snacks she found in the pantry. She opened the fridge and grabbed two apples, then returned the chicken to the freezer.

Her phone rang. She glanced at the caller ID and rolled her eyes before punching the speakerphone button and placing it on the countertop. "Hey, Lance. What's up?" She continued packing for the trip, washing apples, filling water bottles.

"Ozzi called me. You're going to Santa Fe? What's going on?"

"Nothing. Turns out Mom had to go down there to help out a friend, probably that lady who fell off the trail when they were hiking a while back. She's old, probably took a turn for the worse."

"But why are *you* going?"

Hmm. She wasn't entirely sure of that herself. "Because I'm already all the way here and it's just four hours. It's not a big deal. I invited you to come, remember? But you said you had to work."

"Yeah, some of us have to *actually* fight crime every day, Space Case. Not just write about it."

"You're just jealous that I get to take spur-of-the-moment road trips whenever I feel like it." *Or whenever I can't reach Mom on the phone.* "You better get back to it. Those jaywalking tickets won't write themselves."

"Remind me to show you my medal for shutting down the most lemonade stands in one day."

"I stand corrected. You should get a key to the city. As soon as I get back, I'll lobby your chief." Charlee checked the charge before shoving the phone back in her pocket. It was at sixty-three percent, but she'd charge it in the car while she drove just to be safe.

An uncharged cell phone was something she took to heart in her personal life after she received unflattering comments from her critique group because a major plot point in one of her early thrillers hinged on the bad guy forgetting to charge his phone. Charlee had whined to her agent, pointing out that people forgot to charge their phones all the time. Her agent had responded, "But this is fiction, Charlee. Things can't be that easy." At the time she was annoyed, but after she reworked and strengthened the manuscript, she realized her critique group was absolutely correct. She sent them each a muffin basket with a note that read, "Thank you for never sugar-coating things!"

So now Charlee and all her characters—good guys and bad—never have the excuse of an uncharged cellphone.

She placed the grocery bag next to the overnight bag. When she straightened up, Skyler stood directly in front of her. "I'm going with you."

"You don't need to do that."

"I think I do. I grew up in Wisconsin. I know my way around a snowstorm."

"I grew up in Colorado. I'll be fine."

They stared at each other for a beat too long. That extra beat sent them into frenemy territory.

"Dena told me about Georgia, that friend of hers who had the hiking accident," Skyler said. "Why'd you tell your brother this has something to do with her?"

"Because it might. Plus, I had to tell him something. I've met most of my mom's friends, so I'll just make the rounds and see if anyone knows anything."

"Why don't you just call them and ask if Dena's there?"

"Because I don't know their last names. But Mom took me to some of their houses at Thanksgiving, and I know some of her favorite places. It'll be fine. Someone will know something." Charlee really hoped that was true. But Skyler made a good point. And she did know Georgia's last name.

She pulled out her phone and searched "Georgia Peach Santa Fe." A long list of recipes popped up, along with many links to and photos of an exotic dancer in San Diego.

Not helpful.

Charlee had also visited an art gallery managed by one of Dena's friends. She couldn't remember the name of the artist, but he specialized in grotesques. Another search, this time of "grotesque art Santa Fe" brought up a ton of hits, none of which helped Charlee, and she didn't have time to sort through all the internet chaff. Definitely faster to drive to Santa Fe.

Charlee grabbed her keys from her purse and dropped them on the counter while she put on her coat.

"You must be tired. I'll drive." Skyler made a grab for the keys.

Charlee beat her to it and scooped them up. "I'm fine. I'm driving. You really don't have to come. Don't you have a store to run?"

"Nobody will be in with this storm. Besides, I can't get my deliveries anyway."

"Neither rain nor sleet nor dark of night. What if your deliveries get delivered?"

Skyler waved away the thought. "I'll call Hugo. He'll take care of things for me."

Charlee sighed. It sounded like Skyler was serious about accompanying her on this road trip.

"Listen," Skyler said. "Your mom means a lot to me. My mom's not around—"

"Oh, I'm sorry."

"She's not dead. Geez. She's in Wisconsin. But Dena is kinda like my Colorado mom. I want to go with you. Maybe I can help."

"Fine. I'm happy to have the company and … in case … but she's my mom and I know what I'm doing. I have a plan."

"Do you?"

"No, not really. But I have four hours to think of one."

Skyler

SKYLER KNEW Charlee didn't particularly want her to go to Santa Fe with her, and maybe they got off on the wrong foot. But in Charlee's agitated state, Skyler couldn't in good conscience let her go alone, especially in this weather. Maybe the storm was going the other way, but still, who knew what she was going to find in Santa Fe. If it was Dena just gone down to help a friend, then great, they could go down and then be able to drive her back home. But if she wasn't there … or worse …. Skyler couldn't even presume what would happen if they couldn't find her.

Skyler was only a few years older than Charlee, but she was convinced Charlee needed her. For what, she wasn't quite sure, but they'd find out in due course.

As Charlee gathered up the two bags she'd packed, Skyler stopped her. "Do you have your Ten Essentials?"

"I peed and I'll stop for gas first place we come to."

"Good. But that's not what I'm talking about. I went snowshoeing with this guy—Jake, my cheese supplier—"

"Ooh la lah."

"And he makes it a point whenever he goes out hiking

or something to make sure he packs his Ten Essentials. He even did it when we went snowshoeing in the forest, just across the river from town."

"We'll be in the car. On the highway. Not out in the boonies. And you saw me pack water and snacks. Would else would we need?" Charlee hefted the bags again and headed for the door.

Skyler counted off the items on her fingers as she listed them. "Map and compass, hydration, real food, extra clothing, fire starter, first aid kit, pocketknife, flashlight, sun protection, and an emergency shelter."

Charlee gaped at her. "We know how to get to Santa Fe. It's a straight shot down the highway. You saw me pack water, food, and clothes. First aid kit in my glove compartment. Doubt we'll need sun protection." She opened one of Dena's kitchen drawers and pulled out a box of matches which she held up. Then she held up her phone. "Flashlight, map, and compass. And like it or not, my car doubles as an emergency shelter. But we won't need it, because we're just going down a busy interstate highway. There are roadside motels all along the way." She stared at Skyler. "Remember, you don't have to come."

"And we need to tell people where we're going."

Charlee sighed. "I already told my boyfriend and my brother. But I guess I can leave a note for Mom, just in case." Charlee pulled over the notepad where Jain had written to Dena. On a different page Charlee wrote, "Mom, you weren't answering your phone and you FREAKED ME OUT so I came down here. And now I'm heading to Santa Fe (for reasons I'll explain later) with Skyler. Call me and call Lance and I hope to see you very soon. ox ox Charlee."

Skyler was on her phone when Charlee had finished. "And please ask Kober to keep Twist until Dena gets back.

Thanks, Hugo. See you soon!" She turned to Charlee. "All set. Kober and Hugo will take care of things at the Marketplace."

"Thanks, Skyler," Charlee said quietly. "It didn't even occur to me to deal with the bookstore and the dog."

"You have a lot on your mind. And you're tired. Are you sure you don't want me to drive?"

"I'm fine."

Skyler thought she saw a hint of agitation cross Charlee's face, but maybe it was to be expected. Snow days were always weird and this one particularly so.

They loaded the bags into Charlee's trunk, then got to work brushing the snow off the car. Charlee started the engine to begin to warm it up.

"What's this color?" Skyler asked.

"Not sure. I call it olive red." Charlee patted the car lovingly. "My theory is that it had some body work done and they had some leftover red and green paint, maybe a little brown, and mixed it all together for this old girl."

"It's … unique."

"Never seen another like it." Charlee caressed the quarter panel.

Skyler asked her to pop the trunk and retrieved the bag of snacks. She wouldn't survive this trip without the Oreos she knew were in there.

Evelyn

"MAX! LOOK AT THIS!" Evelyn said. She'd wiped a layer of dust from the top of the box and was rubbing her hands on her mint green polyester pants.

Balaam pushed toward her and wound himself around her ankles. She scooped him up and relocated him.

Balaam immediately returned and began batting at the box.

Evelyn realized he was interested in it and not her ankles. She again scooped him up and walked him six feet away where she turned one of the empty boxes on its side and placed him in. She rejoined Max standing over the third box.

"What is it?" Max asked.

"If it's what I think it is, it'll make a great prop. Hold the box while I try to get it out." Evelyn grabbed the leather handle of a case wedged into the box. Max pushed down on the box while she lifted out an old carpet bag valise. She held it aloft and turned it from side to side. "It's beautiful!"

She placed it on the prop bales of hay and turned the

clasp. Pulling out a full-length dress, she drew an intake of breath as the garment unfurled. It was sumptuous fabric in a rich moss green with a gold shawl collar, matching wide belt, and enormous pockets. Tiny gold buttons up the forearm and down the bodice. She handed it to Max and then dove back into the valise. Another long woman's dress, this one pink and full of frothy layers instead of slim cut. A pair of boys' breeches with matching jacket. Sailor suit. A couple little pinafore dresses. Two pairs of uncomfortable looking leather shoes for children, and a tall pair of women's boots. Evelyn held one of the boots and ran a hand over the soft fabric upper. With her thumb she wiped away the dust on the patent leather of the shoe and chunky heel.

"Max, these are vintage clothes, not cheap costumes. Look at the stitching." Evelyn held the garments close, inspecting them.

"They're costumes now!" Max said, gleefully. "These are a great addition, especially the kids' sizes. No more Velcro to hold stuff together." He lifted the valise and walked over to one of the velvet settees they used as props. He placed it on the floor in front of it. "It fits in perfectly. And a nice pop of color."

"Since when did you get such an artistic eye?" Evelyn teased.

"I've been watching you." Max placed the carpet bag in various positions around the props. "This looks great everywhere."

"It does. And these clothes are beautiful." Evelyn's face clouded. "But why would someone give us a fully packed traveling case? Whoever dropped it off might want it back. They obviously didn't look inside."

"It was wedged in that box pretty tight. Maybe they just didn't want to bother with it."

"Max, this obviously came to us by mistake."

"Unless this is our payment for having to deal with the other two boxes of junk."

"Then why wouldn't whoever dropped it off hand it to us themselves?"

Max shrugged. "People are weird."

"We have to figure out who dropped this off."

"Now, Ev, don't be so hasty. I say Finders Keepers is in order here. You know those TV shows where people buy abandoned storage units of stuff, sight unseen? Maybe this is something like that." Max said excitedly.

"Except we didn't buy anything."

"No, I mean maybe back in the day—like what are these, from the turn of the century, maybe even late 1800s?—maybe back then, if stuff was left at a … a … a train station, people bid on them, sight unseen the same way."

Evelyn stared at him for a moment. "You mean like *Storage Wars Victorian Edition?*"

"Yes!"

"No." Evelyn began to check the pockets of all the clothes they'd pawed through. "This is a bag that's been in someone's attic for a hundred years, completely forgotten. And this box it was in." Evelyn pointed. "Didn't Montgomery Wards close decades ago? Now we just have to figure out whose attic it came from."

"Party pooper."

"Help me look."

She and Max searched every pocket and sleeve of every garment but found nothing. Evelyn searched the pile of clothing in front of Max again.

"Don't trust me?"

"Well, it wasn't me who invoked the Finders Keepers rule."

"That's fair."

But still she came up empty.

"I don't know what else to do. I'll ask around, maybe put a notice in the paper. But until someone comes forward, I guess these are ours."

Max jumped up for hangers.

"But we're not going to use them as costumes right away. Let's give someone a chance to claim them. We don't want to ruin anything."

"Fine. I'll hang them over there," he pointed, "away from the rest of the costumes."

Evelyn put the two pairs of children's shoes back in the carpetbag, after feeling to see if anything was shoved inside. She did the same thing to the women's boots.

She dropped one of them with a squeak.

Max raised his eyebrows. "Don't tell me there was a foot in there," he said dryly.

"Ew. Gross. What is wrong with you?" She pulled out a yellowed piece of paper and unfolded it.

Max thrummed with impatience. "Out loud, please? Or are we on a TV show scheduled for a commercial and the dramatic unveiling will be in three minutes?"

Hugo

HUGO HUNG up the phone after talking to Skyler. He had a bad feeling about the conversation, even though it was clear she was trying to keep it light-hearted. *That's the beauty of owning your own business*, she'd said. *So you could have a mid-week adventure if you want.*

Adventure. More like death wish.

Hugo hadn't told her about Boyd or that he was at the hospital in Colorado Springs and not even at the Marketplace. She didn't need him to heap any more worry on top. He'd take care of things.

First this storm, then Boyd, and now Skyler? Hugo didn't do well with chaos. He was a planner, liked a schedule.

He woke at the same time every day.

Worked out—Monday legs; Tuesday yoga; Wednesday arms; Thursday yoga; Friday core; Saturday yoga; Sunday recovery.

Ate breakfast—Monday poached eggs; Tuesday avocado toast; Wednesday oatmeal; Thursday homemade granola; Friday Greek yogurt with berries; Saturday bacon, spinach, and onion stir fry; Sunday whole grain waffles.

Took a shower and opened the store by eight o'clock, even though the Marketplace didn't open until ten. He had specific tasks he needed to do each morning, then he ate his lunch—which alternated between soup or a sandwich —between customers. Then his afternoon chores until it was time to close up.

Sometimes it irked him when customers came in and ruined his flow. He even went so far as to complain to Evelyn once, "If these customers weren't always bothering me, I could get my work done." Evelyn had laughed until she realized he wasn't joking and said, "Hugo, dear, without customers you wouldn't have any work."

So now he was able to be patient with his customers, even the ones who didn't know what they wanted and had a million questions to ask him about the chocolates. He sometimes spied on Kober and tried to emulate how she dealt with those kinds of customers. She seemed to know what she was doing. At least in that regard.

But today. Sheesh, today. How was he going to survive today?

He glanced through the window at Boyd all wired up in a hospital bed. The three of them—Hugo, Boyd, and Pham—had been shooting the breeze and it felt exactly the same as earlier in the vendor room at the Marketplace. Except now Boyd was in a hospital gown and had no qualms about walking around, flapping his naked butt in the wind, whenever he got tired of being in bed.

Hugo stowed his phone and returned to the room.

"Everything okay?" Boyd adjusted his position in the bed, trying to get comfortable.

"I don't know. Skyler is on her way to Santa Fe with Dena's daughter."

"How come?"

"Not really sure. I got the idea she didn't want me to know. Kept dancing around it. Just asked if I'd keep an eye on the cheese shop until she got back."

Boyd began struggling to get out of bed. "Then we should get back."

"Quit it, you big lump." Hugo tucked the blanket around Boyd's legs again, both for Boyd's comfort and so his own eyes didn't get scorched again from that flapping gown. "We're here and we're waiting for the test results. Get over yourself."

"What if it takes forevah?" Boyd whined.

"Then we wait forever," Pham said.

"You know, my dad had four hawt attacks before he died," Boyd said. At their alarmed looks he added, "Cah accident killed him, though."

"Geez, Boyd." Hugo shook his head and frowned at him.

"I haven't had a heart attack, but I've survived many, many, *many* parent-teacher conferences," Pham said with a smile.

"Nevah had the pleasure," Boyd said.

"Me neither," Hugo said.

After a short silence, Boyd said, "I survived plantar fasciitis."

"Never had the pleasure." Pham pointed to his nonexistent foot. "But my odds are half of yours." He must have seen the discomfort on Hugo's and Boyd's faces. "Oh, come on. That was at least a little bit funny." When they didn't laugh, he added, "Listen, guys. I don't have a leg. It's perfectly fine. I'm not embarrassed or mad about it. It's been over forty years. Please don't make it weird."

They were quiet for a moment. Then Hugo said, "I guess I've survived this awkward conversation."

"Attaboy."

"I survived a bout of mumps as a kid," Boyd said.

Pham pointed to his chest. "Measles."

They went back and forth trying to "one up" each other on childhood illnesses. Finally, Boyd guffawed. "We must have had terrible parents to have let us catch all that!"

Hugo said, "I survived my parents."

Boyd's laughter hung heavy and unwelcome in the air. "Oh. I'm so sorry."

"And both your parents? They must have been young," Pham said.

Hugo shook his head. "No, no, no. They're both alive. I just meant they weren't the best parents."

Boyd laughed. "Raise your hand if your parents weren't perfect." His hand waved in the air.

Pham kept his hand down.

"I didn't need them to be perfect," Hugo said. "Just … engaged, interested. In me. Don't get me wrong, they were filthy rich and I got the best the world had to offer a skinny little runt like me. The very best education, finest houses. Traveled everywhere, saw everything. But they were … distant. Literally and figuratively. I spent more time with nannies than with them."

"Some of that sounds wicked awesome."

"Some of it was," Hugo said. "And I didn't even realize how weird it was until I was older and found out not everyone received invitations to the Royal Palace of the Netherlands." He looked at his friends. "I never went to a slumber party. Never played basketball in someone's drive-way. Never raced home after school on my bike to watch old sitcoms on TV." Hugo paused. "How old were you when you went to your first movie?"

"Ten," said Boyd. "Saw *Butch Cassidy and the Sundance*

Kid. Desperately wanted to be a cowboy right then and there. Begged my parents for chaps and a black hat."

Pham thought for a moment. "I was fourteen."

"I would have thought the war disrupted the movie biz in Vietnam," Boyd said.

"I was in a US Army hospital. They played *True Grit* with John Wayne for us."

"Another wicked awesome cowboy." Boyd frowned. "Wait. You were fourteen in a US Army hospital? I think there's a lot more to this story."

Pham smiled. "There is. But I think Hugo was trying to make a point."

"I was. My point is that you guys were young and I was nineteen—nineteen!—before I saw my first movie. Can you imagine? I saw more operas before I was twelve years old than ninety-nine percent of the population ever does, but movies? I had to sneak out to see my first one. *Love, Actually*, actually." Hugo gazed into the distance at the memory. "My parents thought movies were too low-brow and vulgar for our family. I get jealous when I see good parents like Dena or Kober. And Skyler tells some funny stories about her parents, but they're close. I wish ..." Hugo trailed off.

Pham nodded. "I understand that jealousy. My parents were good, but I didn't have much time with them. My father died when I was a baby. He didn't survive imprisonment in Vietnam in 1956."

"Your father was a communist?" Hugo asked.

Pham shook his head emphatically. "No. But he was a professor and free-thinker so the government said he was dangerous. What did your dad do?"

Hugo knew Pham was trying to change the subject. "My dad always called himself a nabob. When I was a kid, for some reason I decided that meant he was a swimmer—

you know, bobbing around—so that's what I told all my friends. It made sense at the time. To be honest, I'm still not entirely clear on how he spent his time. What about you, Boyd?"

"My parents were spies."

Boyd

BOYD LIKED the looks of intrigue on Hugo and Pham's faces, but he knew he had to tell them the truth.

"My folks weren't *spy* spies. They owned a business providing undercover shoppers for stores around the Boston area. They spied in the sense that they watched for shoplifters as well as light-fingered employees."

"That's almost as exotic as working for the FBI or CIA," Hugo said.

Boyd cocked his head, curious. "Ya think?"

Hugo nodded.

"You're not pulling my leg?"

"No. Why would you think that?"

"Because when I was a kid, it embarrassed the heck out of me. One time my mom caught my third-grade teacher stealing a cashmere sweater."

"Oh, man. That's rough. Hadn't thought about that." Hugo made a *tsk-tsk* sound.

"At least your parents were doing the right thing, on the right side of the law, Boyd. You should hear some of the things my foster kids tell me." Pham let out a low whistle. "Talk about being embarrassed by your parents."

"It wasn't until I was older that I understood it was honorable work and they weren't just trying to entrap people or be all sneaky about stuff. But believe you me, the rest of third grade was pretty hahd on little Boyd-a-reeno!" Boyd bugged out his eyes and made a crazy face.

Hugo and Pham laughed.

"Did you ever work for them?" Hugo asked.

Boyd roared. "Seriously? Ya think I could sneak around anywhere in this ridiculous meat suit?" He gestured up and down his body. "I've always been this big and this loud. In fact, let me tell you a funny—"

The nurse interrupted, coming in to check on him, adjusting this, reading that, jotting something in the chart hanging off the foot of his bed.

Suddenly, they all remembered why they were there. The levity disappeared from the room, replaced by a heavy foreboding.

"Shouldn't be too much longer, Mr Drummond," the nurse said as she left.

Nobody said anything for a few moments until Boyd said quietly, "I can't thank you guys enough for … you know … all this." He waved his arm around. "You're my only friends."

"You just moved here. Give it time," Pham said.

Boyd knew better. He also knew that when the two of them found out who he really was, their friendship would end abruptly, like one of those film strips in school that suddenly snapped and went *fwapp-fwapp-fwapp*. It was third grade all over again. Everyone simply had to move on.

He listened with half an ear as Hugo told Pham about his travels to southeast Asia. Boyd hated himself for being so pathetic. The thought crossed his mind that maybe he subconsciously *wanted* to drop dead from a heart attack. There was absolutely no need for him to be outside shoveling snow in the middle of a blizzard. Or even after it was over. There were plenty of neighborhood kids he could pay to handle that particular chore for him.

So why had he done it?

Evelyn

"WELL, it *is* dramatic. Listen to this." Evelyn read to Max from the paper she pulled from the woman's boot.

A Pirate's Prayer

Understand, my acts are not criminal.

Navigating stormy seas, I simply seek safe haven.

Defeat is not an option in my attempt for a better life for me and my fellow pirates.

Escaping king and crown is foremost on my mind. I shall disguise my crew; they shan't find us.

Refugees, far from home, we seek a friendlier, more fulfilling life, perhaps on the ocean side.

Treasure has been buried forty paces from shore, jewels and gold to start anew.

Homecoming seems impossible, yet I yearn for dear mama and worry about stern doting papa, knowing

Escape is mine only option.

Sails arise! I am

Undaunted. My cause is valiant, though my quest a

Gamble, and each step

Arduous.

Rebirth, like a drab caterpillar's transformation into a ruby red butterfly, remains our one and only option.

Miracles will be fervently beseeched, before, during and after our travels.

Independence, our aim and constant guiding Light.

Lasting peace to those who read these words. You are ever in my heart.

"I'll give you the dramatic. But what is it?" Max asked.

They both read it again, silently.

Finally, Evelyn said, "It's a … prayer … from a pirate, I guess."

"That clears it up."

"Okay, let's put our thinking caps on," Evelyn said.

Max mimed putting on a bonnet and tying it in a big bow.

"A pirate, the captain of the ship," Evelyn said. "Stormy seas, looking for shelter. Worried about their crew being caught."

"They're tired of the pirate life, going to live on a beach somewhere with all their buried loot," Max added.

They read silently again.

"Since when are butterflies ruby red?" Max asked, pointing to the line in the poem.

"Probably just poetic license. I mean, look how fancy the script is. And how the first letter of each line is bigger and fancier—" Evelyn ran her index finger down the margin of the paper, crossing each first letter. Suddenly she frowned and ran her finger down the margin again, slower. "Max! Are you seeing this?"

"Your finger? Yes, I'm not blind."

"No. Look at each letter I'm pointing at. This is an acrostic poem."

"Across what?"

"Acrostic." Evelyn enunciated slowly. As she pointed to each fancy first letter, she named it. "U-N-D-E-R T-H-E—"

"Good gravy! This *is* dramatic!" Max finished naming the letters as Evelyn pointed at them. "S-U-G-A-R M-I-L-L. Under the sugar mill." He and Evelyn stared at each other with wide eyes. "But what's under the sugar mill?"

They reread the poem.

"I don't know," Evelyn finally said. "But let's go look for a secret door!"

They hurried out to the promenade in front of their photo studio and stood in the center. All of the businesses formed a rectangle with their back doors opening into the vendor area. The promenade formed a bigger rectangle all around them.

Evelyn gestured to the shops. "All of these were added

when they refurbished, so there's not going to be anything there."

"And upstairs is the same, just without any shops." Max looked toward the enormous two-story picture windows. "But this part of the mill, these brick walls, have always been here."

There were exterior doors set on the diagonal at all four corners of the building. They hurried to the closest but didn't exit. They walked along the short side of the rectangle. The windows were smaller on this side, and they peered closely to see if anything was amiss with the brick-work. Max ran his hand along the bricks.

They ended up back where they began, with no sign of any secret door.

"Well, that's disappointing," Evelyn said.

"Remember, though, that this refurbished Marketplace is just one small part of the original sugar mill. Let's look outside."

"Max, there's a blizzard out there."

"You're going to let a little bit of snow put the kibosh on this mystery?"

"It's not a little bit of snow, but point taken."

They bundled up and Evelyn grabbed an umbrella. Max ran up to the storeroom on the second floor and found a shovel.

"Ready, spaghetti?" Max pulled the hood of Evelyn's parka over her head and tied it under her chin.

"As I'll ever be," Evelyn replied, doing the same for Max.

Max did a little jig in the promenade. "We're having an adventure, we're having an adventure!" he sang.

Evelyn laughed. "What are you, eight?" but then she did a version of the same jig and sang along.

Max pulled open the door and a rowdy swirl of snow blasted their faces.

Evelyn opened her umbrella and stepped outside. It was immediately pulled from her grasp and went dancing away across the parking lot. She turned to go back inside.

"Oh no you don't!" Max shouted over the wind. "An adventure, remember?"

Evelyn took a deep breath and snuggled down into her coat. She felt for the pirate poem in her pocket and held it tight, wondering if wind this strong could actually dip into her pocket and steal it from her grasp.

With faces downturned to keep the wind out of their faces, Evelyn tromped close to the Marketplace wall following Max who carried the shovel. Every so often he moved closer to the brick wall and studied it.

Again, they made it all the way around the building without so much of a hint of a hidden door. They huddled out of the wind, heads touching. Max still had to shout to be heard. "It's gotta be over in the old part."

Evelyn knew the "old part" was the more decrepit part of the sugar mill, the part deemed not attractive or useful any longer. She also knew it wasn't meant to be tromped through by a couple of old people. Young people, sure. Everyone knew that was the kind of secluded, magical place where kids liked to hang out, and adults rarely followed. Her own son spent too many hours— "Max, you're not thinking we should—"

"C'mon, Ev!"

She pulled his sleeve and shouted directly into his ear. "Let's do it after the storm!"

"Nonsense," he shouted back. "After the storm we'll be busy with customers again!"

Evelyn knew he was right. This was the sweet spot. And she was as curious as Max.

"Okay. But don't you move from this spot without me, old man. I'll be right back."

She hurried to the nearest diagonal door and pulled it open. She caught her breath for a moment then rummaged through a drawer in the studio to find a flashlight. She shoved it in her coat pocket. On her way back to Max, she stuck her head in Kateri's office. "Hey, Kateri?"

"Just the friendly face I was hoping to see," Kateri said. "I wanted to show you something."

"Can it wait? Max and I are going over to the outbuildings. We want to check on something. I didn't want you to worry about us if you couldn't find us."

Kateri stood. "I'll go with you."

Evelyn waved her back down. "No need. We won't be long. But if we don't come back, I just wanted someone to know where to look for our bodies." At Kateri's alarmed look, Evelyn laughed. "We'll be fine. Back in a jif." She turned back to Kateria. "But if we're not …" she said ominously, then laughed.

"Are you on drugs? Should I call someone?" Kateri stood again. "Wait. Are you going to kill Max and I'm going to turn into the prime suspect somehow?"

Evelyn laughed again. "Probably not today, but if I don't get back out there, he might freeze to death. Can you make a fresh pot of coffee, though? We'll definitely need some when we get back."

Evelyn returned to Max.

"Took you long enough! I'm an icicle!"

"Do you want to go warm up and then try again?"

"Wrangle my boots again? No way. We're doing this now."

They linked arms and Max used the shovel as a walking stick. Evelyn kept her hand in her pocket, holding tight to the pirate poem.

Despite the raging storm, it didn't take them too long to cross the parking lot and the field where the other buildings of the sugar mill stood. Some parts of the mill had been demolished due to their age and structural integrity. The townspeople all knew that this remaining bit of the old sugar mill was an attractive nuisance for the kids in town, but everyone also knew that anyone—including Sheriff Johnson and Deputy Chavez—walked through randomly. Sheriff Johnson ran a tighter ship than did her predecessor, so the kids who would be tempted to frequent the old buildings only did so to scare each other with spooky ghost stories and seances.

When they reached the brick building, they pulled open the creaky door and leaned against the wall, catching their breath, warming up, and allowing their eyes to adjust.

"Wish we thought to bring a flashlight," Max said.

The room was immediately illuminated. "You're welcome," Evelyn said.

"You've always been the brains of this operation."

"And don't you forget it."

They made a pass through the space, investigating every inch of the walls for evidence of some hidden staircase or secret room. Evelyn also kept an eye out for any booze containers or drug paraphernalia in case she needed to alert the sheriff. She was pleased as punch to find nothing to report in that regard, but disappointed they didn't find a way to get under the sugar mill, as the pirate poem teased.

"There's nothing here, Max."

"Seems that way. But I want to try one last thing."

"What?"

"This place processed sugar beets, right?"

"Right. So?"

"So, there must have been some sort of root cellar,

right? They'd need to keep the beets——"

"Yes, they would!" Evelyn popped Max's hood over his head and tied it, then held out her chin for Max to tie hers. "Follow me."

They hurried outside and Evelyn stopped in the doorway to get her bearings. "I used to work in the office over there," she murmured, pointing toward the parking lot that replaced it. She closed her eyes, taking a quick trip to the past. Suddenly her eyes snapped open. "This way! Bring the shovel."

She walked right up next to the outbuilding, bumping it with her shoulder occasionally. After every twenty steps or so, she'd close her eyes and access her memory before hurrying forward. Finally, she stopped. "I think it's around here," she shouted, pointing at the snow-covered ground.

"What, exactly?" Max shouted.

"The door to the root cellar!"

"It's underground?"

Evelyn rolled her eyes. "It's not a *roof* cellar! Where did you think it was going to be?"

Despite the reprimand, Max had to laugh. "We're having an adventure, we're having an adventure," he sang.

Evelyn bent and tried to scoop snow away with her hands, but it was futile, like using a teaspoon to clear a beach.

"Let the man do it," Max said with forced bravado.

"Be my guest." Evelyn clapped her gloves together to remove the snow as she leaned against the wall.

Max began shoveling snow in a small area not too far from the wall. After clearing a two-foot square, he took a giant step parallel to the building. Evelyn did too. After he cleared another two-foot square, Evelyn said, "Take a break. Let me try."

"You're not the man," he said, handing over the shovel.

Now *he* leaned and Evelyn took a giant step away from the cleared area and began shoveling.

Nothing. She tried again. When it yielded no evidence of a root cellar, she joined Max against the wall. "I'm sure this is the place," she said. "It has to be."

"We'll keep looking. Unless you want to go in? Are you okay?" He looked at her with concern.

Evelyn checked her watch. "Fifteen more minutes. Then Kateri will be calling the sheriff to report your murder."

"You told her you were going to murder me?"

"No, but it's a solid guess."

"True." Max grabbed the shovel. "My turn."

On his second jab with the shovel, he stopped short. "Found it!" He dropped to a squat and used his hands to move the snow from the metal handle he hit with the shovel.

Evelyn helped him clear snow from the root cellar door. It was exactly how she remembered, albeit a little further down the building. She leaned the shovel against the wall and they both tugged on the handle. They heard the rusty hinges scream in protest even over the roar of the wind. They lifted the door and leaned it backward so it rested against the building.

Standing in front of it, Evelyn suddenly got a case of the willies. "Anything could be down there after all these years," she said.

Max put a hand on her sleeve. "Do you want to wait here and I'll go down alone?"

Evelyn looked across the field and parking lot toward the Marketplace. "No, I'll be fine."

"Okay. Hold my hand."

"Besides, if anything creepy is down there, I just have to be able to outrun you, right?"

Dena

BACK IN GEORGIA'S CAR, Dena was listening with half an ear to yet more manic anecdotes about Georgia's water aerobics class. Was she there morning, noon, and night?

The road had gotten worse, if that was possible. Dena gasped and clutched at the dashboard every time Georgia fishtailed on the slippery road, which was all too often.

Georgia didn't seem the least bit worried about the road conditions, although at one point when they fishtailed, she placed a hand on her belly and laughed, saying, "That gave me the collywobbles!"

Dena knew that meant Georgia was queasy but didn't know how exactly she knew that. She'd never heard Georgia use that phrase, and honestly, it felt a bit extreme for her vocabulary. Georgia didn't typically go in for folksy sayings. It must have been an expression her grandmother had used.

When they had left the truck stop and Dena saw the highway hadn't been closed like the trucker said, she got some collywobbles herself. If it *had* been closed, they would have been forced into a shelter somewhere, maybe a church basement or a high school gym, and she could have found help for Georgia. Maybe even delivered her to a doctor or hospital.

Dena regretted not making a huge scene at the truck stop. But that might have totally backfired. Perhaps then Georgia would have bolted back out into the storm without her. Who knows where she would have gone or what she would have done. No, better to have stuck with her, through this ridiculous kidnapping, to keep Georgia if not safe, at least in sight. There was still every chance to get Georgia some medical intervention.

Each time they passed a highway sign pointing out the exit for a hospital in one of the small towns nearby, Dena had tried to get Georgia to take it.

"Georgia, I think I'm having a panic attack. Please stop at that hospital."

"Georgia, these handcuffs have cut off my circulation and I think I have a dangerous situation here. You don't want me to lose my hands, do you? Please stop at that hospital."

"Georgia, holding our pee for so long probably gave us both UTIs. We better get to that hospital."

"Georgia, my heart is beating really fast. I'm probably having a heart attack. Please stop at that hospital."

Georgia never even considered it. Dena might as well have told her she needed to stop because a fly landed on her knee.

It might have been for the best, though, because none of the exits had been plowed and Dena couldn't actually see the lights from any towns. Who knew how far they'd have to go to get to a hospital and how long it would take in these conditions?

Dena wasn't sure any more what worried her most—

being kidnapped by a crazy woman or sliding off the road in a blizzard.

And Dena was now convinced that Georgia was indeed a crazy woman. Something was really, truly, substantially wrong with her. She'd lost track of how many of those blue pills Georgia had popped. Dena kept asking, but Georgia wouldn't tell her why she was kidnapping her and shuttling her off to Santa Fe in the middle of a blizzard.

Perhaps Georgia *couldn't* tell her why she was kidnapping her. Crazy, remember?

Dena began to feel chilled, and not just from the cold. Georgia spoke about her water aerobics class with the same casualness she had when she'd accused Dena of pushing her off a mountain last year. Georgia's grasp on reality was tenuous no more; she had let go entirely. With every mile they drove, sanity slipped further and further away.

What was all Georgia's chatter about Dena pushing her off that trail, anyway? Dena knew that's what other people thought at the time, but it wasn't remotely true. She thought Georgia knew that by now.

But even if Georgia was convinced Dena gave her a shove, why hadn't she called the police from the hospital after emerging from her coma? Or when she was released to recover at home? Or at any time during the last four months?

Maybe Georgia *had* called the police, Dena mused. And if she had, they would have politely listened to her rant and discovered it was simply an old lady's fever dream.

Dena glanced at Georgia.

"—and then we all took our bathing caps off, but Mildred misunderstood and started taking off her suit—"

The police would have reminded Georgia—as per the

incident report—that she simply slipped on loose gravel and that Dena was the one who went for help and that was the end of it for them and their investigation. But maybe that's why Georgia felt she needed to kidnap me and take me back to Santa Fe, Dena thought. Perhaps her plan was to offer me up to the police like some crazed bounty hunter. Here she is, she'd scream, Santa Fe's Most Wanted! And I had to go collect her in a snowstorm. Gimme a medal, she'd demand.

Instead, they'd snap pink fuzzy handcuffs on *her* for kidnapping across state lines and charge her with some big fat felonies.

Dena listened to a couple of minutes of some story involving the almost topless Mildred and Georgia's boyfriend, who seemed to Dena more and more imaginary with each tidbit she told her.

"—the deep end is too deep for Catherine—we call her Catherine the Great because of her double-H cups—so she was just bobbing along—" Georgia plucked her phone from her bra. "Yeah? Oh, good idea." She hung up then popped another pill in her mouth. "But she boobed, ha ha, how Freudian, bobbed too far out and later when I told my boyfriend—"

"What did you just eat?" Dena asked.

"Vitamin. Pretty sure."

"You're pretty sure?" It occurred to Dena that she hadn't heard Georgia's phone ring or buzz or anything. She couldn't remember a time when Georgia silenced her phone. She was so busy and knew so many people it rang nonstop. At least in all the time Dena hung out with her in Santa Fe.

"This boyfriend of yours. Do Beige Ann and Cassandra like him?"

Georgia shook her head forcefully. "His Drishti is too

… you know. Different paths and all. Those women are full of toxins and simply can't … manifest. You know."

Dena definitely did not know.

The more Georgia talked—and it was nonstop now—the less she was actually communicating. Georgia was like one of those toddlers who picked up a toy phone and began babbling with exactly the right intonation and cadence as an adult, but using nonsense words. Dena remembered Charlee doing that as a baby, pausing as if it were a true telephone conversation, even throwing her head back and laughing as she'd seen Dena do a thousand times. Dena found it a bit alarming.

But not as alarming as what was going on in this Volvo.

Was all of this worse than Dena recognized? Was this boyfriend of Georgia's simply a figment of her imagination? Had she invented him? Was she deep into some sort of manic psychotic episode?

It was dawning on Dena that she needed to get Georgia to talk about what was really going on. Not water aerobics. Not her imaginary boyfriend. Not her fantasy of being pushed off a mountain trail. But what was actually going on. Dena's communication skills were going to be the only thing to get her out of this mess.

She remembered how uncommunicative she'd been over the years, especially after her husband died. She didn't want to talk to anyone about anything. It was too much to bear. Her brain only had one thought and she did not want it to be the only thing she could say. Otherwise, people would look at her the same way she was looking at Georgia with her broken record about water aerobics.

That lack of communication was the biggest regret of her life. To this day it shamed her that she was not strong enough for her kids, pawning off Lance and Charlee to others. Lance went to boarding school. Charlee was taken in by the parents of her best friend until she graduated early and went off to college. Dena ran away to Santa Fe where she didn't know anyone and was able to wallow in secret, never having to discuss or explain her husband's murder, or listen to any of his fellow cops proclaim his guilt and betrayal.

When all that noise pummeled you from every side, it was almost impossible to know what to believe and what to tune out. She had tuned it all out. She was thankful that Charlee and Lance turned out okay. Although when she brought it up with Charlee recently, she had quipped, "You think I'm okay? You realize I kill and terrorize people for a living, right?"

But Charlee's tremor went away after she learned the truth, and while Lance was a stoic cop just like his dad had been, they all had solid relationships with each other and came out the other side unscathed. Maybe a couple of scars, but not deadly ones. Just reminders.

Was Georgia going through something similar that took her in a different direction, a true break from reality rather than just a temporary blocking out of reality?

Was there a difference? Had Dena acted this same bizarre way but hadn't realized it because she hadn't taken a weird road trip with a friend during her … episode?

Georgia's headlights illuminated the road sign that said, *Santa Fe, Next Four Exits.*

A chill ran through Dena.

What happens now?

Charlee

CHARLEE GRIPPED the steering wheel so tightly her hands began to cramp. They were almost to the southern Colorado border, near Walsenburg. There hadn't been many cars. In fact, Charlee couldn't remember the last time they'd seen one traveling in either direction.

They'd been moving slow and steady, like the tortoise, and Charlee had fallen into a rhythm during the drive. There were faint tire tracks in front of them the entire way so far. She focused on them so fervently she knew she was in danger of becoming hypnotized. She'd driven on plenty of snow-covered roads in her life and knew that a driver could become mesmerized by tracks in front of them. You couldn't simply plow forward because what if the other car ahead of you had ran off the road? You'd run off the road right behind them. But what else could she do? There were no visible lines on the road, so she had only a vague idea of where the shoulder might be. Of course, she was assuming there *was* a shoulder. The reflective lettering of the mile markers was always a welcome sight.

Often the land next to the road dropped away from

them completely. Charlee could picture the rolling hills and ravines she knew were out there in the darkness because of her drive to Santa Fe a few months earlier, a much more pleasant journey.

Charlee had to constantly calibrate where she was on the road, where the tracks were, where the shoulder was. Even though it was eerie to be a lone car out in the middle of nowhere like this, she was thankful there were no cars behind her because she could drive in the center of the highway.

But it took all her attention.

Skyler had tried to fill the silence with conversation, but when Charlee responded only with grunts and *mm-hmms*, she'd finally given up. Every so often Skyler would offer to drive but Charlee declined each time, mainly because she was afraid to stop.

Charlee began flexing first one hand and then the other in an effort to get some blood flowing back into them. She didn't want to get to Santa Fe and require surgery to remove her hands from her steering wheel.

Suddenly, red flashing lights appeared in front of them.

Charlee was well aware that slamming on her brakes would be a very bad idea in this weather. While Skyler took quick little gasps and braced herself with one palm on the dashboard and the other gripping her door handle, Charlee pressed her foot gently on the brake, easing up when she felt the rear end of the car begin to slide.

They half-rolled and half-slid to a stop in front of a highway closure gate. The flashing lights lit up the evening, casting a spooky glow over everything, like it had been bathed in blood.

Charlee shook her head to erase the morbid thought, but was torn, because it would be an evocative image in one of her books.

The idea of a road closure gate was not a foreign concept in general to Charlee. But seeing one in reality was unexpected, to say the least.

"Well."

"Yeah."

Skyler's phone lit up when she tapped on it.

Charlee continued to stare at the gate.

"They want us to take this exit back to Walsenburg. This says I-25 is closed from Walsenburg to … maybe Las Vegas."

Charlee gasped. "Las Vegas?"

"New Mexico, not Nevada."

"Oh. That makes more sense. How long are they closing it?"

"Doesn't say."

"Like all night or just an hour or something?"

Skyler lowered her chin and spoke slowly. "It doesn't say."

"I'm thinking we go around it. We've come this far," Charlee said.

"I'm thinking we don't."

"It can't be any worse up ahead than it's been back there."

"Sure it can. Hence the road closure."

Charlee turned sideways in her seat so she was facing Skyler directly. "If my mom came this way, she didn't get stuck behind this gate."

"How do you know? She could be holed up in some Marriott in Walsenburg right now."

"She could be, but she's not."

"How do you know?"

"Because she would have called me by now." Charlee waggled her phone at Skyler. "No calls, no texts, no nothing."

"Maybe she called your brother."

"Then *he* would have called me."

They stared at each other until both their phones went dark. The red flashing lights made them look like they were in a cartoon. Or maybe a Batman movie.

"Skyler, listen. You invited yourself along on this trip. I didn't ask you to come. I have to keep going."

"I get that you want to, but do you see that gate in front of you with all the flashing lights that says Road Closed?"

"The road in front of us is exactly the same as the road behind us. And my mom is in some kind of trouble up ahead."

"You don't know that."

"I do. And so do you, or you wouldn't have made this trip with me."

Skyler took a deep breath. "You're sure?"

"Absolutely."

Skyler took another deep breath. "Okay."

Charlee gripped the wheel and glanced in her rearview mirror, even though she knew there were no cars for miles. She peered through the windshield then placed the car in Park. Bracing herself, she stepped out into the storm. The wind buffeted her, and she quickly zipped her coat and raised her hood.

She tested the crossing arm, trying to see if she could lift it, either all the way, or at least enough to drive under it. She wasn't surprised when it didn't budge. She used the flashlight app on her phone to light up the shoulder. Was there enough room to drive around?

She moved to the other edge, where the brace held the crossing arm, again lighting up the shoulder. After a bit of study, she decided she had plenty of room to drive on the shoulder and around the gate on this side. The snow was deep and there were no tire tracks to guide her, but she felt confident she could picture what was under the snow. She gave the snow a bit of a kick, as a test.

Back in the car, she told Skyler the plan.

"You're sure?"

"I am."

"But are you?"

"I told you, I am."

"But really … are you?"

Charlee took a deep breath and held it. Shifted from Park to Drive and crept toward the hinge of the gate arm. She moved slowly, trying not to think about what would happen if the highway patrol saw what she was doing.

Inch by terrifying inch she drove along the shoulder. The passenger side dipped down and Skyler braced her hands on the ceiling of the car. Neither one of them breathed.

The rear end slid. Skyler whimpered and immediately clamped a hand over her mouth. Charlee felt like her heart was going to explode out of her chest. The car moved achingly slow in the direction she pointed it, but at this moment Charlee felt like she had absolutely no control.

When the tall metal brace was directly next to her door, she steered a bit to the left as they continued to inch forward, aiming back to the road.

Inch by inch. Another iota to the left. Two inches. Four inches. Six.

The brace was at the rear door. No sliding. Still inching toward the road.

Skyler's hand shot out to Charlee's taut forearm but stopped before grabbing it. "I think you're doing it!"

Charlee gripped the wheel tighter, concentrating. She didn't want to blow it now. They were so close.

Creeping and creeping around the gate. "Slow and steady," Charlee murmured.

Charlee breathed a sigh of relief when they finally cleared the gate. It felt like it had taken three hours, but it was probably only three minutes. She and Skyler shared a high five.

"Nice!"

Skyler's smile froze on her face, morphing to wide-eyed panic as the car began sliding sideways down the embankment.

Skyler placed her palms flat on the ceiling, again bracing herself, eyes squinched tight.

Charlee pressed the brake slowly at first, but when it made no difference, she slammed it hard. The car continued its slide down the embankment, like butter melting down a stack of hot pancakes.

Charlee tried turning the wheel. Nothing.

Stomping the brakes. Nothing.

The car had gained momentum and now was by anyone's definition, completely out of Charlee's control.

She shut her eyes. Hands clenched on steering wheel.

Both women let out animal noises until the car slammed into a snowbank.

Then everything was silent.

Charlee opened her eyes. The red flashing lights behind them continued to light up the dark sky. "Are you okay?"

"Yeah. Are you?"

"Yeah."

Skyler still had her hands braced against the ceiling. She pulled them down slowly, and turned her head to the right, following Charlee's gaze.

The entire passenger side of the car was dark,

including half the windshield and half the rear window. Snow was packed, crushed against the windows.

Charlee had to push hard on her door to get it open at that sharp uphill angle. She finally stepped out and Skyler clambered on all fours after her. They huddled close, bracing against the heavy, swirling snow.

The snow was up to her knees except where the car had pushed it out of the way on its trip down the ravine. There it was only up to mid-shin. They took giant steps around the front of the car to assess the damage. She couldn't see anything troubling except, of course, that they were wedged into a snowdrift at least eight feet high. The snow had filled the ravine. A cattle fence created the perfect edge to collect and compact the snow.

Charlee felt Skyler's breath right behind her.

"How did you not see that?" Skyler said.

"It looked solid to me. I thought it was the road." Charlee pushed past her to check the rear end.

Again, no visible damage to the car. Snow was soft, after all. Most of the time.

But there was no denying it. Half the car was wedged into the snowbank.

Charlee opened the back door on the driver's side and rooted around for the long-handled combo snow-scraper-and-brush Ozzi had given her for Christmas. She attempted to brush some of the snow away from the trunk, but more fell and took its place. She brushed that away too and was rewarded with a solid chunk of snowbank landing with a thud on the trunk.

She seemed to recall some information she read about slab avalanches while researching a book, how they're made of tightly packed snow, but are triggered by the collapse of the weaker snow underneath.

You know, like what she just brushed away.

She walked backward toward the driver's side of the car, sweeping Skyler with her.

If she moved any more snow, she'd make it worse.

She leaned against the driver's door and assessed the route back up to the road. The flashing lights from the road closure arm continued to strobe into the swirling snow.

"It doesn't seem all that steep, even looking up from the bottom of the ditch," Charlee mused out loud.

"Ditch? This is a crevasse!" Skyler said.

"Maybe to someone from Wisconsin. You don't have mountains there, do you?"

"We're not in the mountains. If we weren't at the bottom of this crevasse, you'd be able to see that."

"I think we can get back up there."

Skyler stood next to her and turned her gaze in the same direction. "Seriously?"

"Yeah. Pretty sure." Charlee didn't sound convincing even to herself. "But we don't have much choice, do we? We can't stay down here all night."

"Okay. So what's your plan?"

Again with the plans! Why was Skyler so hung up on having plans for everything? Charlee thought for a few minutes. "I'm going to crank the steering wheel away from the snowbank. You're going to the back, as close as you can get to the snowbank, and when I press the gas, you're going to push. We're going to get the car un-wedged from the snow, then drive back up to the road."

Skyler looked at the snowbank at the rear of the car. "Sure. That'll work."

"That's what I th—Oh. You're being sarcastic. Got a better idea?"

"Nope." Skyler pulled her gloves from her pockets and put them on. She moved to the back of the car and positioned herself at the far corner of the trunk, as close as she could wedge herself. "Ready when you are."

"Get ready to run out of the way if any more snow starts coming down."

Skyler moved to the other side of the trunk, away from the snowbank, giving it the side-eye the entire time.

Charlee returned to the driver's seat. She turned the key, enormously relieved when the engine turned over. She cranked the steering wheel all the way so the front tires were pointed as far to the left as they could go. Tapped the gas and felt the back of the car rock a bit.

This was going to work!

She continued cranking and tapping while Skyler continued pushing and rocking.

The car inched forward little by little. Charlee gave it a little more gas and the car slid a few inches further from the snowbank.

THUNK.

The rear window was still covered so Charlee couldn't see what was happening behind her but tapped the gas again.

THUNK.

The car wasn't moving. There was no more inching, pushing, or rocking.

Suddenly Skyler's face loomed up in Charlee's window. She did not look happy. The driver's door was yanked open.

"We're stuck even worse now!" she said.

"What? How is that possible? We were moving forward!" Charlee jumped out of the car and groaned when she reached the rear.

A huge part of the snowbank had fallen on top of the car, covering more of it now. Avalanche 101.

Without another word, Skyler climbed across to the passenger seat and Charlee returned to the driver's seat.

They sat silently in the glow of the flashing lights. Snow swirled in their headlights. Charlee shut off the ignition. Before she did, she checked her gas gauge. About a quarter tank.

She didn't mention this to Skyler.

Kober

SEVERAL MONTHS AGO, when the cracks in her relationship with Nic began to show, Kober had seen an apron that said, "I'm not upset about my divorce. I'm only upset because I'm not a widow." She immediately adopted the sentiment as her personal motto, but because it was a little too darkly funny and she didn't want her kids to think anything was wrong, she didn't buy the apron. Nor had she ever spoken her new motto out loud.

Besides, she knew enough about murder investigations to know that if Nic had some sort of accident, she'd be the first suspect rounded up. With her luck, she'd probably be wearing the apron when the detectives banged on her door. *I'm not sure there's a Snarky Apron Defense on the books in the Colorado Revised Statutes,* she thought darkly. No, better just to file her motto away in the back of her mind.

She did, however, consider divesting herself of all wedding customers. No wedding cakes. No groom's cakes. Nothing for the reception table.

But then she did some math.

Wedding cakes were lucrative, her bread-and-butter, pardon the pun.

So instead of trying to ban wedding cakes from her bakery, or talk brides out of getting married, she recently opted instead to subject the brides to lengthy interviews, asking pointed questions about their intendeds and the matrimonial lives they anticipated for themselves. If they gave answers that satisfied Kober, she agreed to bake them a wedding cake. For an exorbitant price, of course.

Brides hadn't yet balked at the price. In fact, they seemed so pleased that they had passed Kober's test they probably would have paid even more. But Kober didn't want to take advantage. Not too much, anyway.

While she sat sadly on her sad little stool, thinking about her sad little marriage in her sad little bakery, staring at her sad little menu board, she thought again about Rattlesnake Kate and all the men who took advantage of her over the years.

"Men. Ugh." Kober jumped off the stool and went to the sink. She returned to the menu board, again with the corner of a wet rag wrapped around her index finger. "No more weddings. No more brides. No more wedding cakes."

She reached out to erase the line that said, "Wedding Cakes At Owner's Discretion," but then pulled back her finger.

Nic was gone. That meant Nic's income was gone too. Kober was suddenly a single mother of four. There was no way the bakery would survive if she didn't make wedding cakes.

She slumped back on her stool, gazing across the bakery and through the floor-to-ceiling Marketplace windows. The snow swirled and fell all over Sugar Springs. She stared at it for so long, it began to look like frosting to her. She imagined Sugar Springs was one gigantic cake covered in white cloud frosting.

Had Rattlesnake Kate ever had a wedding cake?

If Kate had been subjected to her bridal interrogation, would she have taken up with the men in her life? If someone would have interrogated Kober about Nic, would she have gone through with her wedding?

Kober began to get angry. Why was it always up to her to fix things? Why did Nic think it was okay for him to sneak away from his marriage just because he found someone younger, thinner, hotter, and less opinionated than his wife of all these years? At least Kober imagined his new plaything was younger, thinner, hotter, and less opinionated because otherwise, why bother? Even Nic wouldn't be so stupid as to exchange a cherry pie for a blueberry pie. A brownie for a blondie. The mother of his children for a … a tart.

She couldn't begin to understand what was in Nic's mind because all he told her was that if he was going to get snowed in, he didn't want it to be in Sugar Springs, with his ugly shrew of a wife, although Kober might have misremembered that last part.

What would Rattlesnake Kate do?

Kober thought about it for a while, then opened two new documents on her laptop. She titled one of them *Questions for Grooms*, and the other *Questions for Parents*. If brides were to be subjected to endless soul-searching questions about marriage, then why shouldn't grooms endure the same interrogation? And was there any reason not to assess the quality of the marriages of their parents?

No, there was not.

Kober typed furiously, only stopping to call the kids and tell them she'd be home soon and there was frozen pizza in the garage freezer if they got hungry.

When she had listed all the questions she wished she would have asked Nic, his parents, and her parents, she stopped.

Then she went to the price list she kept under the cash register and doubled the amount for wedding cakes. Again.

Evelyn

WITH ONE HAND holding on to Max's, and the other gripping the flashlight, Evelyn descended the stairs to the root cellar with Max. They left the door open so they wouldn't get trapped and hurried down, out of the storm. At the bottom of the stairs, she turned on the flashlight.

They wrinkled their noses against the dank, musty odor of the rough underground room and moved further into the interior where the snow couldn't reach them.

"Can you smell the beets?" she asked. "Kind of a faint sugar smell?" It was a familiar scent to Evelyn. She shined her flashlight around. The cellar was so large that the beam didn't penetrate to the other wall.

Max grunted. "Wish we'd brought that poem. Now that we've figured out what *under the sugar mill* means, I can't remember what else we were looking for."

Evelyn produced the poem and shined the light on it. "You're welcome."

"You're gonna get a big head if this keeps up."

They read the poem again, then Evelyn ran her finger

under the line, "Treasure has been buried forty paces from shore, jewels and gold to start anew."

"Forty paces," she said.

"Treasure," Max said, waggling his eyebrows. "But is this the shore they're talking about?"

"I guess we'll find out." Evelyn shined the light around the room again. "But where to start pacing?" Without waiting for a reply, she hurried back to the bottom of the stairs. Placing her heels in the center of the step, directly against it, Evelyn began counting off forty paces. The light bobbed in front of her. Max followed behind.

She ended far inside the room, where the flashlight hadn't illuminated. Without moving, she surveyed the area. There were large wooden boxes on stands back here. She stood directly in front of the first one. "This must be it," she said excitedly. She dropped to one knee. "I don't see anything, though. Could something have been buried underneath all this?"

"If it is, I don't know how we'd ever get to it. This dirt is packed as hard as granite."

"Oh no! All this work for nothing? That can't be!" Evelyn scuffed the dirt with her boot.

"Don't be giving up just yet, you!" Max took her hand. "You've figured it out so far, no reason to think you can't find buried treasure too."

Evelyn sighed as she half-heartedly shined the light around, taking in the brick wall to her right. "I doubt I'll —" She focused the light on an area of the brick wall. "Do you see that? Does that look weird to you, Max?"

Evelyn walked toward the wall, straight out from where she ended her forty paces.

Max followed.

She placed a palm on the wall for balance as she took a

knee, then rubbed her hand on a brick four from the floor. "This one doesn't match."

Max slowly lowered himself, using the wall for support. "Looks the same color to me."

"Not the color. Look here, it's not even with the others on this side."

Max rubbed his hand where she pointed. "You're right." He pulled his keys from his pocket and jabbed one into the space. Using it as a fulcrum, Max easily moved the brick. He grinned over at Evelyn.

They both got a grip on the brick and pulled it out of the wall. Evelyn shined the light inside, then gently nudged out a long, narrow wooden box.

She placed it in Max's open palms and gently traced the delicate carving of a tree on the top. It was set inside a circle. A symmetrical chain of flowers was carved around it. The negative space was painted seafoam green. "So pretty."

They looked at each other with jittery anticipation.

"Open it." Max encouraged her with a nod.

Evelyn slid the bronze swing arm latch to the side. "Here goes noth—"

"Wait. Don't open it yet. I've gotta stand up," Max said. "Some pirate I am."

They stood and bounced a bit, getting the kinks out of their legs and the blood flowing again.

"Okay, Creaky Peg-Leg Peter, you want to do the honors?" Evelyn asked.

"No, Captain Cold Toes of the High Seas. You got us this far. You do it."

Evelyn took a deep breath and lifted the lid. The interior was painted the same seafoam green. Nestled inside were two pouches made from handkerchiefs. One was tied with a blue satin ribbon. Evelyn held it in her palm and pulled one end of the ribbon to untie it. The hankie fell away, revealing numerous gold coins. So many, in fact, some rolled from her hand to the floor.

Max inspected one of them. "This is a double eagle!" he said excitedly. "Twenty bucks each in the early 1900s."

They picked up the coins that fell and dropped them into the box. They quickly sorted them into piles.

"Twenty double eagles—that's four hundred bucks back in the day—and twelve of the ten-dollar coins," Max lct out a low whistle. "That's five hundred and twenty smackaroos! We can buy you a new umbrella now."

"That's a ton of money back then," Evelyn said. "Who would have hidden it here?"

Max scrolled through his phone. The signal was weak and kept dropping, but he kept at it and was able to keep the connection long enough to confirm his opinion. "If these are real, this coin website says those double eagles are worth nine hundred bucks each! And at the high end, nine million."

"Dollars?"

"And the eagle ten-dollar coins? Up to six hundred thousand."

"Dollars?" Evelyn's hands trembled. She dropped her voice. "Oh, dear me. This is making me very nervous."

"Open up the other one." Max gestured toward the other handkerchief in the box.

"You do it."

Max gently slid the bundle from the box and placed it on his palm. "It's not coins, that's for sure." There was no ribbon on this one. The hankie was simply folded around the object, probably to protect it. Max carefully lifted the corners of the hankie away, one by one, until a brooch shaped like a butterfly was revealed.

Evelyn stared at it. "I've seen this before," she murmured.

"Yeah. It's a butterfly." Max leaned close and aimed the flashlight directly at it. "Are those real rubies?"

"They can't be!"

"Why not? Those are real coins. This is the real *under the sugar mill.*"

"I mean," Evelyn struggled to find the right words. "I just … they're so … they can't be!"

"But, Ev," Max said softly. "I think they are."

"Are you kidding? Pirate treasure?"

Max's eyes sparkled. "Pirate treasure."

Kateri

———

"FINALLY! First Dena goes missing and now you two?" Kateri met Evelyn and Max at the outside diagonal doors on the opposite side of the Marketplace from their photo studio. "I was about to come looking for you."

Evelyn and Max shook the snow off themselves.

"Is that coffee ready?" Evelyn asked.

"Get in here. You don't look so good." Kateri hustled them through her office into the vendor room. She helped them off with their coats then sat them down and brought them coffee. "Now, tell me what was so all-fired important for you to freeze outside in a blizzard."

Evelyn lifted her mug to her lips with shaky hands. She took a sip then jumped up. "I'll be right back." She grabbed her coat and hurried into the studio.

Kateri raised her eyebrows at Max.

He shrugged, said, "Women," as if that was a reasonable explanation and continued to sip his coffee.

When Evelyn returned a couple of minutes later, she didn't have her coat, but handed Kateri a piece of paper

203

and placed a handkerchief on the table, smoothing it out in front of her.

"What's this?" Kateri scanned the poem.

"We found it in an old shoe," Max said.

Kateri turned to Evelyn and repeated her question.

"It's true. We found it in an old shoe. It's a poem, called an acrostic, which has—"

"I know. The first word of each line spells out something." Kateri read down the margin. "Under the sugar mill? What's under the sugar mill?"

"That's what we were out there doing." She slid the handkerchief toward Kateri. "We found this."

Kateri traced the faint outline of stitches in one of the corners. "Looks like a monogram that someone picked out the thread."

Evelyn and Max pulled it close to them and put their heads together studying it.

"I think I see it," Evelyn said.

"Me too."

Kateri began reading the poem out loud. "*A Pirate's Prayer. Understand, my acts are not criminal. Navigating stormy seas, I simply seek safe haven. Defeat is not an option in my attempt for a better life for me and my fellow pirates. Escaping king and crown is foremost on my mind. I shall disguise my crew; they shan't find us. Refugees, far from home, we seek a friendlier, more fulfilling life, perhaps on the ocean side.*"

"What in the world does that mean? On the ocean side? The ocean side of what?" Max said.

"Maybe it means Oceanside. Like they're going to California," Kateri said.

"Pirates going to California?"

"Why not? It's as good a place as any." Kateri continued reading. "*Treasure has been buried forty paces from shore, jewels and gold to start anew. Homecoming seems impossible, yet I yearn for dear mama and worry about stern doting papa—* Shouldn't it be stern BUT doting papa? And what kind of pirate talks about his mama and papa?"

"A female pirate, that's who. I was just talking to a customer this morning about female pirates," Evelyn said. She began telling Kateri about them.

After a few minutes Kateri stood up. "This has been fun, Evelyn, and I hope you enjoy your antique hankie. I'm glad you weren't murdered, Max, but I've got to get back to work. When Dena gets back, I don't want her to think I was goofing off."

"I'm sure she wouldn't, dear."

Kateri shrugged. "I haven't made much of a mark around here." She began to walk toward her office but turned and said quietly, "I'm just glad I have at least two friends here."

"Give yourself a chance, dear. You've only just started. And from what I can tell, everyone here likes you," Evelyn said soothingly.

"Leave your door open once in a while, why don't you," Max called as she was closing her door. "Attagirl," he said under his breath when it swung open again.

Dena

GEORGIA REACHED up and hit the button that opened her garage door. "Home again, home again, jiggedy jig!" she sang out.

Inside the car, Dena ducked when Georgia began to drive in before the door had barely cleared the roof. As flinchy as she was all the way from Sugar Springs, she was more than relieved to be at Georgia's house. Now she could concentrate fully on what exactly Georgia's deal was right now.

"Out you go!" Georgia kept using that sing-song voice which confused Dena.

Is she ready to murder me or play patty-cake? Dena wondered wryly.

She hoped for patty-cake, but planned for the murder thing. Who knew anymore?

Georgia kept the pink fuzzy handcuffs on Dena and they weren't any looser than when she first snapped them on her. During the entire ride Dena had been pulling, prodding, and pushing against them, hoping to wear out the mechanism.

It never happened. Maybe they weren't from the party store like Dena assumed. Was there a law enforcement outlet somewhere that catered to seventy-two-year-old kidnappers with a penchant for girlie restraints?

Dena led the way into Georgia's house. At the doorway Georgia slapped the mechanism that lowered the garage door.

Blessed silence.

No howling wind. No staticky radio. No more anecdotes about water aerobics.

Dena slumped against the washer/dryer unit in the mudroom and closed her eyes. But only for a few seconds until Georgia pushed her along.

"Not here, you silly goose! Let's get you into the living room!"

Yes, please, Dena thought wearily.

She'd been in Georgia's living room countless times and knew there was a plethora of comfy furniture in there. She made her way to the velvet settee, past the four-paneled Chinese screen that divided the room, one-third of the area behind it, two-thirds where guests gathered.

Dena's exhausted brain wasn't too exhausted to wonder about that screen, just as it did every time she saw it. Why did this room need to be divided in the first place? Dena always assumed Georgia bought it to support the artist who she'd most likely met at some gala or another. Perhaps he or she visited Georgia often enough that she wanted it to be conspicuous. There were several other rooms in Georgia's house where the Chinese screen would make more sense, though. At least to Dena.

She knew her thoughts flitted around because she was tired, or perhaps because she was coming completely unhinged. She giggled and waved to the hideous—Georgia's description—oversized vase that stood next to the screen. When Dena had helped Georgia carry it into the house all those years ago, they both made fun of the earnest and much too humanoid woodland creatures romping with some evil-looking cherubs all painted in pastels around the circumference. Georgia had rotated it inch by inch all the way around, trying to find the least atrocious angle. She finally sighed and gave up. "I'll just put it here."

"Why in the world did you buy this?" Dena had asked.

"Because he was such a nice man and hadn't sold anything yet. I didn't want him to be completely demoralized."

Somehow it comforted Dena to see that at least Georgia's living room hadn't changed. It reminded her of the old Georgia. That was the Georgia Dena wanted back. Not this manic kidnapping one. Maybe they'd both be back to normal after a nap.

After Dena had settled in, snuggling into the comfortable couch, Georgia grabbed her by the arm and pulled her to her feet. "Nope. Over here." She dragged over a wooden chair from the dining table that seated twelve.

Dena had eaten at Georgia's dining table countless times and knew these mahogany chairs—while gorgeous and carved ornately—were also the most uncomfortable money could buy. At every dinner party at least one guest mentioned how much their back hurt by the dessert course. And every time Georgia said, "I bought this dining set for a princely sum from a Thai artist who I think actually was a prince. He hand-carved each chair uniquely. Not one is the same as the other … go ahead, look!"

"Can I please sit on the couch?" Dena pleaded. "Or at least the wing chair? That drive was brutal."

"Don't be silly. I can't tie you up over there."

"Why do you have to tie me up? I'm already handcuffed and there's a blizzard raging outside. Where do you think I'm going to go?"

"No reason to take chances, is there?"

Georgia picked up a long coil of blue-and-white striped nylon cord from the top of the wet bar.

Dena looked at her incredulously. "You knew you were bringing me all the way back here? All this was premeditated?"

Georgia quirked her mouth. "Um … duh?" She pushed Dena into the chair and began uncoiling the rope.

"Georgia, you really don't have to do this. Let's make some tea and have a nice chat on the couch. You can finally tell me what this is all about."

"You know what this is all about." Georgia didn't sound angry, but she also didn't sound as much like a raving lunatic like she had so much of the day.

Dena couldn't quite put her finger on it, but for the last half-hour or so Georgia almost sounded like herself again. Less manic, and she was speaking in sentences instead of paragraphs now. Maybe those pills were wearing off.

Dena began to feel hopeful. If Georgia wasn't on medication, maybe her mind could clear and Dena had a chance to get through to her.

"Georgia, I want to ask you something."

"Shoot."

"What are you doing?"

Georgia waved the rope at her while she circled Dena in the chair, winding it around her torso. "Tying you up."

Dena squirmed, figuring if she slouched, the ropes would be looser. But maybe if she sat tall with good posture, perhaps the chair wouldn't be so uncomfortable. In the end, she did a little of each, which probably rendered both theories moot.

"No, I mean, why did you go to Sugar Springs like that and drag me down here? You were acting crazy."

Georgia stopped in front of her. "No crazier than you agreeing to get in the car with me." Georgia began circling her with the rope again. "You know, being so rash is a big flaw of yours."

"A flaw? Of mine? That wasn't a rash decision anyway! That was friendship."

Georgia simply shrugged and continued tying her to the chair.

Dena squirmed ineffectively.

"I should have taken you to the doctor in Sugar Springs."

"Doctors don't understand my pain." Georgia tucked in the loose end of the rope and stepped back to admire her handiwork. "But I'll tell you who does ... my boyfriend. He understands that doctors refuse to acknowledge women's pain. Thank goodness!"

"Is he a doctor?"

"No! I just told you. Doctors refuse to acknowledge women's pain. But he does. He sees me. Really sees me." Georgia placed a hand over her heart and her face went all gooey. "He takes such good care of me."

Georgia had been talking about her boyfriend all day —when she wasn't talking about water aerobics, that is— but never mentioned him by name. If he took such good care of her, would he really let her drive to Colorado and back in a blizzard with a hostage?

"Georgia," Dena said softly. "Can other people see your boyfriend, or just you?" She glanced around the room to see if there were any framed snapshots or any sign at all of a man in Georgia's life.

"I can't wait for you to meet him. You'll see how much

he loves me and you'll realize you pushed me for no reason. You'll get a severe case of the collywobbles." Georgia giggled and left the room.

She used that word again. Dena still couldn't remember where she'd heard it before, but it didn't matter. She'd never heard Georgia say it until today. Which she did twice. Maybe she's not as lucid as Dena had imagined, not back to herself after all. Dena hadn't seen nor spoken to Georgia in more than two months, which could be a lifetime to someone with a traumatic brain injury.

Georgia returned to the living room with two glasses of red wine. She held one out to Dena, who wiggled her fingers.

"Thanks! Gotta untie me first, though."

"Oh, right. Never mind." Georgia sipped from one glass and then the other before settling into the comfy wingchair.

Dena watched as Georgia polished off both glasses of wine. She'd hoped Georgia would explain herself and this escapade, but every time Dena began to speak, Georgia raised one finger to silence her. Normally Dena wouldn't be silenced so easily, but this was a weird day. Plus, she didn't know what to say that she hadn't been saying all day.

Finally, Georgia spoke. "You know, I didn't appreciate it when it was pointed out to me you were trying to steal my boyfriend."

"Steal your boyfriend? What are you talking about?"

"You know exactly what I'm talking about."

"I don't. Who pointed this out to you?"

Georgia shook her head, as if she just found out Dena couldn't even count to ten. "You poor dear. How long are you going to keep up this charade?" She pronounced it *shar-odd*.

"Georgia," Dena said firmly. "I honest to goodness do not know what you're talking about. Why don't you start at the beginning and tell me everything."

"You already know everything."

"I don't. Believe me, I really don't." Dena tried to make her face neutral, no judgment, no anger. "Tell me why you brought me back to Santa Fe."

"Duh, because this is where I live."

"True, but I don't. Why couldn't we have done all this —" Dena wiggled her fingers — "in Sugar Springs?"

"Because I live in Santa Fe." Georgia shook her head and checked to see if there was any wine remaining in either glass. "Why is this so hard for you to understand?" Georgia collected both glasses and left the room, tossing an "Honestly" over her shoulder.

Honestly, indeed. Dena went back to her earlier assumption that Georgia was not in her right mind, mainly due to her pronunciation of charade and liberal use of the word collywobbles.

Georgia returned with a single glass of wine and launched into another anecdote about water aerobics that was not funny in the least but made Georgia double over in laughter in the wing chair. She spilled the entire glass of wine on her hand-woven Navajo rug and didn't even bother to clean it up. Just watched it soak into the fibers.

Dena was out of ideas. She couldn't get Georgia to tell her why she'd been kidnapped. She couldn't get her to believe Dena had nothing to do with her fall during their hike. She couldn't get Georgia to tell her about this boyfriend of hers. And if Dena heard one more story about water aerobics, she might just lose what was left of her sanity. She let the sound of Georgia's voice wash over her.

Suddenly she jerked to attention.

Dena remembered where she heard the word collywobbles before.

Boyd

BOYD, Hugo, and Pham were just beginning another round of "Two Truths and a Lie" when Boyd's cardiologist walked in.

"I don't see any permanent damage, but I want you to start taking these prescriptions." He handed a list of medications to Boyd.

"What are they?" Boyd asked.

"The nurse will give you a list of everything with instructions." He made some notes on Boyd's chart. "And you need to lose weight. You might not be this lucky next time. A nurse will be in to get your discharge started."

After he left Hugo said, "Well, wasn't he just a cuddly 'ol bear?"

"Doesn't matter. Told you I was a survivor."

"We're all survivors," Pham said. "We'll help each other get strong and stay strong."

Boyd guffawed. "You're both such skinny minnies you couldn't possibly help me, but I'm wicked delighted to have your friendship."

Pham wagged a finger at Boyd. "What does that matter if we're thin?"

"Neither one of you know what it's like to lumber around like a refrigerator."

"You won't have my friendship much longer if you keep pointing out how skinny I am. It's rude," Hugo said.

"It is? I wish I was so—" Boyd clamped his mouth shut. The last thing he wanted was to hurt anyone's feelings.

"Geez, don't cry about it. I'm just sayin. You don't like it when people comment on your weight, do you? So you shouldn't comment on theirs. Men or women." Hugo narrowed his eyes. "But especially not women."

"Definitely not women," Pham agreed.

"Tell you what," Hugo said. "Pham and I can teach you to eat healthier." Pham nodded enthusiastically. "I will make you healthy dark chocolates, naturally low in sugar, that you can eat in moderation." Hugo stressed each syllable.

"And I'll teach you to make both ramen and pho. I taught all my kids, I can teach you too," Pham added with a laugh.

Hugo asked Pham how fast he could name his kids in age order and Pham began rattling off their names and ages.

Boyd listened for a bit, but then his mind wandered. Earlier today he'd wondered if he subconsciously tried to cause his own heart attack, but now, he couldn't imagine such a thing. It had been a very long time since he'd had friends.

Maybe this time he wouldn't screw it up.

Hugo

HUGO BEGAN WORRYING ALL OVER AGAIN. He'd been distracted by the chaos of the hospital and the immediate concern about Boyd, but now the doctor gave Boyd the all-clear. Almost the all-clear. How Boyd was supposed to lose weight when he truly believed ice cream was medicine was a complication to be figured out later.

Now Boyd was third on Hugo's list of things to worry about and Skyler was at the top. His constant anxiety about the chocolate shop pretty much always earned the number two spot.

Hugo wondered where Skyler was. He checked his phone but there were no new texts or missed calls. No news must be good news, he hoped. Skyler, Dena, and Dena's daughter were probably holed up someplace cozy and warm, waiting out the storm. And couldn't be bothered to let anyone know?

He texted her. "You ok?" He stared at his phone waiting for a reply, but none came. Texted again. "LMK when you get back."

Hugo's feelings for Skyler were complicated. And Boyd's promise to help him woo her mildly horrified him. Boyd and Hugo were at opposite ends of the spectrum, as far as subtlety went.

Besides, his wooing train had probably already left the station. He should have come clean about already knowing her the first minute he saw her at the Marketplace that day. It would have been so easy. "Wow! Small world! We met at the FrouFrouFood show, remember? What are you doing here? … A cheese shop? No way! I'm opening a chocolate shop here!" Done. No weirdness. No secrets. No Dena calling him a stalker.

But no. That's not what he did.

And now he would have to confess all this to his new friends. He watched Boyd and Pham play Rock, Paper, Scissors for control of the remote.

Hugo wasn't too sure about all this camaraderie. It felt weird, but not entirely terrible. When Boyd had called him this morning it felt good to be needed. But how long would that last?

Hugo watched them flip through channels, trying to find a televised spring training baseball game.

"Who's your team, Hugo?" Boyd asked. "I'm Sawx all the way."

Hugo knew enough to recognize there were both White Sox and Red Sox teams, and fairly certain they played baseball, but didn't know which one Boyd meant. He also knew enough not to ask.

"I'm a Rockies fan, myself," Pham said.

"Not much of a baseball fan, I'm afraid," Hugo said.

"Oh. Well, we don't have to watch baseball. What tickles your fancy until they spring me from this joint?" Boyd handed Hugo the remote.

Hugo hadn't had too much luck with friends or father figures.

Maybe that was about to change.

Skyler

SKYLER PULLED OUT HER PHONE. "Who should we call?"

"Nobody!"

"You realize we're stuck in a ditch, right?"

"Skyler, we drove around a highway barricade. I don't think we—"

"Technically, *you* drove around a highway barricade. Pretty sure I'm innocent."

"Pretty sure I'm not." They had a stare down, but Charlee lost by speaking again. "Someone will come along to pull us out. We won't be here for long, I know it."

"You know it? How?"

"I just do. You know these Colorado storms. They don't last long and then it's back to business as usual. Some highway crew will be by soon to raise this gate. They'll see us, winch us out, and we'll be on our way. No cops, no citation, no hefty fine, no court appearance."

Skyler kept staring at her.

"Okay, I'll tell you what. If nobody comes by before the sun is up, you can call 911. We can certainly survive a night in a car. We have water, food, blankets, and gas in the tank."

"How much gas?"

"Plenty."

It wasn't lost on Skyler that Charlee hadn't even glanced at the gauge.

After a bit she said, "Fine," knowing she could call 911 any time she pleased.

"Thank you. You'll see," Charlee said. "Everything will be okay. We'll get out of this mess and reach Santa Fe, find my mom, and laugh about all this in a few weeks."

Skyler didn't share Charlee's optimism. "If you say so." She settled back in her seat and glanced at her phone.

Charlee gasped. "You said—"

"Relax. Just checking my messages." Automated text from her dentist reminding her of her cleaning tomorrow. She'd completely forgotten. She texted back. "Need to reschedule. Something came up."

There was also a text from Hugo that she hadn't seen. Probably came in when she was trying to push the car out of the snowbank. She sent him a thumbs up emoji. That would cover both "I'm okay" and "Thanks for closing up for me."

She'd love to call and have a long talk with him. He always calmed her down. She wasn't sure if it was his Eeyore personality or what, but she could use a little dose right now. Unfortunately, she'd have to tell him all about this fiasco with Charlee while Charlee wasn't two feet away from her. Plus, she didn't want to wear down her battery because she hadn't brought her charger.

Thumbs up will have to do for now.

Skyler leaned her head against the headrest and tried to sleep. Comfort didn't seem to be an option. Plus, she began to worry that if they slept, they might not know if the highway crew came by. "You should put the emergency blinkers on."

"Why? It'll drain the battery."

"In case we fall asleep when the highway crew comes to raise the barricade."

"I'm not going to fall asleep."

"You might."

"I won't."

"You might."

"Pretty sure I won't. Will you?"

Skyler pondered that. "Probably not. No offense, but this car isn't very comfortable to sleep in."

"That wasn't on my list of must-haves when I was shopping for it."

They settled back into their seats once again and resumed their silence. Skyler kept sneaking peeks at Charlee and watched at various times as she chewed her lip, chewed her thumbnail, and tapped her index fingers on her legs.

Despite Charlee's optimism from before, Skyler believed Charlee was beginning to wallow in their predicament. As a chatterbox, this oppressive silence was going to give Skyler nervous diarrhea. She was sure of it. People complained that she was a "close talker." Imagine what they'd say about that.

She poked Charlee in the arm with her index finger. "You're sure quiet."

"Sorry. Just processing my rage for getting us stuck here. I guess I take after my mom like that."

"Like what? Getting stuck in a snowbank?"

"No. For being uncommunicative."

Skyler laughed. "Dena? Uncommunicative?"

Charlee turned on the ignition and fired up the heater to warm the car, then ran the windshield wipers.

"Did my mom ever tell you how she ended up in Santa Fe?"

Skyler shook her head.

"After my dad was killed, she ran away to New Mexico. She made sure Lance and I were taken care of first, but yeah. No real communication for a while, just superficial stuff. Did we need money. How was school going. That kind of stuff. It was a long time before I understood that she was just afraid of the truth, didn't want to face it. Worried that anything she'd say would scare us kids, maybe make it impossible for us to move forward."

"That must have been rough."

"Yeah, but we muddled through okay. But then this past Thanksgiving this stalker thing really made her mad and it's like a dam broke. Ever since, she's been telling me and Lance everything, even stuff we're not interested in." Charlee turned to face Skyler. "That's why I know something happened to her. She would have told us if she was planning a trip, even an impromptu one."

Skyler was quiet for a moment. "Maybe she hasn't been telling you everything."

"That thought has crossed my mind. But why?"

"She felt she needed to protect you back then, maybe she started feeling that way again." Skyler gazed out the windshield at the storm. "Your mother and I are different in so many ways. She's elegant, I'm a hippie. Her motto seems to be *Let's just try*, while mine is *Let's think about everything over and over and over and over until I can't remember what I was supposed to be deciding*. I eat my weight in cheese every day and she has self-control. But we're alike in one important way."

"You like talking my ear off?"

"No, well yes, but that's not what I was going to say. Dena and I both have trouble asking for help. We'd always rather do things for ourselves. Even when it's hard. Even when we can't. You should have seen how much arm twisting we had to do to get her to hire a Marketplace manager. Finally, Evelyn just told Kateri to show up and she'd get the job."

"I don't want to call you a liar or anything—"

"But I feel like you're going to."

"But my mom told me you're always asking everyone's advice on everything, like you're constantly second-guessing yourself."

Skyler tensed, ready to push back. But then she took a breath and considered Charlee's secondhand assessment. "You know, you're right. I do that. I think it's because of that stupid calf."

"Balaam? Evelyn and Max's cat? Yeah, he's a real—"

"Not cat. Calf. Like, a baby cow? When I was a teenager, I fell through an icy pond on our dairy farm trying to rescue one of the calves."

"Yikes!"

"You're telling me."

"Did you save it?"

"I did. And everyone praised me to the skies for my quick thinking and bravery." Skyler snorted with derision.

"Sounds like there's more to this story." The car had warmed so Charlee turned off the ignition.

"I never told anyone, but the reason the calf was out in the first place was because I tried to pawn off my job to a ranch hand. I was supposed to gather the calves up before a storm that was blowing in, but I asked him to do it. I had this project to finish for my science class. I was doing it with a partner, but she completely dropped the ball and didn't tell me until the last minute. We were supposed to make a solar oven from a pizza box and be able to cook s'mores. I had to figure out the entire project myself.

Problem was, the ranch hand that I tried to delegate the calves to got busy with his own chores and forgot. I was so lucky the desk in my bedroom overlooked the pond. I went racing out there like I was on fire. Jumped through the ice and pulled that calf to safety."

"How'd you do that? It must have weighed ten times more than you."

"I don't know. Adrenaline? Like how mothers can lift cars off their babies? I hurt like heck the next day. But the point is, that's when I learned to always do for myself. Never ask for help." Before Charlee could speak, she added, "But, it also always makes me second-guess myself. And that science project? Totally screwed it up. Tried to do my part and my partners' part but I would have been better off just doing something different on my own and ratting her out to the teacher. And the calf? Not two weeks later I saw with my own eyes how the calves would wade in the pond and wade right back out. Turns out they could swim, a little factoid unknown to me. So I wrenched my knee for no reason."

"Wow. That's some story." Charlee was quiet for a minute. "What was the point you were trying to make again?"

"That your mom and I don't like to ask for help. Even when we probably should. Maybe she hasn't been telling you everything. Like when you were kids."

"We're not teenagers anymore."

"No … but you're still her kids. Whenever I go back to see my parents on the farm, they treat me like I'm eight years old again. Last time I went home—"

Then Skyler screamed.

Evelyn

EVELYN AND MAX returned to the studio.

"Where'd you hide the loot, matey?"

"The box is in the carpet bag." Evelyn unlocked the cash register and pointed. The coins were in the spot where pennies would go, if anyone ever used pennies anymore, and the brooch was nestled on top of the ones. Evelyn rubbed a finger on it. "This is an heirloom, Max. We have to figure out who it belongs to."

"But do we?"

"Maxwell Zachary Milligan. You know as well as I do that we can't keep these."

"You always were a goody-goody," Max said with a grin. "Remember that time Oscar brought home that mangy cat and you didn't sleep until you figured out where it belonged?"

"I remember it very well. But it wasn't because I was a goody-goody. It was because I didn't want us to go blind from looking at that hideous creature."

"Ha! And here I thought your petition for sainthood was going to come through any day now." He looked at her slyly. "But you know, that brooch and those coins aren't hideous. No chance of us going blind looking at them."

"You are incorrigible." Evelyn shut the cash register and smoothed the handkerchief out on the counter. They both stared down at it.

"Is that an O? Or maybe a B?" Max squinted at the faint pinholes of the missing embroidery.

"I can't tell. But I'm pretty sure that's an S." Evelyn pressed a fingernail near some of the stitches.

Max rubbed his eyes. "I'm not sure what it's going to tell us even if we figure out this monogram. If that's truly what it is."

"It has to be a monogram. What else could it be? Oh!" Evelyn jumped like she'd been stung by a bee. "I know!"

She scurried over to her fancy camera and brought it back to where Max stood at the counter. She fussed with the settings then lifted it to her eye, snapping photos of the handkerchief. When she was satisfied she'd taken enough, she held the camera at arm's length where both she and Max could see them.

She slowly paged through close-ups of the hankie, then did it again, stopping at one photograph. "Hm." Again, she fussed with the settings. When she showed Max the photo, it had been enhanced. "Do you see it?" She pointed at the screen, her finger shaking with excitement.

Max squinted again and moved the camera closer to his face. "S ... D ... P?"

"That's what I see too!"

"Okay. So ....?"

"So, let's ask the All-Knowing Being." Evelyn hurried to the computer and typed in "SDP" in the search bar.

Max read over her shoulder. "Sand Point Airport. Session Description Protocol. Software Defined Perimeter. School District of Philadelphia. Sundance Printing."

Evelyn's face fell. "This list goes on forever!"

Max placed one hand over Evelyn's. "Hang on, now. Don't get your knickers in a twist. We just need to do some refining. Let's think."

"Oh! What was it Kateri said?" Evelyn typed in *SDP Oceanside*.

Max squeezed Evelyn's hand a bit too tightly when a blog post from the Oceanside historical society entitled, "The Tragic Tale of Silas Dietrich Pfeiffer" immediately popped up.

Evelyn gasped and stared at Max with wide eyes.

Max pointed slowly at the nearly invisible monogram on the handkerchief while he spoke. "Stern. Doting. Papa. SDP. Silas Dietrich Pfeiffer."

"The guy who built the sugar mill?"

Shoulder to shoulder, they silently read the article.

"I never knew any of that," Evelyn said when they'd finished. "Did you?"

Max shook his head. "Maybe it's not the same family."

"How many Silas Dietrich Pfeiffer's do you think owned sugar mills in 1899?"

"But—"

Max was interrupted by Evelyn scrambling to open the cash register. She grabbed the brooch and hurried into the promenade and around the corner where there was a short history of the mill, along with some photos. Evelyn triumphantly held the brooch near the black and white photo of the sugar mill groundbreaking. A woman wore it pinned to her coat. "I *knew* I'd seen it before!"

"That article said Silas Dietrich Pfeiffer and his wife Mary had a daughter, Susan Diane—"

"Her initials were SDP too," Evelyn said excitedly. "She would have stitched them on her handkerchiefs. That's what they did in the old days."

"Susan disappeared in—what did it say? 1917?—with a couple of kids?" Max studied the group photo of the sugar mill groundbreaking. It was dated 1899.

"A boy named Frank, Jr who was four, and a girl named Roberta who was three."

"So, at this groundbreaking, Susan must have been about that same age." They both peered at the grainy photo. "That must be her." Max pointed to a little girl standing between a man and woman holding shovels. That must be Silas and his wife, and that must be Susan."

"I want to read the article again." Evelyn held the brooch up next to the photo again. "But this is that brooch, right?"

"Definitely looks like it."

They returned to the studio and reread the blog post.

Evelyn pointed at the screen. "Silas tracked Susan to Oceanside, California. But when he got to the hotel she worked at, she must have gotten spooked and fled again with her kids."

Max pointed to the screen. "Here it says the two kids were boys, according to the other employees at the hotel." He scrolled. "But here it says Silas was looking for a boy and a girl."

"Typo? Bad reporting?" Evelyn suggested.

"Maybe." Max kept reading. "But if this really was Susan his daughter that he'd tracked down, Silas never saw her again. He died in 1927."

They were silent, each feeling the pain of that information.

"I can't believe I've never heard anything about this before," Max said. "Have I just forgotten?"

Evelyn shook her head. "It's not part of the town history, as far as I can tell."

"Silas must have been ashamed. Or scandalized by it

and kept it quiet," Max said. "He was rich enough to call in some favors, I bet."

Evelyn looked stricken. "There aren't too many reasons adult daughters grab their kids and run away from their fathers."

"Susan had married, though. Wasn't the boy named Frank Jr?" Max skimmed the article again. "Yep. There it is. Frank, Jr. But I don't see anything in here about Susan's husband."

"Maybe that's who she was hiding from," Evelyn said.

Rattlesnake Kate, the pirate poem, and this blog post began to twist and turn in Evelyn's brain. All the stories sounded like survival to her. Keeping safe, disappearing, reinvention, buried treasure, a better life for children.

Evelyn picked up the carpet bag and began laying out all the items they'd found inside of it. She set the carved box aside. When she'd set a pair of shoes on each pile, she said, "Two sets of clothing for Susan, two for Frank, Jr, and two for Roberta." She placed the pirate poem in between Susan's upright boots and took a step backward to take it all in. "For whatever reason, Susan packed this bag, but ran from Sugar Springs with her kids in tow without grabbing it."

"Something scared her."

Evelyn nodded. "But she must have thought that might happen, which is why she wrote this cryptic note. The forty paces, the ruby red butterfly. She was leaving clues for someone—maybe her parents, maybe her kids—about that buried treasure. She must not have had time to dig that up either. If she had, she wouldn't have had to work at a hotel. She definitely left in a hurry."

Max mulled that over, but shook his head. "You're assuming this bag wasn't found in Oceanside."

"If it was, how would it make its way back here if nobody ever saw Susan again?"

"The article didn't say *nobody* ever saw her again, just that Silas didn't. Maybe she brought it back with her and buried the coins and brooch later."

"I don't think so, Max. If she came back to Sugar Springs, don't you think we would have heard about that in the town history? I don't remember ever hearing that Silas and Mary had a daughter, just sons. Three, I think. They ran the sugar mill after Silas died up until it went bust. I'm convinced this poor girl had to disappear herself so quickly she couldn't even grab her suitcase or those coins. The treasure was left buried, and this bag was left hidden somewhere." Evelyn was quietly drumming her fingernails on the counter. The rhythm quickened the more she spun Susan's story. "She must have lived near here someplace with that man—that Frank, Senior—who was abusive in some way to her, her kids, or all three of them. She snuck that bag over to her parents' house one day when she realized at some point she'd have to get away, and stashed it in the attic so her husband wouldn't find it. She knew it would be a town scandal if it came out her parents allowed her—or worse, maybe encouraged her—to marry this terrible guy, so she made a plan to disappear. She amassed those coins. She stole that brooch from her mother—"

"How do you know she stole it?"

"If it was hers, she'd just grab-and-go. Besides, if she was the only daughter, she knew it would be hers eventually."

"Maybe her mom was in on the plan from the start," Max said.

"Maybe, but I doubt it. Women of that era didn't have much ... what do you call it ... you know ... freedom. Independent action."

Max gestured toward the promenade. "In that photo she's holding a shovel for the groundbreaking of the sugar mill. That's not very delicate of her."

"True. Maybe there's more to Mary Pfeiffer than we know." Evelyn looked at Max. "Regardless, you know who we have to call, right?"

Max nodded. "Mary Pat."

"Mary Pat."

Charlee

CHARLEE DIDN'T KNOW why she was screaming, but since Skyler continued to scream, so did she. She followed Skyler's panicked eyes to the car window behind Charlee.

Light flooded the interior of the car. A murky figure loomed up out of the dark. Charlee scrambled across the car toward Skyler, but got stuck over the center console.

They heard a knock on the window and the light bobbed inside.

"Is everything okay in there?" a man's voice shouted.

They didn't answer right away. The driver's door jerked open. Illuminated by the flashing red light from the highway closure arm stood a Colorado state trooper.

"Are you both okay?" The trooper bent down, reaching for Charlee.

"Officer! Oh my gosh, yes! We're fine!" Skyler shouted in Charlee's ear.

Charlee scooted back to the driver's seat. "Thank you! We've been here for hours."

"Why don't you get out of the car." He didn't ask it like

a question, but Charlee was all too happy to comply. "You too," he said to Skyler.

He directed both of them to stand in the front of the car. "Whose car is this?"

"Mine," Charlee said. She glanced toward the sky. The storm was definitely letting up.

"Did you drive around the barricade?" The trooper gestured up to the road where his cruiser flashed red and blue lights unsynchronized with the guard arm lights.

"I had to," Charlee said.

"Why?"

"My mom is ahead of us on the road somewhere on the way to Santa Fe and I think she's in trouble."

"What kind of trouble?"

"I … don't really know. But trouble. I'm sure of it."

"She is," Skyler said, nodding her head emphatically at the trooper.

He stared at them for a moment. "I'll need to see both your IDs and the registration for this car." He watched them closely while they dug through their purses and the glove compartment, shining his spotlight on them the entire time. He studied their documents while Charlee and Skyler stood in front of the car again.

He used his shoulder radio to call in to his dispatcher to check out the information. While they waited, he walked around the car, shining his flashlight inside the back seat and around the trunk to where it was wedged into the snowbank.

"Looks like you got yourselves into some trouble here."

"Yes, sir. We tried—"

"I wonder if it could all have been avoided if you hadn't tried to circumvent the road closure." He narrowed his eyes.

Charlee and Skyler both knew what a scolding sounded like and didn't respond.

The mic crackled at his shoulder. He high stepped through the deep snow until he was far enough away for a bit of privacy. He kept his light shining on them the entire time. They heard his voice but couldn't make out what he was saying. Finally, he made his way back to them.

"Are you Charlemagne Russo the writer?" he asked.

Skyler grabbed the sleeve of Charlee's coat.

Charlee wanted to reassure her, that this was almost always a good question. Unpleasant trolls hid behind the anonymity of the internet. If someone wanted to talk about your books in person, they were usually perfectly lovely people. She hoped that was true this time as well. "I am."

"Cool, I think I've read all your books. I really liked that one with the arsonist."

"Oh, that' so nice to hear," she said. She refrained from asking what his problem was with her other books.

"You say your mother is out in this storm? Whereabouts?"

"I'm not sure. To be honest, I'm not *completely* sure she was heading to Santa Fe." Despite the fact he was a fan, Charlee felt another scolding was heading their way. She added, "But that's why I drove around the gate. I'm ninety-three percent sure."

"Ninety-three."

"Maybe as high as ninety-four-and-a-half."

"How do you fit into this?" he asked Skyler.

"I ... um ... came along for the ride." At his frown she quickly added, "I'm a friend of both Charlee and her mother. I came to ... help."

"Help with what?"

"Honestly? I'm not sure anymore."

He stared at them for a moment. "My jurisdiction ends in a few miles, at the New Mexico border. I've been told there are no stranded cars between here and Santa Fe. Seems not everyone thinks it's a good idea to ignore safety barriers." He gave them his Police Officer Look, infinitely worse than the Mom Look. "Is there anyone I should contact in New Mexico about your mother?"

"I wish!" Charlee said. "But the truth is, I don't know the names of any of my mother's friends—she used to live there until a few months ago. But I've been there and I know where some of her friends live. Not street names or anything, but I think I can find them once I get there."

"So, your plan was to drive to Santa Fe in a blizzard and then drive around until you found your mother?"

"Well, it sounds stupid when you say it like that," Charlee said.

"Sounds stupid no matter which way you say it," Skyler muttered.

"There's not much for me to do, except write you a ticket."

"Can you help us get out of here?" Charlee asked.

"No." The trooper dragged the word out long enough for Charlee to regret asking the question. "But the storm seems to be winding down and the plows will be along at some point—"

"Soon?" Skyler asked excitedly.

"At some point." He gave them another Look. "You are to wait here inside your car. I will tell them to look for you. When they get here, they will tow your car up to the road again. When they do so, you will thank them profusely, and if you have any cash upon your persons, you might consider offering them that as well. When you are on the road again, you will travel behind the snowplows— far behind the snowplows—at a safe distance. You will not pass them, even if you think they are going too slowly. They will exit near the state border, and I cannot vouch for the road conditions in New Mexico. But if there is another highway closure or detour, I trust you will not be this stupid again. You will wait at the gate, or take the detour as you are told. But you will not—and I can't state this emphatically enough—you will not attempt to drive around the gate. Even if it is on flat land with dry road as far as your eyes can see. Do you understand me?"

"Yes, sir," they both said.

"Good. Now, please tell me what your next book will be about."

Charlee gave him a brief synopsis of the manuscript she was working on and took his business card with a promise to send him a signed copy the minute it was available. That pleased him and somewhat alleviated her guilt at getting a scolding from a state trooper.

"You're still getting that ticket, though."

Before he left, he made sure their tailpipe was not buried or clogged with snow, and made them prove they had plenty of food, water, and warm clothes. He seemed somewhat mollified in his concern when Skyler rattled off the list of Essential Ten items, demonstrating she knew something about winter safety.

He turned back to them before he attempted the climb up the ravine. "Who are you going to wait for?"

"The snowplows," they said in unison, like schoolchildren reciting their multiplication facts.

"And what will you do when they come?"

Charlee said, "Tip them heavily" at the same time Skyler said, "Follow them at a safe distance."

"Both of those things. Good luck with your mother and the rest of your journey, ladies."

Charlee and Skyler watched him make a U-turn on the highway, traveling north in the southbound lane.

"Geez, now I'm worried about him," Charlee said.

"Don't worry. The road's closed."

Charlee shot Skyler a look.

"Oh, yeah. I'm sure he'll be fine. He has his emergency lights on."

———

They pooled their extra cash together as a "thank you" to the snowplow drivers, then sat biding their time until they showed up. They continued to run the heater every so often to take the chill off. They ate cookies and drank water, which Skyler had stuck in the snowbank next to her window to chill.

Charlee wanted to keep her mind off her mom but when Skyler asked if she wanted privacy to talk on the phone to Ozzi, she demurred. "I texted him a while ago. If I talk to him, I'm sure I'd blurt out something that would worry him."

"Like you're stuck in a snowbank near the Colorado state line waiting for snowplows to rescue you?"

"Yeah, like that."

"Tell me about him."

"About Ozzi? Hm, let's see. He's hot. Really hot."

"Ooh la la."

Charlee proceeded to tell Skyler all the great things about Ozzi, and then a few of the less-than-great things. Then she asked Skyler, "What about you? Are you seeing anyone?"

Skyler thought about it for so long that Charlee laughed. "I didn't think that was such a hard question."

Skyler sighed. "You know Hugo? The guy that owns the chocolate shop?"

Charlee nodded.

"He has a little crush on me, but I just want to be friends. I'm not sure he's getting the picture, though."

"That's rough."

"But there's this other guy, Jake. He's my cheese supplier. He has an exotic animal ranch not too far from Sugar Springs."

"Ooh, a cowboy."

Skyler nodded so hard Charlee was afraid her head would dislodge.

"Picture the hottest cowboy you can imagine—"

"Ozzi in a Stetson."

Skyler told Charlee all about him and his llamas, alpacas, sheep, and goats and that he was looking into raising yaks as well. She had just launched into their recent snowshoeing excursion, when they heard a loud rumble and saw white and yellow flashing lights mingling with the red. The sky suddenly seemed very festive.

"The cavalry has arrived." Charlee grabbed the stack of money from the dashboard.

Dena

COLLYWOBBLES.

Memory slammed Dena back to the restaurant where she had sat with Andy Fatalov who'd she'd gone to high school with. Or at least who she *thought* was Andy Fatalov.

He said that the speed dating event had given him the collywobbles, which was something his grandmother used to say about getting queasy. He seemed surprised Dena had never heard the word before.

She'd never heard that word before or since, until Georgia said it today. Her skin suddenly felt electrified. Was it possible her stalker was the mysterious boyfriend Georgia had been going on about? It couldn't be. Could it? Was he dating Georgia to somehow continue his weird plot against Dena?

She shook her head to try to clear it. No. She was just exhausted, allowing irrational thoughts to make connections that weren't there.

Dena hadn't heard from the Santa Fe police since she'd given them her report that night. They said they'd look into it, but it was exactly as she had suspected. He hadn't done anything. Nothing violent. Nothing criminal. Sure, he'd appropriated someone's identity, but hadn't done anything nefarious with it. And Dena didn't even know his real identity. How did she expect the police to find him?

Dena's imagination was working overtime. But what if it wasn't? What if he really was the person Georgia had been talking to on the phone on the drive? If it was, he might be on his way there right now!

She had to figure out a way to get them out of there.

"Georgia," she said sharply. "I have to pee. Right now."

"Okay. I do too." Georgia unwound the nylon cord binding Dena to the chair.

"And unless you want a repeat of the truck stop, you're going to have to get these handcuffs off me. I could have run off a thousand times today, but I didn't. And I won't. Get them off."

"Fine." Georgia reached into her bra and pulled out the tiny key which opened the cuffs. With a tinny click, they popped open on the first try.

"Why didn't that work at the truck stop?" Dena asked suspiciously.

"No idea." Georgia looked at the key in her hand as if seeing it for the first time.

Dena followed Georgia's route through the house, getting flutters in her stomach every time they passed one of the crystal candy dishes holding rainbow-wrapped PeppaMints. It seemed that these days Georgia had the mints all over her house. At Thanksgiving they were solely in a bowl in the foyer.

"I thought you didn't like PeppaMints. Have you changed your mind about them?" Dena asked suspiciously.

"Oh, goodness, no. But guests seem to like them."

Georgia's voice seemed sleepy to Dena. Earlier Dena

would have been thrilled if Georgia suggested getting a good night's sleep, but now she had to think of a way to get them both out of the house.

They walked across the plush carpet of Georgia's bedroom toward the master bathroom, passing through the enormous closet lining the walls. Dena used to jokingly refer to it as Georgia's "clothes pantry" because that was the vibe it gave off. Floor-to-ceiling shelves of various heights, drawers, rods, shoe racks, a vanity with a poofy little bench, jewelry stands and hangers of all kinds.

Dena stopped and did a double-take.

Hanging on a gold hook was a long boho necklace with nine turquoise pendants of varying lengths attached to the end of a copper multi-strand chain. Dena reached out her hand and let the delicate chain drape through her fingers. She hadn't seen this necklace since she'd put it in the birthday gift bag for Georgia the day after Thanksgiving.

It had been stolen before she could give it to Georgia.

"Georgia, where did you get this necklace?"

"I thought you had to pee." Georgia pivoted to see what Dena was referring to. "Oh, that. Isn't it beautiful? My boyfriend gave it to me." Georgia let it cascade over her hand.

"You've never told me your boyfriend's name."

"Drew. Now, do you have to pee or not? Because I do." Georgia stepped around the corner into the bathroom but didn't close the door.

Dena's head was splitting. Not enough water, not enough food, not enough sleep, and too much danger and secrecy. "Do you have any aspirin?"

"In the medicine cabinet," Georgia called.

Dena pulled open the mirror and was face-to-face with several prescription bottles. She picked one up and frowned, then studied two more. "Georgia, whose prescriptions are these?"

"Mine, of course."

"Your name isn't on any of the labels."

"Oh, that. My boyfriend started picking them up for me after I got released from the hospital. One day the pharmacy made a mistake and it just stuck that way."

Dena heard the toilet flush. "A mistake? So these aren't your meds?" Dena gathered all the prescriptions.

Georgia came around the corner, stepping to the sink area. "Of course they're mine. Right meds, wrong name. No big whoop." She yawned.

"Um … pretty big whoop."

"What time is it?" Georgia asked with a start, sounding concerned. "I think my pills are wearing off. I better call Drew and ask."

Dena panicked. "Wait. Are you telling me that your boyfriend, this Drew, controls your medication?"

"I wouldn't say he *controls* it. Just picks it up for me and tells me when to take it, is all."

Dena brushed past Georgia and dumped all the medication into the toilet. Lids and plastic bottles flew everywhere.

"What are you doing?" Georgia screeched. "I need those!"

Dena flushed but the pills simply swirled around the commode since the tank hadn't properly filled from Georgia's earlier flush. They stood side-by-side watching the colorful pills and capsules dance around the water. Georgia made a move, but Dena stretched her arm out in front of her blocking the way.

"Don't you dare!" Dena said.

"What?" Georgia tried but failed to sound innocent.

"You *weren't* going to fish those pills out of there?"

"I told you. I need them."

Dena wouldn't put it past Georgia to do something stupid, so she made sure the pills would remain out of her temptation. She locked eyes with Georgia as she lowered her lounge pants and then herself to the toilet.

"You're not going to—" Georgia's eyes widened and she left the bathroom in a huff.

While Dena waited for the second flush to clear away all traces of Georgia's bogus medication, she knew that her "Andy" and Georgia's "Drew" had to be the same person. But even if he wasn't, whoever he was, he was drugging Georgia and keeping her in a loopy state. The fact that Georgia was becoming more lucid and less manic must mean that the drugs were clearing her system.

When the toilet tank had refilled and none of the capsules remained, Dena left the bathroom and went to find Georgia. As she passed the series of windows stretching across the front of Georgia's house, she saw the storm had wound down.

Georgia had returned to the living room and was busily scrubbing at the wine stain on her Navajo rug. "Look at this! Someone spilled something on my rug!"

"Georgia, that was you. You spilled wine a little while ago."

"Don't be ridiculous. Who spills wine on an expensive rug and leaves it to soak in?"

Who indeed.

The handcuffs and nylon cord had been placed on the kitchen counter. Since Georgia didn't seem to be interested in handcuffing or tying up Dena any longer, Dena went to the kitchen and found some club soda and a rag. She dropped to her knees and helped Georgia with the stain. The soda fizzed into the stain. As they worked, Dena tried to formulate what she wanted to say to Georgia.

"Look, it's working," Dena said. The carbonation had begun to dissolve the red pigment from the wine.

"Whew. Thanks for your help."

Dena sat back on her heels. "Georgia, are you as hungry as I am? The storm seems to be over. You wanna go to Geronimo? It's still your favorite, isn't it?"

"Yes, I love that place. I'm going to have the Mexican prawns. No, the Tellicherry elk. Maybe both." She scrambled to her feet and assessed the stain. "Can't even see it. Thanks for helping."

"You're welcome. Let's get our coats. I'll drive, if you want. And it's my treat." Dena felt it was imperative to get Georgia out of the house. She was sure this so-called boyfriend was going to show up any minute and she didn't want either of them to be there.

They'd get to the restaurant, Georgia's brain would clear the rest of the way, and Dena would tell her the whole story about her stalker and her history with him. Of course, she'd told all of this to Georgia before, but Georgia had been so angry for so long, and recovering from her fall, that she clearly hadn't processed any of it.

And after she got the chance to carefully detail the entire story *again* to Georgia, then she'd ask Georgia to do the same with information about this boyfriend of hers. Dena had to figure out how everything was related. And maybe it wasn't going to be. But she wouldn't find that out until they got to the restaurant and she could relax.

Dena hurried Georgia along, helping her with her coat and finding her purse. She began to trust herself to breathe again. All they needed to do was get into the car, back out of the garage, and be on their way.

She clutched Georgia's car keys and opened the door to the garage.

As she began to step out, someone stepped in.

Evelyn

EVELYN AND MAX debated how to contact Mary Pat.

"She must have been the one Hugo saw dropping off those boxes. This stuff came from her. We have to get it back to her," Evelyn said.

"We are not showing up on her doorstep in a blizzard," Max argued.

"We have to get out of here at some point. We'll just stop by on the way home."

"Mary Pat's house is way out past the county line! No way."

"I need to show her that brooch. See if she recognizes it."

"Remember that class I took about sales tax?"

"Yes, but what does that have to do with—"

"It was on the computer. I sat in my lounge chair. I listened, I asked questions, without having to leave the comfort of my home." Max was already dialing up the program on the computer. He tapped the keyboard for a bit, then said, "We need her email address."

"I don't have it. I'll call her." Evelyn dialed the phone.

"Mary Pat? Hi, It's Evelyn Milligan…. I'm fine, how are you?…. Yeah, we spent today at the Marketplace…. no…. no…. actually we did have one customer. They were—"

Max cleared his throat.

"I'll tell you about that another day. The reason I'm calling is to get your email address…. Yes, I do realize we're talking right now, but I want to do a video call with you…. I know, it's truly a remarkable world we live in…. I'm going to email you a link. All you have to do is click on it and you and me and Max can talk face-to-face. Okay, see you in a bit."

They stared at their computer screen waiting impatiently for Mary Pat to dial in. Evelyn had the brooch, the hankie with the monogram stitches picked out, and the coins on the desk in front of her. The carpet bag with the wooden box inside sat on the floor next to her chair. She nervously rubbed one of the shiny coins.

The computer tone of a doorbell made them both jump. Max pushed a button and Mary Pat appeared on the screen in front of them. Her mouth was moving but they couldn't hear her.

Max leaned in close and said, "You're on mute."

Mary Pat continued to talk.

"You're on mute!" Max said louder.

Mary Pat looked flustered, leaning in so close Evelyn could see every pore on her nose. "Click the button that looks like a microphone!" Evelyn shouted.

While Mary Pat searched, Evelyn looked deep into Mary Pat's nostrils. Finally, Mary Pat grinned and Evelyn counted four fillings in her teeth. She was about to mention one looked cracked, but then Mary Pat said, "Got it! Can you hear me? Evelyn? Max? Come in, Houston … have we got lift-off?"

"We can hear you just fine. We don't want to look up

your nose anymore. Oh, and next time you're at the dentist, have him look at your fillings. I think you've cracked one. Now lean back."

She laughed. "Okay, you guys do the same. Max, did you shave today? Looking pretty scruffy, there."

The three of them settled back into their seats.

"Now, what exactly are we doing?" Mary Pat asked.

"Did you drop off three boxes for us a couple weeks ago?" Evelyn asked.

The smile slid off Mary Pat's face. "Evelyn, I am so sorry. It's just that we needed to make some room in that attic. It's so full I'm afraid that old floor is going to collapse. My however-many-greats grandpa built it. But I really thought you could use some of our old hippie clothes. I noticed you didn't have a 1970s section. That nice guy from the chocolate shop helped me carry them in. But if you can't use them—I'm really, really sorry. We heard other people were bringing you things and—"

"Mary Pat, I'm not mad. It's absolutely fine, dear."

"But don't do it anymore," Max said.

Evelyn elbowed him.

"What?" He rubbed his ribs.

"Then what?" Mary Pat's face clouded with concern.

"Did you look in those boxes before you brought them?"

Mary Pat shook her head. "I asked John to bring them down for me. Oh no … what did he bring you? Not that dreadful box of cords for electronics we no longer have."

"No. No cords." Evelyn lifted the carpet bag so Mary Pat could see. "But this."

"What is that?"

"You've never seen it before?"

Mary Pat shook her head, squinting and leaning toward her screen.

"It's an old carpet bag, we think from around the turn of the century. The last one, the 1900s."

Mary Pat's forehead wrinkled. "*That* was in a box I gave you?"

Evelyn nodded. "And not only that, but inside this bag were some clothes and shoes." She turned to Max. "Go get them and show her." Evelyn pulled the wooden box from the carpet bag. "We found this too."

Max brought back the clothing and held the pieces up one by one.

"None of this looks familiar to you, dear? The clothes? That box?"

"No. Are you sure it was in the stuff I gave you?"

"Everything but that wooden box. Max and I have been playing detective today. We think this bag belonged to your—" Evelyn squinched her eyes and counted generations on her fingers— "great grandmother, Susan."

"Susan?"

Evelyn and Max exchanged worried glances. "She was Silas and Mary Pfeiffer's daughter." Still no recognition on Mary Pat's face. "Aren't you related to Silas? The guy who established the sugar mill? Isn't he the one who built the house you live in?"

Mary Pat nodded slowly.

"Dear," Evelyn said softly, "I don't mean to be rude, but don't you know your family history?"

"I don't. Well, I kinda do. Nobody ever talked about Susan. I don't know much."

Max started to say something, but Evelyn placed a hand on his forearm and said, "Would you like to hear what we found?"

"Absolutely!" Mary Pat perked up. "I'm sorry, I'm just so surprised. I haven't heard Susan's name in forever. This is just really weird." She called to her husband. "John, come here and listen to this. Evelyn and Max have a story to tell us."

After John joined them and pleasantries were exchanged, Evelyn said, "Now, we may not have this completely correct, but we think we have the major puzzle pieces put together. Jump in if you think something is wrong." Evelyn took a breath and composed her thoughts. "We found a poem about pirates in Susan's shoe and—"

"Wait. Did you say pirates? I have two volumes of pirate stories that were handed down to me when I was a kid. I got them from my grandmother Bobby, er, Roberta. I was told the books were originally Susan's, but nobody would tell me hardly anything else about her. Just that she loved pirate stories. Bobby did too. In fact, Grandma Bobby named my mother Bonnie Anne, after a female pirate—"

Evelyn said it with her. "Anne Bonny."

"Wait," Max said. "If nobody ever saw Susan again, how did you know your grandmother?"

"Grandma Bobby, er, Roberta and her husband, my grandpa Jimmy, moved back to Sugar Springs when my mom was about four years old. She remembers meeting Mary, but Silas had been dead for a long time. I'm named after Mary … Mary Patrick Pfeiffer … Mary Pat."

"What do you know about Roberta's father?" Evelyn spoke carefully. She didn't want to besmirch anyone to their ancestor's face. "He was Susan's husband."

Mary Pat's face clouded. "First husband. His name was Frank. Nobody ever told me any specifics, but I get the impression he was a terrible man. He disappeared soon after Susan did, apparently." She was quiet for a moment. "For a long time I just assumed he killed her. But I got a bee in my bonnet a while back and did some detective work of my own. Found out that in the 1920s Susan had remarried—a good guy, by all accounts. They had three boys together. They lived in the Pacific Northwest, can't remember where. But it was the three boys who reunited Roberta with the family again."

"How?" Evelyn asked.

"After Susan's funeral, in like the early 1940s, they were all sitting around talking, sharing stories, like you do. Susan never really spoke of her previous life, apparently—maybe because she was afraid Frank might track her down, or just because she was ashamed—but all of them had a couple of tidbits she'd told them over the years. They kinda put two and two together and it led them back to Silas and the sugar mill. They told Roberta—she would have been their half-sister—what they discovered, and she came back to Sugar Springs."

"What about her brother, Frank Junior?" Max asked.

"Killed in the war, I think," Mary Pat said. She turned to her husband for confirmation. He nodded. "But that's about all we know."

Evelyn and Max looked at each other. Max gave a slight nod.

"We think we can fill in a few more pieces for you. If you want to hear our theories."

"By all means!" Mary Pat scooted forward in her seat. Evelyn had her complete attention.

"Based on some things written in this Pirate Poem" — Evelyn waved it in front of her— "we think Susan took her kids—your grandmother Roberta and your great uncle Frank Jr—and fled from her abusive husband. She ended up in Oceanside, California—"

"California? I've never heard that."

"We found a blog post written a few years ago by the historical society there," Max said. "The gist of the blog was unsolved cases in the area. Oceanside mysteries. There were some minor mistakes in the blog, like that Susan's kids were both boys—"

"Why didn't I see that in my research?" Mary Pat said.

"Because blogs weren't invented back then," John said.

"Oh, yeah." Mary Pat frowned, thinking for a minute. "Boys, you say …. You know, once when I was little, I got gum stuck in my hair and my mom had to cut it really short. I was devastated because I looked like a boy. I remember crying and crying, completely inconsolable. My grandmother Roberta told me that when she was little, she got *her* hair cut so short that she looked like a boy too. But she liked it. She said her mom Susan told her how lucky she was. They pretended that Roberta *was* a boy. They called her Bobby for years, she told me. She wore boy's clothes and played only with her brother Frank Jr and his friends." She cocked her head. "I never believed her, thought she was just making it up to make me feel better. But now I wonder if that actually happened."

"Maybe that blog wasn't wrong after all," Max said.

"If someone was looking for a woman with a boy and a girl, they'd completely overlook a woman with two boys," Mary Pat said. "Maybe Susan did that to throw people off the scent."

"It didn't work, though," Evelyn said. "Because Susan figured out that her abusive husband had found her, so again, she grabbed the kids and ran away. I guess that's where she met her next husband, the good guy."

Mary Pat was nodding slowly, but it seemed to Evelyn that her thoughts were far away. She waited for Mary Pat to come back.

She finally did. "Susan's husband didn't find her. Her father Silas did. I remember hearing a story involving a Pinkerton detective—"

"He must have been the one who found Susan in Oceanside," Evelyn said excitedly.

Mary Pat didn't share her enthusiasm. "There's more to that story, though. Susan's mom Mary never trusted that Frank. Susan only married him because Silas wanted her to. Thought he was some upstanding citizen, but he was really a gambler and a jerk in every possible way."

"Stern doting papa," Max murmured.

"What?" Mary Pat asked.

"In the pirate poem, that's how Susan referred to him, using the same initials as his name. It was one of our main clues," Evelyn said. "And if he pushed Susan into a terrible marriage, no wonder he never wanted to talk about it. Think of the shame and heartbreak that man must have endured."

Mary Pat nodded. "And being one of the bigwigs in Sugar Springs at the time …"

"He was able to sweep it under the rug," Max finished for her.

They all held a moment of silence, each with their own thoughts.

Evelyn was the first to speak. "I wonder whatever happened to Frank Senior. You said you thought he killed Susan, until you did that research. But what if—"

"Susan killed *him!*" Mary Pat finished Evelyn's sentence.

"It could explain why she left in a hurry," Max said.

"It could also explain why the Pinkerton detective got involved. Maybe he wasn't hired by Susan's parents after all," Evelyn said.

"And why Susan never talked much to her second family about her life. Her kids were so young, they probably didn't have a clue what was going on." Mary Pat looked at her husband with wide eyes.

John nodded. "That makes sense."

Again, each of them silently sorted the information for themselves.

"Thank you both for telling me this," Mary Pat said.

"Oh, there's more." Max rasped out a loud laugh. He scooped up a handful of coins. "There was buried treasure too."

Mary Pat and John both opened their eyes wider than seemed possible.

Max told them the story of how the pirate poem led them to find the coins under the sugar mill. He ended by saying, "I think you've come into some serious money."

"And this, too." Evelyn lifted the ruby brooch so they could see it.

Mary Pat gasped. "The Ruby Red Butterfly!"

Evelyn gasped too. "That's what she called it in the poem too!"

"Practically all of the photos of Mary show her wearing that brooch," Mary Pat said. "In fact, there's one hanging on the wall of the Marketplace of the groundbreaking where she's wearing it. I saw it at the Grand Opening."

Evelyn and Max nodded.

After a bit Mary Pat said, "I'd like to think Mary gave that to Susan to fund her getaway."

"That's what I thought too," Evelyn said. "But in the end Susan didn't need it. She navigated her stormy seas all on her own. A true survivor."

Dena

DENA STARED at Georgia's boyfriend. He stared back, seeming as if he'd never met Dena. Never went out to eat with her, never video chatted. No recognition in his eyes whatsoever.

Georgia pulled Dena backward through the laundry room and into the kitchen.

"Excellent timing, Drew!" Georgia said. "We were just heading to dinner. Dena's treat." When they were all in the kitchen, she said, "I'm glad you two are finally meeting."

Before Dena could say that they'd already met, Drew saw the handcuffs and pile of nylon cord on the table. His eyes grew wide and he set a pharmacy bag next to them before turning to Dena with concern. "Are you okay? What has she done?"

The feeling of electricity shot through her again. She was suddenly disoriented. Had she jumped to yet another wrong conclusion? Had she built up this boyfriend of Georgia's so much in her mind that he couldn't possibly look like anyone but her stalker?

Drew asked again, "Are you okay?"

The concern in his eyes was real and Dena began telling him the story, starting with Georgia waking her up at four o'clock that morning. Had it only been that morning?

He interrupted Dena to say, "This sounds like a long story. How 'bout I make some tea? You two go sit in the living room. I'll be right in."

As they made their way to the comfortable furniture, Drew called out. "Georgia? I can't find the tea."

Georgia pivoted back the way they'd come and Dena collapsed into the arm chair, suddenly exhausted mentally and physically. She hadn't realized how hard she'd been trying to hold it all together and get Georgia the help she so obviously needed. And now the cavalry appeared, even though it was not in the form she expected. Relief that someone was here to help with Georgia coursed through her, replacing the tingly electricity. She tipped her head back and closed her eyes.

Drew tapped her on the knee and handed her a cup of tea before settling in next to Georgia on the velvet settee. "Okay, go on with your story."

Dena saw Georgia's eyes begin to droop and her head sag against Drew's shoulder. She realized Georgia had an even longer day than she had. She walked Drew through their day.

He took in Dena's story with a thoughtful, worried expression, then finally turned toward Georgia, who sleepily opened her eyes to look at him. He stood up, gently leaning Georgia against the back of the couch where she began snoring. "You were listening, after all. Good girl." He smoothed her curly hair. "I didn't really think you'd do it in a blizzard, but whatever."

Before Dena knew what was happening, Drew had pulled the pink fuzzy handcuffs from the back of his jeans and handcuffed her again. He pushed her roughly back into the chair when she struggled to stand and began binding her feet to the legs of the chair.

Dena yelled to Georgia as she struggled against Drew's binding. "Georgia! Wake up! Give me that key!" but Georgia was dead to the world.

"She's out," Drew said with a smile. When he finished lashing Dena to the chair, he disappeared into the kitchen.

Dena struggled, testing the handcuffs and bindings. They didn't budge. Same as before. She was held tight.

Holding the pharmacy bag, Drew emerged from the kitchen. He walked over to Georgia and fished out two plastic prescription containers. He popped the lid on one and dropped a capsule on the table, before doing the same with a tablet from the other bottle. He roused Georgia and gave her two capsules which she took without question before dropping back to sleep.

They were different from the blue pills Georgia had been popping on the drive. "What are you giving her? She doesn't need those!"

"She most certainly does. How else will I get her to do what I want?"

Charlee

CHARLEE AND SKYLER scrambled out of the car and began yelling, to make sure the two snowplow drivers knew they were down there. Their voices sounded unnaturally loud in the stillness of the aftermath of the howling storm. The drifts of snow caused the noise to bounce and muffle all around them.

The men kept their plows running while one of them disabled the road closure gate and the other slipped and slid down to meet them.

"You the two who are stuck in the snow?" he asked.

Skyler and Charlee exchanged a giddy glance. It was a question that begged for a snarky response, but they were too overjoyed to see the men and their plows. They could only manage nodding crazily like bobblehead dolls.

He told them his name was Eddie, then took his time walking around the car and inspecting it, presumably formulating a plan to get them out of there in the most expeditious manner. Or really, any manner. Charlee didn't care.

Eddie glanced over at her. "What do you call that color?"

Skyler coughed, but Charlee knew she was stifling a giggle, because that's what everyone did when they saw her car. They wouldn't giggle if they knew what a screaming deal she'd got on it.

"I call it Olive Red. I don't think it's a factory color, though."

Eddie responded with his eyebrows.

The other driver joined him and they discussed their options, finally deciding on the winch in the back of one of the plows. "If it pulls her bumper off, then we'll have to figure something else out."

"Wait. This is going to pull off my bumper?"

Eddie shrugged. "Might do."

"I'd rather that didn't happen," Charlee said.

Eddie conferred quietly with the other man.

Charlee was relieved they were trying to figure out a better, less bumper compromising solution.

They began scrambling up the ravine.

"Well?" Charlee asked. "Is my bumper going to be safe?"

Eddie didn't turn around. "Probably," he called over his shoulder. "Maybe."

Charlee took a deep breath. *Probably* and *maybe* were two entirely different beasts. "If you yank off my bumper, can I still drive my car?" she called.

"Probably," Eddie said.

"Maybe," the other one said.

Skyler watched studiously as the men worked. She asked a dozen questions, but only received two answers. Mostly the men were grunting and concentrating on getting this job done. One of the questions Eddie answered was, "How many times have you done this?"

Charlee was dismayed to hear him say, "Never."

The other question he answered with a "Yep," was to Skyler's delighted, "You've named your snowplows?" She pointed out the painted script on the side of the plows to Charlee. One was named "Eisenplower" and the other "Darth Blader."

The men readied their winch with the enormous hook on the end, along with many fat canvas straps and chains with jumbo links.

When they revved up the winch on the back of the snowplow, Charlee covered her eyes. Hearing only the creaking and groaning and Eddie's shouts of encouragement, warnings, and instruction was worse, though, so she watched through her fingers.

After several minutes that felt like hours, Charlee's face began cramping due to her completely unnatural expressions behind her fingers. She turned away to rub her face, and a few moments later spun around to wild shouts.

She expected to see her bumper flying across the highway in a perfect lobbing arc, perhaps with her car close behind. Instead, she was thrilled to see her car up on the road, pointed in the right direction.

As the men unhooked the winch and all the chains and straps, Charlee and Skyler scrambled up the slippery embankment.

Skyler pressed half the money into Eddie's hands. "We honestly can't thank you enough." She also pressed money into the other man's hands, along with a package of Fig Newtons, explaining, "It wasn't an even amount, so I added this to yours."

They mumbled their thanks and went back to their real jobs, climbing into the snowplows. Before they drove off, Eddie stuck his head out of Darth Blader's window. "Keep your distance and don't even think about passing us."

Charlee saluted and watched them drive off, Darth Blader in the passing lane, a bit ahead of Eisenplower in the other lane. Eisenplower pushed his snow to the shoulder plus what Darth Blader threw in front of him. They were a perfectly synchronized team.

Charlee and Skyler stayed behind the snowplows, and just like the trooper said, they plowed to the state line then took the next exit, tooting their airhorns as they passed the women going back north.

New Mexico plows hadn't been out yet, but the highway remained blessedly open. Charlee drove along at a very cautious forty miles per hour. They took the first exit they reached advertising gas and food.

Charlee filled the tank while Skyler made a dash for the restroom. By the time Charlee made it inside, Skyler was chatting with the man behind the register at the mini-mart.

"Road should be open into Santa Fe," he was telling Skyler. "Plows are out, I hear, but haven't seen one yet. You girls should wait it out here. They'll be in to fill their thermos soon enough."

"We're in kind of a hurry," Charlee called on her way to the restroom.

"Never pays to be in a hurry during a storm," he called after her.

Charlee knew he was right, and at any other time she would take his advice. But as she washed and dried her hands, she vowed to be careful. Everything would be fine. It had to be.

She returned to the mini-mart and was surprised to see Skyler taking a selfie between two burly men in coveralls. "Charlee, get in here! Guess who I found? New Mexico snowplow drivers!"

Charlee stepped behind Skyler, noticing each man

carried a large, battered Thermos. She grinned just as Skyler snapped the picture.

"We're going to buy your coffee," Charlee said, taking each man by the elbow and steering them toward the coffee station.

"Mario gives it to us for free," one said, indicating the cashier.

"We take a turn around his parking lot for him when we come out," the other said.

"Then we're going to buy you whatever else you want. Get some donuts, get a sandwich. Snickers bar? T-shirt? Go crazy. We're just so happy to see you," Charlee said.

The men looked at each other and shrugged. One of them scooped up some packages of mini-donuts, the other a Roswell UFO themed t-shirt. "My mom in Florida will get a kick out of this. Thanks."

They filled their Thermoses, Charlee paid for everything, then she and Skyler dashed back to the car. They waited while the men cleared snow from an acceptable area near the gas pumps and the front of the building, then headed back to the highway.

Charlee kept a healthy distance behind them and finally felt her breathing return to normal. She still didn't know what she'd find in Santa Fe, if anything, but she finally believed they'd actually get there.

The plows zipped along, faster than the Colorado plows she thought, but staggered in the two lanes in the same manner.

She held her breath as they traveled over Raton Pass, which she knew could be treacherous in bad weather. The elevation wasn't particularly high, not like the Colorado mountain passes, but it was still tricky navigation in the snow. Even through plowed snow. Plowing doesn't get to the roadbed, so it could still be problematic up and down hills.

Skyler had been telling Charlee the differences between goat cheese and the cheese Jake brought her from his llamas, but trailed off when she realized Charlee wasn't listening.

When they were on the Santa Fe side of the pass, Charlee looked over and grinned at Skyler who raised a hand. They high-fived. Skyler said, "You're driving like a boss!"

Their happiness was short-lived, though, when the plows took an exit. Charlee had assumed they'd plow all the way to Santa Fe. When she thought about it, though, that didn't make sense. She slowed down to account for the unplowed road in front of her. Suddenly she realized the road in front of her had already been plowed and laughed. Of course it had! There were teams of snowplows all over the state working to clear the main roads. She'd seen it happen all over Colorado during storms too.

She and Skyler both whooped and Charlee nudged the gas pedal.

Dena

"GEORGIA, I've been trying to tell you!" Dena shouted at her to try and rouse her to some kind of action. "This is the guy who put the rat in your birthday gift. That beautiful necklace? Don't you remember when we saw it in the store window and I told you it would look terrible on you? I was fibbing to make it a surprise. I went back the next day and bought it for you. This guy, Andy—" Dena pointed angrily "—switched it out for that dead rat to get back at me for my husband putting him in prison. I told you all this!"

Georgia looked at her through slitted eyes. Totally out of it, Dena realized.

Dena struggled uselessly against the pink fuzzy handcuffs. How were they so sturdy? Her ankles ached from being wrapped so tightly to the legs of the chair. Her torso wasn't tied, but she knew if she attempted to stand, she'd fall right over. A growl of frustration boiled over. It's two against one, I'm tied up, nobody even knows where I am, she thought in despair. And she had been so close to getting out of there with Georgia.

"Andy isn't even his real name. He's been lying to you all this time."

"I don't know any Andy." Georgia raised a limp arm. "That's my boyfriend, Drew."

It infuriated Dena to see the smug look on Andy/Drew's face while he sat there so calmly. She didn't know what he was planning for her or for Georgia, but she knew he hadn't tied up Georgia or restrained her in any way. If only Dena could break through her drug-induced haze.

"Drew isn't his real name either. Just two versions of his fake name. I think he's lying about everything. I mean, think about it, Georgia. Have you ever been to his house? Does he do any errands for you besides going to the pharmacy? Does he ask you a lot of questions about me? Does he seem to be overly interested in what happened on that mountain trail?" Everything Dena wanted Georgia to understand came tumbling out of her mouth. But Georgia couldn't hear it, she was too far gone. "I've always told you the truth, Georgia. I'm telling you the truth now." Dena watched Georgia fade the rest of the way out of the conversation.

Earlier Dena knew that her survival depended upon her communication skills. She was blowing it.

"Georgia, open your eyes!" she shouted. "He's medicating you! You told me yourself the doctors didn't want to prescribe more meds for you."

Andy stroked Georgia's hair. "Doctors don't understand women's pain."

Georgia looked up at him with liquid eyes. "I tried to tell her that."

"You just repeat what he tells you!"

"What do you know about it?" Georgia said listlessly,

slurring her words. "When I fell off that trail, I was in the hospital for a long time. Lots of pain. And you just ran off. Drew was there to help me."

"I told you a hundred times. I didn't *run off*. I went for help because there's no phone service out there. You know that." Dena slammed her back against the chair in frustration.

"You didn't even try to call for help." Andy/Drew frowned, scolding Dena on Georgia's behalf.

Dena snapped her head toward him. "How would you know that?" She saw a flicker of alarm pass over his face, but it was gone almost immediately.

"Because you wanted her dead," he said.

A realization swept over Dena. *He had been there that day.* He was the one who had pushed Georgia. They hadn't been hearing squirrels in the underbrush, it had been him, tracking them. Trying to keep her voice casual, she asked Georgia, "Who did you tell we were going hiking that day?"

"Only Drew," she said sleepily. "Everyone else hated you." Georgia slumped against Andy/Drew who then stood up and let her fall the rest of the way to the couch.

Dena noticed he didn't even put the pillow under her head or drape the throw over her.

"I'm right, aren't I?" Dena asked him. "Georgia told you I was coming back to town and where we were going to hike that day. You followed us and when I was far enough ahead so I wouldn't notice, you pushed her."

He moved to the other wing chair and after manspreading, said smugly, "If you didn't always have to be line leader, I never would have had the chance."

"You would have just pushed me, then."

"What would be the fun of that? I assumed that

Georgia was going to tell the cops you pushed her, but she had to go and get herself a brain injury and couldn't remember what happened. I finally convinced her you were in love with me."

Dena made a retching noise. "Gross. Why? How?"

He laughed. "It was easy. I showed her my call history, pointing out all the times you called me."

"I wasn't calling *you*! I was calling … you. Andy."

He laughed again. "See how easy it was? I just told her you were always contacting me, even when I tearfully explained to you that she and I were dating, and I was in love with her. Then you got so jealous, you lured her out to that trail and pushed her, you harpy, you."

"Why bring her into your little game?" Dena cocked her head. "What is your game, anyway?"

"My game is what it's always been—messing with you. I can't imagine having more fun than this."

"Don't you have anything better to do than drug an innocent woman and try to frame me?"

"Nope." He laced his fingers behind his head and grinned.

The bottom dropped out of Dena's stomach.

"It was so gratifying when all your friends turned against you. That was a real bonus. But I didn't expect you to move from Santa Fe. Plot twist!"

Dena tried to keep her voice steady, pretending she wasn't scared of him. "Why haven't I had any problems with you in Sug—where I moved?"

"Sugar Springs, yes. It did cost me some time to reconnoiter, but I knew you'd be back in Santa Fe eventually. Besides, small towns have nosy cops and nosy residents. Better to just keep gaslighting you through Georgia."

"Considering this is the first I've thought of you since you walked out of that restaurant that night—"

"No, it's not."

He was right. Nobody who had a brush with a stalker put it out of their mind completely. But Dena didn't want him to know that. "Yes, it is. You were just a blip on radar I never had to look at again. And besides, you're not technically gaslighting me. You're just drugging an old, trusting woman."

He shrugged. "I'm playing the long game, something I learned both from your undercover husband and from prison. It's just so much easier for me to get Georgia to mess with you for a while than for me to do it." He glanced over to her snoring softly on the settee. "I'm not greedy. Happy to share the fun."

"If you didn't keep her drugged, she wouldn't do any of this."

"Sadly, I think you're right. Thank goodness for crooked doctors who over-prescribe, right? While it has been a hoot getting Georgia hooked on both uppers and downers, *and* getting her to trust me completely, mostly I just wanted to brainwash her enough that she'd tell the cops and finally get you arrested for pushing her off the trail. I tell her to call the cops every so often and ask about the status of the case, just to keep it all fresh in their minds for when the big day comes."

The hair on Dena's arms stood on end. That feeling of electricity had returned. "What big day?"

"Today, of course," he said in a chipper voice. "The day you broke into Georgia's house in a jealous rage to try and kill her." He stood and pulled plastic gloves from the front pocket of his jeans. "It's a good thing I got here in time to witness everything. It's sad that poor 'ol Georgia has to die, though. She was a good sport."

"You're going to kill her?"

He shook his head. "No. I think they'll find it was you."

He pulled a small gun from his back waistband. Before Dena knew what was happening, he'd grabbed her by the handcuffs and placed the gun in her hand, pressing so her fingerprints were clearly on it.

Charlee

CHARLEE AND SKYLER whooped again later when they saw a road sign proclaiming "Santa Fe Next Four Exits."

"We made it! I knew we would," Charlee said.

Skyler gave her the side-eye. "Did you?"

"No," she admitted sheepishly. "But I really hoped we would. Otherwise …" Charlee finished her sentence with a shrug, refusing to think about failure then, or now.

Charlee took the exit that she hoped would lead them to the Canyon Road art galleries.

When she'd been at Dena's at Thanksgiving, they had created a treasure hunt for Georgia's birthday. Georgia lived near Canyon Road somewhere, and Charlee was sure she'd be able to determine Georgia's address by recreating the route they walked and the memory of Thanksgiving dinner at Georgia's.

But walking wasn't driving, and daytime wasn't dark. Charlee crept through the unplowed streets getting more and more worried. Nothing looked familiar to her in the dark and covered with three feet of snow.

Several times Skyler began to speak but thought better

of it. Charlee could only imagine the expression on her face if it stopped Skyler from speaking to her. If it were any other time, though, she'd like to find out. A face like that could come in handy on an airplane or when she rode the light rail trains around Denver, or when she didn't want to get hit on in a bar.

They'd crept up and down some of the same streets so many times that it fooled Charlee into thinking she was on the right track, only to realize it seemed familiar because they'd already driven there tonight.

More and more cars were moving around the city, now that the storm was over. Charlee wondered where everyone was going because she knew in Denver if there was a storm, the last thing she wanted to do was go out into the unplowed aftermath. Of course, she wasn't a parent who might have run out of diapers or baby formula, or a nurse needing to relieve someone on a hospital shift, or an addicted gamer searching for wifi.

Finally, she slammed on her brakes hard enough to skid. She saw the artist's gallery with all the grotesques that one of Dena's friends managed. It was dark and obviously closed, but Charlee drove into the parking lot anyway. She pulled into a space and put her car in park, but left it idling. She closed her eyes and tried to envision the day she and Dena were here.

After a bit, she turned to Skyler. "I think I've got it."

"Let's hope so."

Charlee remembered when they'd been on foot for the treasure hunt, they'd passed through what she thought at the time was someone's yard. But now, as they rolled slowly behind the block of buildings, tires packing down the snow, she saw it. An alley. Or at least she hoped it was an alley.

She pointed the car in that direction and was rewarded with a residential street in front of her. She hadn't found it earlier because this was at the cul de sac at one end. They'd been passing Georgia's street back and forth by one house without knowing it.

Charlee sat idling.

"Well?" Skyler asked. "Is this it?"

"This is the street. Now I'm just trying to remember what the front of the house looked like and envisioning it covered in snow." Charlee knew it wasn't any of these three houses at the end. She pulled out of the alley, or whatever it was, and turned right. She drove slowly along the street studying each house.

"What do you remember about it?"

"The front had a big circular driveway with a really pretty stamped concrete design."

"Probably not helpful."

"No, probably not." Charlee squinted into the night. "It reminded me of a hacienda from a movie set."

"That's what all these houses look like."

"It had curved windows on the second story."

"Okay, that's something." Skyler rolled down her window and stuck her head out, craning upward. "Oh! Like that one?" She waved her finger at it.

"Kinda." Charlee continued to creep along the street.

"That one?" Skyler pointed again.

"Nope."

"This could be going better, I think," Skyler said. "Are you *sure* we're on the right street?"

"I was until you just now said that."

They reached the corner and Charlee still hadn't been able to identify Georgia's house. She sighed and made a U-turn. "It's gotta be here," she muttered. She passed two houses then swerved to the curb, or at least where she thought the curb might be. "Maybe if I walk."

Skyler got out too, but stood next to her open car door

and watched as Charlee walked in the center of the street, availing herself to the packed snow of one of their tire tracks.

"Lose a dog?" someone yelled from a porch.

"No, but I'm looking for someone's house. Do you know a woman named Georgia?" Charlee called.

"Georgia Pisch? Yeah, up there, just past where the road curves." He pointed. They hadn't driven far enough. "Looks like a hacienda, arched windows on the second floor."

"That part I remembered. Thanks!" Charlee hurried back to the car and they both hopped in. She executed another U-turn, gunning it a little too enthusiastically causing wild swinging and lurching until she regained control.

Charlee almost sobbed when she recognized Georgia's house.

"Look." Skyler pointed. "Tire tracks into the garage."

"Let's hope it's them."

Dena

WHILE GEORGIA SLEPT on the settee across the room,
Dena stared at Andy/Drew sitting in front of her in the
other chair. She'd said all she needed to say to him.

It seemed he'd said everything he needed to say to her
as well and, still wearing the latex gloves, walked to the wet
bar on the opposite side of the room. He placed the gun
on the top of the bar.

Dena turned to watch him, trying to figure out what his
next move might be. She struggled again, trying to loosen
her restraints to no avail.

"Georgia! Wake up! Get up!" Dena knew they were
both sitting ducks, no matter what Andy/Drew had in
mind.

He glanced at Georgia, unmoving on the settee. He
once again turned his back on the women and picked up
the receiver of Georgia's landline. He held it aloft for a
moment. "Gotta get into character," he said with a laugh.
He dialed then spoke breathlessly and a bit hysterically. "A
woman named Dena Russo pushed Georgia Pisch off a
hiking trail in January. You guys have been investigating it.

She's here at Georgia's house right now and she has a gun —" He set down the receiver then picked up the gun from the bar and turned, aiming it at Georgia.

In slow motion, Dena followed the trajectory of the bullet she knew would slam through Georgia. In her mind's eye she saw Georgia's body jerk and a floof of feathers as the bullet tore through the pillow behind her body.

But when Dena's gaze reached the settee, Georgia wasn't there.

Dena looked back at Andy/Drew. His entire face wrinkled in confusion. He took a step closer to the empty settee across the room.

Dena had been staring so intently at Andy/Drew, she hadn't seen Georgia get up either.

But Dena saw her now.

She was half-hidden behind the Chinese screen, reaching for the hideous vase. She silently hoisted it above her head and sneaked up behind Andy/Drew, who had continued to slowly drift toward the settee, as if Georgia had simply shrunk down and he couldn't see her.

Georgia bashed him over the head with the vase. Those cherubs and woodland creatures looked positively gleeful at the action.

Dena gasped as Andy/Drew slumped to the floor, surrounded by shards of pastel porcelain.

Georgia turned to her with a grin, flexing like a bodybuilder. "Water aerobics. If you hadn't come with me in Sugar Springs, I was going to whack you just like that. I'm glad I didn't have to. This was much more satisfying. I've never liked this vase. Remember when I needed you to help me carry it in?"

Dena stared at her, dumbfounded. Georgia looked full of energy, fresh as the proverbial daisy.

She dug in her pocket, then stepped toward Dena.

Dena flinched.

Georgia opened her palm to reveal the capsule and tablet Andy/Drew had given her earlier. "I heard every word the two of you said."

"You spat out your pills." Dena gazed at her friend with admiration and relief. Lots of relief.

Georgia toed Andy/Drew in his side. He didn't budge. "I should probably apologize, Dena. I wasn't in my right mind."

"When have you ever been?" Dena smiled weakly.

Georgia had reached into her bra again and dangled the key to the handcuffs in front of Dena, still lashed to the chair. "Maybe I'll just leave these on you," she teased.

Dena held her handcuffed wrists in front of her. "Where did you get these, anyway? They're sturdy."

"At the pink fuzzy handcuff store, of course."

"Of course."

Georgia began fiddling with the key into the mechanism when the doorbell rang. She handed the key to Dena to see if she could do it before going to answer the front door.

Dena heard women's voices in the foyer as she concentrated on the handcuffs.

"Mom!"

Dena was so startled at hearing Charlee's voice that she dropped the handcuff key in her lap.

"Charlee! What are you doing here! And Skyler? What's going on?"

"Um ... we wanted to ask you the same question."

Skyler saw Andy/Drew's body on the floor and screamed.

Suddenly Charlee took a step back. She saw Dena restrained in the chair. A gun on the wet bar. A body. And

Georgia roaming around. She began hollering, moving fast toward Georgia. "What have you done? Is he dead? You killed him?"

Georgia hurried over to the chair where Dena was tied up.

Skyler started screaming again.

Georgia began digging her hands all around Dena's thighs, trying to find the handcuff key.

Dena looked at Skyler and Charlee from over the top of Georgia's head, yelled at them both to hush up so she could explain. Her words were drowned out by Skyler's screaming.

Charlee rushed over and began struggling with Georgia to get her away from Dena.

"Skyler! Grab the gun!" Charlee yelled.

Skyler lunged for it on the bar and held it with shaky hands, first pointing it at Georgia, then swinging it toward Andy/Drew, then back at Georgia, then to a sound behind her.

"Drop that gun! Everybody freeze!"

Skyler immediately dropped the gun and raised her hands in the air. "It's not mine!"

Two Santa Fe police officers stood in the doorway, weapons drawn.

All four women froze.

One of the officers continued to aim his gun at the scene. The other holstered his and began patting down the women, except Dena, since he saw she was restrained and wouldn't be a danger.

He motioned Georgia, Charlee, and Skyler to the settee. "Don't move. Don't talk," he commanded.

He took a knee next to Andy/Drew. Searched for blood or bullet holes. "Sir?" He shook him and

Andy/Drew began to rouse. The officer helped him sit then said, "Can I see some ID, sir?"

Andy/Drew looked at Dena, then the women on the couch, trying to quickly assess the situation. "I don't have my wallet on me, Officer. I rushed right over here to rescue Georgia"—he pointed at her— "from the evil clutches of this woman. I got her tied up, but I guess that one" —he pointed at Charlee— "hit me and knocked me out."

"That's not at all what happened," Georgia said calmly. "And check his pocket. He has his wallet."

The cop stared at Georgia for a moment, then rolled Andy/Drew to get at his back pocket. He walked to the edge of the room where he could continue to keep an eye on the situation with his partner. He read the information into his shoulder radio. After a staticky reply, he grinned. He motioned to his partner in some shorthand way, causing him to immediately step closer to Andy/Drew, who hadn't moved from the floor. The officer trained his weapon directly at Andy/Drew's chest instead of at the women.

The officer who spoke on the radio grinned then slapped non-pink-and-fuzzy handcuffs on Andy/Drew. "Why, if it isn't Douglas Gregory Basham in the flesh! We've been looking for you."

Kateri

"DO YOU WANT SOME COFFEE, DEAR?" Evelyn held the coffee carafe aloft in the vendor room as Kateri walked in. "I've had so much today I'm about to float away."

"That's just what I was coming for." She held out her cup to Evelyn. "I thought you and Max would be long gone by now. Or did you get all caught up in your detective work?"

"We did."

Kateri had been joking, and her surprise must have registered on her face because Evelyn told her the most remarkable story.

"We just finished telling Mary Pat everything."

"Wow … just wow. That's some story. Everyone's going to be bummed they missed all the excitement around here today. Speaking of which, have you seen Dena? I have a million things for her to sign. I wanted to talk to her before I left for the day."

"No. I haven't heard a word." Evelyn pinched her lips so tight they turned white. "I'm worried."

Kateri knew that if *she* took the day off and didn't bother to call anyone, she'd be sacked pronto.

"I wanted to tell you I was impressed with the way you handled that obnoxious teenager earlier," Kateri said. "I caught her vaping in the restroom. Told me to leave her the heck alone. Except she didn't say heck." She gave Evelyn a knowing and judgmental look. "As my grandmother would say, she's a real pip."

Evelyn sipped her coffee. "I think she was just disappointed that she got stuck here in Nowheresville with her mother when she could have been off skiing in Aspen. That might turn me into a pip too."

"Well, I was ready to throttle her—I wouldn't, of course—"

"Of course."

"But then I poked my head into your studio to ask you something and heard her laughing and joking with you and her mom, I couldn't believe it. I had to look closer to see if it was the same girl. How'd you do it? She seemed like a contrite little kitten."

"I don't know. She didn't like my costume choices. Thought they weren't feminist enough, so I pulled out my Rattlesnake Kate dress—"

"You know Rattlesnake Kate?" Kateri realized the way she was grinning showed her crooked front tooth and clamped her mouth shut.

"I do. And now Deondra and her mother do too. Maybe they even have a new role model." Evelyn sipped her coffee. "What did you want to ask me?"

"Oh. I'm redoing the website—"

"You're redoing the website?"

Kateri bristled. "I am. I believe that's what I was hired to do, even though I have yet to see my official job description."

"That's great!"

"It is?" Kateri wasn't sure if Evelyn was mocking her. It had happened before. Not with Evelyn, though, but the memory was still fresh.

"Can I see?"

Kateri shrugged, bracing herself. May as well get this over with, she thought, resigned. "Fine." She turned on her heel and Evelyn followed her through the back door into her office. Kateri swiveled her laptop so it faced Evelyn across the desk.

Evelyn bent her knees a bit and squinted, staring at it.

Here it comes, thought Kateri. "It's rough. I'm not finished, just playing with some designs. I'll probably change it back the way it was."

Evelyn crossed Kateri's threshold and called across the vendor room. "Kober! You've gotta see this!"

Kober hurried into Kateri's office and stopped short when she saw the two women sans emergency. "Son of a ham sandwich! Evelyn, quit hollering like that. You made me spill the sugar! I thought I was here alone!"

"Look at this." Evelyn pointed to the computer screen.

Kober lifted the laptop to see it better.

Kateri felt heat rising through her chest. "That's enough. I don't need your—"

"Okay. I stand corrected. That might have been worth your histrionics and a little spilled sugar. This is fantastic!"

Kateri unballed the fists at her sides.

"Isn't it? While you and I were yukking it up over cookies and rattlesnakes, Kateri was in here working some magic."

"You ... like it? I was afraid ..." Kateri trailed off, suddenly unsure of what exactly she had been afraid of. That she'd taken initiative? That she put her skills to good use? That she demonstrated some talent?

"What did you want to ask me, though?" Evelyn said.

Kateri couldn't remember. The idea that she could maybe survive in this job without a chip on her shoulder erased every other thought from her mind.

Dena

SKYLER HAD CALLED Hugo last night from Georgia's house and asked him to tell everyone they were all safe and going to be spending the night in Santa Fe, but they'd be on their way back to Sugar Springs bright and early. Dena heard her give Hugo an abbreviated version of their adventure, but that she was exhausted and didn't want to repeat it to the others. "They'll hear the whole thing—"

"Every stinkin' detail," Dena said with a laugh.

"—when we get back."

Charlee had called Lance and Ozzi to tell them the same.

Dena had called Kober to ask about Twist.

The Santa Fe police officers said they'd contact Sheriff Johnson in Sugar Springs and let her know what had happened.

On the drive from Santa Fe back to Sugar Springs, the sun was shining, the sky was blue, and the highway was only patchy with snow. Drifts still packed the shoulders and ravines next to the road. As they passed the area where they'd been stuck in the snowbank, Charlee and Skyler had saluted it, then high-fived each other.

When Dena asked what the big deal was, after some debate, they told her.

"Are you kidding me? You guys could have been killed!"

Charlee grinned. "But we weren't."

"Not from lack of trying, though," Skyler said with a laugh.

Dena realized she had two directions to go. She could rant and rave and scold. Or she could see the absurd humor in the situation. Ranting and raving seemed like a lot of effort. Besides, if she scolded too much, they might gang up on her and point out all the stupid things she had done in the last twenty-four hours.

If it came up, though, she could argue perfectly logically that she didn't allow herself to be kidnapped because she was stupid, but rather that she allowed herself to be kidnapped because she was a good friend. And it turned out just as well as Charlee and Skyler trying to skirt a road closure. Nobody got hurt, and the added benefit was that Georgia and Dena were friends again.

When they reached Sugar Springs, Dena told Charlee to go straight to Kober's house. They'd called from the outskirts and Kober opened the door as soon as they pulled up to the curb.

A blur of white lightning came at them. When Dena opened the car door, she was knocked backward by the force of Twist's exuberant greeting.

Covered by a spray of snow that Twist had kicked up on her mad dash across the lawn, Dena laughed and hugged her, half in and half out of the car.

"Oh my gosh, I missed you too, sweet girl!"

Twist licked Dena's face over and over, and Dena

allowed it. Both actions, a testament to their love.

Dena held Twist's face in her hands and looked directly into her big brown eyes. "I'm so sorry I left you like that. It'll never happen again. Pinky swear." She put out her hand, pinky up. Twist batted it with her paw. Dena buried her face in Twist's neck.

During Dena's reunion with Twist, Charlee and Skyler walked up to the front porch and stood with Kober and the kids.

Finally, Dena told Twist, "If you get off of me, I'll give you the present I got you in New Mexico."

Twist immediately removed herself from Dena's lap and sat on the sidewalk, tail wagging a perfect arc in the snow.

"Half a doggy angel," Dena said approvingly. She opened the back door and reached into a bag from the truck stop.

Twist stood and did a doggy jig before racing into the house with her gift clamped between her teeth.

Dena watched her barrel up to the porch, then politely thread her way through the legs on the porch to get inside. Dena picked up the truck stop bag and carried it to the porch. After hugging Jain, Wyatt, Leo, and Lincoln, she held out the bag. "I have presents for you guys, too. I truly can't thank you enough for taking care of Twist for me. I hope you like these." Dena pulled out sweatshirts and handed them out.

Dena handed Jain one that said, *Mountains aren't funny ... they're hill areas.* "I got myself one of these to remember my trip."

"You need a sweatshirt to remember all this?" Kober asked.

Dena laughed. "Probably not."

"For Wyatt." She held up one with a funny cartoon

spaceman that said, *Because aliens.*

"Looks just like you," Jain said to her brother with a laugh.

Next Dena pulled out two t-shirts, one red and one blue. As she handed the red one to Leo and the blue to Lincoln, she said "I wasn't sure—"

They immediately traded, and held them up to show everyone. *Area 51 Storm Trooper.*

"Let's go find our blasters!" The twins ran off calling, "Thanks, Miz Russo!"

Jain and Wyatt thanked her too and they all went inside.

Dena brought up the rear with Kober. Dena linked an arm through hers. "Thanks for taking care of Twist for me."

"No funny t-shirt for me?"

"I couldn't find one I thought would go over your hair."

Kober laughed and pushed her nest of hair upward. "We loved having her here. It was a good diversion. For me and the kids."

"Diversion? From what?"

Kober watched Charlee ahead of them, talking to Jain and Wyatt. "Have you ever had to give your kids bad news?"

Dena snorted. "Like tell them their father was shot and killed by an informant?"

"Well, yes, I guess you have." Kober looked at the floor. "Nic left us. Went off with his girlfriend, I guess."

"Oh, Kober, I'm so sorry." Dena embraced her.

"I don't know what to tell the kids."

"Tell them the truth. They'll survive." Dena held Kober at arms-length and looked into her eyes. "You all will. I promise."

Twist

TWIST SNATCHED the gift from Dena's hand and tore across the front yard toward the house, kicking up clouds of snow. She wove her way through everyone on the porch, wondering why they just stood there in her way. Didn't they realize what was happening?

She skidded to a stop in front of the couch where she dropped her present and stared at it. She sniffled every inch of it, then gently pawed at the mini plastic hanger until it slid loose. She used her tiny front teeth and her paws to arrange the gift in front of her. A pair of long white socks with red and green chili peppers of all sizes covering the length of them.

After staring at them adoringly, Twist gathered them in her mouth and dropped them on the top of a rather large pile of socks she'd accumulated over the duration of her visit.

It was an excellent pile, curated with care, and she was proud of it, but she was anxious to get home to Dena's socks. And to introduce these new chili pepper socks to her red ones with the cartoon bones.

She padded over to where Dena talked with Kober. Twist nudged the top of her head under Dena's hand. She stood still, feeling the warmth of Dena's hand while she cuffed her ear.

All was right with the world. Her human had returned.

THE NEXT DAY, Dena again watched as pocket chaff was emptied from a coat pocket. But this time she was the one doing it. It was her own pocket, and she wasn't littering into her Mexican pottery planter. She was at the Marketplace, surrounded by her friends and her daughter.

Over baked treats and coffee, Dena, Skyler, and Charlee filled Evelyn, Max, Hugo, Boyd, Pham, and Kateri in on all the details of their various adventures.

When they finished, Evelyn turned to Charlee. "Didn't I tell you you'd have a nice time if you came to visit your mother?"

"Anything interesting happen around here?" Dena asked.

"Kateri redid the website," Evelyn said.

"It's fantastic, too," Kober said. "Show her!"

Kateri blushed. "She'll see it soon enough."

"Kateri also streamlined all the paperwork for the tenants," Boyd said. "She got me all squared away."

Dena made a face. "I thought I got you all squared away."

"She got me squared-er." Boyd guffawed.

"She got me all set up too," Pham said.

"And you should see his gorgeous restaurant," Hugo said. He looked at Charlee. "Before you leave you must get some ramen." He quirked an eyebrow at Pham. "Or is it phở?"

"I make both. Phở is Vietnamese and ramen is Japanese. Very different. Both delicious."

"I'll have to get both then," Charlee said.

"Wow. All new admin stuff. New tenant. New restaurant. Anything else?" Dena joked.

"Evelyn solved a hundred-year-old mystery—"

"Boyd had a heart attack—"

Dena swung around sharply toward him.

He shrugged. "I survived."

Dena wasn't sure if they were pulling her leg or not. "You solved a hundred-year-old mystery?"

Evelyn nodded.

"Complete with buried treasure," Max added.

Evelyn and Max filled them in. "We gave the coins and the brooch back to Mary Pat, but she wants us to keep the clothes and shoes for the studio. I promised we wouldn't let anyone get their picture taken in them until Mary Pat did. She's coming in next week for a session and she'll wear the brooch. I hope you're around so you can see it. It's so pretty. Then we'll get her picture wearing her great grandmother's clothes up on the wall with the others. She's reworking her family history and the stuff on the wall about the sugar mill."

"Wow. That's some story!" Dena said. After a bit she turned toward Boyd. "And what about you? Did you really have a heart attack?"

"Who would joke about that?" he asked.

"Um … perhaps any—maybe all—of you guys?" Dena

pointed to the whiteboard on the wall behind Boyd. Someone had written "?? days without a murder."

Evelyn shrugged. "You never know."

Dena erased it, being careful not to smudge the haiku written underneath.

Charlee read it over Dena's shoulder and laughed.

> Blizzards bring out the
> Best of the snow but the worst
> Of Dena's stalker.

"You guys enjoy some dark humor here at the Marketplace," Charlee said. She thought for a moment, then counted syllables with her fingers, composing her own haiku.

> You never know what
> Will happen on a drive to
> Visit your mother.

Afterword

Thank you so much for reading my books! If it wasn't for readers, I'd look too much like a toddler banging away on a keyboard for no reason.

I hope you were delighted with your visit to the Sugar Mill Marketplace. If so, check out the rest of the series!

Your reviews help authors drive book sales *and* help readers find new books and authors. Please consider popping over to the BOUND review page and dropping a few words. I'd really appreciate it!

Subscribe at BeckyClarkBooks.com to Becky Clark's *So Seldom It's Shameful* News for free series starters for both the Mystery Writer's mysteries and the Sugar Mill Marketplace mysteries. You'll also find fun short stories, a Christmas play, up-to-the-minute info about releases and sales, and the scoop about becoming a member of my Review Crew.

Acknowledgments

The theme of BOUND is "survival."

As an author, my survival depends on readers so I want to thank you so much for choosing to spend your time with my books. I know there are a zillion other books, TV channels, and fun ways to goof off, so I'm thrilled you're using some of your free time reading this one. It's always humbling and gratifying for me.

My survival as an author also very much depends on my support system. Right now my editor—the incomparable **Jessica Cornwell**—tops my list because she made my frantic publishing pace hers also … with nary a complaint! Not one that I heard, anyway. In all seriousness, I wouldn't be half as successful as I am without her stellar eye for detail and her thoughtful critique. And again, any mistakes that seep through are because I got my grubby fingers all over the manuscript after she signed off on it.

In a tie for second place is (are? where's my dang editor when I need her??) my family and friends. I can always count on them to lend me a shoulder to cry on or to kick me in the butt, whichever I may need. Often both.

Many of these fabutastic people hang out with me in my private Facebook group, Becky's Book Buddies. They're also part of my Review Crew, making sure they shout about my books from their rooftops and otherwise offer some noisy buzz for me. They interact with me in the Cozy Mystery Crew group on Facebook, and they visit our group blog over at Chicks on the Case. If you haven't visited those places, what are you waiting for??

Survival in this world is, let's face it, difficult. Without my band of merry readers and writers, it would be a dismal place indeed.

Thank you for everything you do to brighten it up!

Also by Becky Clark

If you enjoyed this little taste of the Sugar Mill Marketplace series, check out the rest of the series today. And while you're at it, get up to speed with Charlee Russo in the Mystery Writer's mysteries.

Sugar Mill Marketplace mysteries

Booked #1

Plotted #2

Bound #3

Mystery Writer's Mysteries

Fiction Can Be Murder #1

Foul Play on Words #2

Metaphor for Murder #3

Police Navidad #4

Crossword Puzzle Mysteries

Puzzling Ink #1

Punning with Scissors #2

Fatal Solutions #3

The Dunne Diehl Mysteries

Banana Bamboozle #1

Marshmallow Mayhem #2

Nonfiction

Eight Weeks to a Complete Novel—Write Faster, Write Better,
Be More Organized

About the Author

Award-winning author **Becky Clark** is the seventh of eight kids, which explains both her insatiable need for attention and her atrocious table manners. She likes to read funny books so it felt natural to write them too. She surrounds herself with quirky people and pets who end up as characters in her novels. Readers say her books are "fast and thoroughly entertaining" with "witty humor and tight writing" and "humor laced with engaging characters" so you should "grab a cocktail and enjoy the ride."

For entirely too much information about her, visit BeckyClarkBooks.com. While you're there, subscribe to her mailing list for **oodles of fun and free stuff**.

Follow her on Amazon and BookBub to get up-to-the-date info on new releases and sales. Join her private group "Becky's Book Buddies" on Facebook for shenanigans and fun. Put her books on your GoodReads shelf to make all your friends jealous.